Man Friday

The Second Half

(The Life and Times of Robin Friday)

Stuart Kane

First published in 2020
by Helpston Fuller
45 Tamworth Road
Sutton Coldfield
Birmingham B75 6EB

Robin Friday quote is courtesy of *Reading Evening Post*/Reach Licensing.

Photo credit: Mirrorpix/Reach Licensing
Cover design by Kingel Ltd.

British Library Cataloguing-in-Publication Data
A catalogue record for this book is available
on request from the British Library.

ISBN 978-1-8380269-7-4

In loving memory of

Theresa ‘Tess’ Florence Lawrence

(1921 – 2019)

'I reckon I've got twelve years in football from now...after that? I can't think that far ahead. I suppose like everybody else, my ambition must be to play for a First Division club. If you don't think like that, there wouldn't be any point in being in the game.'

Robin Friday, *Reading Evening Post*, February 1974

Author's Preface

This is the second part in a tale of two halves about Robin Friday. It is a fictional account of his life but is laced with fact. The depictions of real people in this book are purely the work of my imagination, informed by research and interpretation.

Man Friday: the second half, along with its prequel, has taken five years of intense study, writing and revisions. I have tried to leave no stone unturned and believe that I have stayed true to the spirit of Robin Friday. I have included the games he played as they are part of Robin's history, and each one tells its own story.

What I have produced in this novel is a written portrait of Robin Friday, woven into the rich tapestry of his life. I have had to make judgements about what to include and what not to include. After all, so many of the stories surrounding him have been embellished over the years. Some have been played down or even made up, whilst others have been hidden for decades.

Robin Friday's life certainly meets the criteria for a Shakespearian tragedy, and it was a life that he led in his own distinctive way. The form I have used to tell his story is biographical fiction, or the biographical novel: a fact-based fiction. Its aim is to take you, the reader, into the mind of Robin Friday. I have really tried to capture the essence of his being in a way that stays authentic to his unique character and the challenges and uncertainties he faced during his life.

We pick up from where *Man Friday: the first half* left off, so lace up your boots and hold on tight.

PART ONE
READING SEASON
1976/77

Robin Friday is now a Third Division player, but his contract remains unsigned.

*

Monday 19 July 1976

Robin trudges into Elm Park, hands in his pockets and his football boots slung over his shoulder. He sees his friend, Eamon Dunphy, and smiles.

'How're you feeling, pal?' asks Eamon.

'Ah, you know, been better. I'd like to say I'm glad to be back, but I'm not. How about you?' asks Robin.

'Cynical and disillusioned with all of this, same as you really.'

'An extra fiver, and they want us just to get on with it.'

'Of course they do, it's them against us,' says Eamon.

'Yeah, I'm meant to be getting married and survive on that. It's poxy.'

'Have you signed yet?' asks Eamon.

'Fuckin' course not, not for that,' he says, shaking his

head.

'Good, we're having a players' meeting at the Spread Eagle tomorrow, you in?'

'Yeah, definitely. We've got to stick together on this, like.'

'Too fucking right we do.'

*

Tuesday 20 July 1976
In the Spread Eagle, there are sharp whispers in the corner, fingers point, heads shake —

'So that's it, a few of us have got an extra fiver and the rest of you nothing. The key is Robin, as they'll not want to let you go,' says Eamon.

'I've said I'm with you all, simple as that. I worked my fuckin' arse off last season, and for what, a bonus, and a paltry extra few quid a week,' says Robin.

'Charlie doesn't give a fuck, and neither does Waller and his cronies in the boardroom. They think they won promotion, that's the arrogance of them. They nicked the beef, and now they're taking the bloody bread from our table,' says Eamon, wagging his finger.

Cumming says, 'I've been here a while, as has Deathie, and it's shoddy by the board. There's a lack of respect, and we'd be better off quitting, or going semi-pro and working full-time.'

'I won't be signing, not a chance,' says Deathie, folding his arms.

'What about you, mate?' asks Robin, looking at Geoff Barker.

Geoff sighs. 'I'll be honest, I think this is it for me. I made thirty appearances last season, and I think I made a decent contribution, but I've got family commitments, and playing football seems like a luxury I can't justify,' says Geoff with sad eyes.

'Have you told Charlie this?' asks Eamon.

'Of course, but he thinks I'm bluffing for a few extra quid,' says Geoff.

'Fucking Charlie,' says Eamon.

'This is a right fucking mess,' says 'Minty' Murray.

'It is, but as long as we stick together we can keep the pressure on them,' says Eamon.

'There'll be more twists and turns before the season starts,' says Robin, draining the last dregs of his pint and standing up. 'See you lot tomorrow.' He leaves and walks the short distance home.

*

Wednesday 21 July 1976

Robin works out on the multigym, or the chamber of terrors as the Reading players call it. He stands and pulls the bar down, lifting the weights, up and down, up and down.

'Why the hell do we need this?' asks Eamon.

'They wanna build us up all big and strong, you know. It's like workin' in a fuckin' factory,' says Robin.

'Yeah, we'll all have bloody hernias before the season even starts,' says Eamon.

'At least it beats running.'

'There's some use there though for your fitness, but not this,' says Eamon, leaning on the multigym. 'I've never known it like this, Robin, never. It's us against them. It's pre-season and we're already up against it. We should be having a laugh, be refreshed, but here we are pissing into the wind,' says Eamon.

Robin nods and keeps pulling on the weights.

Robin pushes and pulls, heaves and works himself over.

'Right, lads, let's get out on a run,' says Charlie.

They run out of the Adwest training ground, move along Henley Road to Shiplake. A lead group of players breaks away. Robin jogs along at his own pace, in his own mind, happy to be trailing at the back. Moves his bow legs along, breathes in heavy spurts and tries not to break a sweat. The lead group moves further ahead. He sees Death a few paces ahead. Looks at Death.

'Deathie, you got any fags?'

'Yes, mate,'

'Can I nick one?'

'Yeah, let's get a bit further down the road, out of sight, and then we'll have a break,' says Death, shouting over his shoulder.

'Sure.'

Robin continues to plod, Death just ahead of him.

*

Thursday 22 July 1976

Charlie Hurley sits with the local press.

'How are things shaping up for the new season?'

'The lads are putting in a tremendous effort, and we're busy getting ourselves ready for Third Division football. I really am fortunate to have such a strong group of players, so committed to the cause,' says Charlie, knowing that this question is the ice-breaker – the easy one.

'Is there any more news on the situation regarding the players' new contracts?'

Charlie fidgets. 'Well, it's not too good in that department. We're hoping it'll all sort itself out sooner rather than later.'

'So how many have signed?'

'We've one so far,' says Charlie.

'Who's that?'

'None of your business. I'll keep you updated in that regard, okay,' says Charlie.

'There have been rumours circulating about Geoff Barker leaving, is this true?'

'I can confirm that Geoff has retired from the game and has returned to Hull to take up a sales post at a building supplies company. It's a shame, he's only twenty-seven, and he probably had another five or six years left in the game.'

'We believe that he quit for financial reasons, is this true?'

'I won't comment on a player's reasons. Geoff is his own man, so you'll have to ask him,' says Charlie, starting to sweat.

'So you're looking for a new central defender?'

'I'm looking for a few new faces to try and bring in over the coming weeks.'

'Is there any update on Robin Friday and his one-match ban?'

'Yes, he'll miss the first league match against Gillingham, but that frees him up to play against Peterborough in the League Cup, which is a bonus. He's also getting married on August the seventh at four o'clock, so he'll miss the friendly against Charlton.'

'That must be a disappointment for you?'

'He tried looking at changing the time, but there's no chance unfortunately. He even suggested playing the first half, but that would have only given him about ten minutes to get washed, dressed and get to church, and I don't think his fiancée would appreciate her groom turning up late…that's her job, isn't it,' says Charlie, grinning.

The reporters scribble into their pads.

'Well, I think that's everything, lads. I've got to get off and make a few enquiries regarding new players.'

'Thanks for your time, Charlie.'

Charlie gets up from his seat, eager to get back to his office and shut the door.

*

Friday 23 July 1976

'Have you seen this, Robin?' asks Eamon, pointing at a newspaper. 'Go on, read it.'

Robin reads the newspaper article:

> *Last season Reading made a loss of £2,575…attendances increased from 119,999 to 172,373, which saw gate receipts grow by nearly £40,000…salaries increased by £28,507…The supporters' club raised £29,500 for the club…Mr Frank Waller said: "We've done our research on player salaries, and what we have put forward to our players is one of the best in the Third Division."*

'They're cunts. I'm not buying it, mate. I don't wanna blow my own trumpet, but I put a lot on the gates 'ere. It makes me fuckin' sick,' says Robin, shaking the newspaper in his hand.

'I don't disagree. The interesting thing for me is the amount the supporters' club raised. What an amount! Without it we'd be fucked…and you know what?'

'What?'

'In the season before I joined, they made nineteen grand profit, and guess how much the supporters' club donated?'

'Nineteen grand.'

'Spot on. Waller and that lot are living in the past. He couldn't run a piss-up in the proverbial, and what's more, he's saying it's down to the team, and that we need to go further in the cups – it's our fault.'

'Cunts. I think I'm done 'ere, Eamon. What's the point? There's no ambition, no investment – it's penny-pinching bollocks.'

'All I know is that I'm not signing that contract as it stands.'

'I'm going to hand in a transfer request. That'll wake the fuckers up, won't it,' says Robin, wagging his finger.

'Without a doubt,' says Eamon, nodding.

*

Robin talks to a local newspaper about his thoughts on Reading FC – he doesn't hold back.

*

Monday 26 July 1976

Robin walks up to Charlie Hurley's office, hovers outside, paces up and down, and knocks.

'Yes?' shouts Charlie from inside his office.

Robin opens the door, pops his head in. 'You wanted to see me, Boss?'

'Yes, take a seat,' says Charlie with a schoolmaster's face.

'Do I talk about you to the press?' he continues.

'Well, you talk to them, like, yeah.'

'What I mean is, do I talk about private matters to the press?'

'No, I suppose not.'

'You've a lot to learn, Robin. If you're pissed off, come in here and lay it out, don't go bellyaching to the press.'

'I'm pissed off. That's why I done it, and I stand by what I said.'

'The number of times I've been asked about you: did Robin do this? Did Robin do that? They'd have had a bloody field day, but I told them to fuck off. If they ever printed anything derogatory about this club, or any player, especially you, they'd not be allowed back here,' says Charlie, prodding his desk with his index finger.

'I appreciate that, but what's gone on isn't right. We got promoted, and I get a few poxy quid more?'

'At least you got a raise, I didn't.'

'Don't give me that, you're doing all right. I want what I deserve. People come 'ere to see me, you know it. Take me out of last season and you're still back in the Fourth.'

'You were brilliant, sure, but this is a team game, and don't ever forget that – you're not easy to manage you know?'

'What d'you mean?'

'Look, what I mean is, you have to be looked after. You've a lot going on outside of the game.'

'D'you want me to leave this club?'

'No, no, of course not, we need you.'

'Then get in that boardroom and fight my cause, and the other lads too. It's not right, and you know it's not.'

'I bring you in here to talk about telling tales, and I'm the one getting the bollocking,' says Charlie, laughing.

'I'm not laughing, Charlie. I'm fuckin' sick of it. Give this to Waller,' says Robin, pulling an envelope out of his pocket and throwing it onto Charlie's desk.

'What's this?' asks Charlie, looking confused.

'My transfer request,' says Robin getting up.

'Come on, don't be like that.'

'No, I'm getting married in a couple of weeks, you know, trying to move forward. We're living on tick at the fuckin' corner shop, barely surviving. I'm fuckin' better than that, Charlie.' Robin opens the door, slams it behind him, and storms down the corridor.

*

Thursday 29 July 1976

Charlie sits down, the local press in front of him.

'Is it true that Robin Friday has handed in a transfer request?'

'Yes, I can confirm that he has put in a written transfer request, and the matter will be discussed at the next board meeting,' says Charlie.

'He's not happy then?'

'Look, anything to do with Robin, or any of my players, is strictly between them and me and will remain private. Full stop,' says Charlie, eyeing his interrogators. 'Now, that's enough for today, folks,' says Charlie, getting up from his seat.

*

Saturday 31 July 1976

Robin travels to Wimbledon of the Southern League for a friendly match. The game passes him by; there's little service from midfield. When he does break, the Wimbledon defence hold their own and won't be bullied or teased into submission. At half-time, he's taken off by Charlie Hurley, and he's glad of the rest. Minty Murray scores; Minty Murray has a point to prove. The game finishes Wimbledon 0 Reading 1.

*

Monday 2 August 1976

The training ground scorches under the summer sun. The grass is as dry as hay. Tempers fray in a training match.

'You want some, Minty!' shouts Robin, rearing up on his man and grabbing him around the collar.

'Hang on, pal, you need to calm down.'

'Don't tell me to calm down, you prick, you need to.'

'Lads, lads, calm it,' says Maurice.

Maurice gets between them and pushes them back.

'Lads, take five minutes out, okay,' says Maurice, looking both men in the eyes.

'But I haven't done nothin',' says Robin.

'Go,' says Maurice, 'five minutes.'

Robin walks off the training pitch, glares across at Minty.

They get back on the pitch and Robin doesn't avoid Minty. 'I'll see you after, son,' says Robin through gritted teeth.

The players go on a run via Prospect Park…along Burghfield Road…alongside the River Kennet, which flows and sparkles in the summer sun…up Elgar Road…towards Castle Hill and back towards Elm Park.

Robin jogs at the back of the pack, eager not do too much running without a ball at his feet. They sit down for lunch at Elm Park and then go back to Prospect Park for the afternoon, for more running and sweating under the summer sun. The day finishes, and Robin pulls on his clothes.

Robin approaches Minty and says, 'I'll see you round the back, okay?' Minty nods and Robin leaves the dressing room.

Robin walks up back around Elm Park, towards his house. He waits.

Minty appears and drops his kit bag, stares at Robin, 'You ready, then?'

Robin looks at Minty and pulls a bottle out from under his sleeve, brandishes it. Minty frowns and keeps his eye on the bottle.

'I was gonna use this, but you're a mate, so let's leave it, yeah?'

Minty looks at the bottle and nods. Robin puts the bottle down on the floor.

'Is this all about some dust-up on the pitch?'

'Nah, it's all this contract bullshit. Sorry, mate, I was out of order.'

'Let's forget about it.'

'Fancy a cuppa?' asks Robin.

'Go on then, so long as you don't threaten me with a milk bottle,' says Minty, laughing.

*

Charlie Hurley's office door is like a turnstile, with players coming in and out, and they only want to talk about one thing. Charlie Hurley rubs the back of his neck and feels like he's high on a tightrope without a safety net.

*

Wednesday 4 August 1976
Bristol City, of the First Division, arrive for a friendly match at Elm Park —

A balmy evening, and the players stand out on the pitch together. The Bristol City players talk about their contracts, and they don't want to sign them either, not enough money, not enough security. Robin and the

Reading players nod, listen, but focus on the game at hand. Robin has a chance to prove himself against First Division opposition. He looks to the stands: he knows and expects scouts to be up there, looking at him.

The first half kicks off. Cumming and Dunphy run the midfield, spraying passes at will. Bristol stand off and sit deep.

Murray breaks and knocks the ball into Gary Peters on the right, who crosses a low ball, which Hiron knocks on, and Robin steps up, sees the goal, and blasts the ball over the crossbar. *Fuck.*

Minty Murray speeds around the park, knocking in shots for fun, comes close. Cumming and Dunphy keep midfield tight. They own it.

Robin walks in at half-time, down the steps and into the dressing room. The players drip with sweat and the smell of liniment fills the room.

'Right, get yourselves a drink and sit down,' says Charlie. 'We should be a couple of goals up by now, lads, at least a couple. We've a good crowd out there, eager to see how we'll cope in the Third Division. You've got to be more clinical in front of goal, Robin; I expect a lot more from you. Cumming, Dunphy and Murray, you've got the midfield sewn up, keep it that way. Now get out there and put this lot to the sword,' says Charlie, waving his team out of the dressing room.

In the fifty-fourth minute, Cumming passes to Murray, who races through and passes the ball to Robin, who casually slams the ball home into the back of the net. Robin raises his arms and salutes the crowd. He runs back to the halfway line and eyeballs Charlie Hurley. Reading 1 Bristol City 0.

After a few minutes, Robin breaks again, goes on a run, and occupies two Bristol defenders. He sends through an inch-perfect pass to Peters, who misses a sitter.

In the seventy-fourth minute, Murray breaks again and puts the ball across goal to Peters, who slams the ball into the back of the net. Reading 2 Bristol City 0.

Murray is having a stormer and is proving a point to Charlie, the board, and some of his teammates.

The final whistle blows, and it's victory. The players shake hands, and Bristol City look to be a team in turmoil. Robin goes to the stands and signs autographs, happy to chat with the fans.

*

Thursday 5 August 1976
Charlie's office —

'Boss, you got a minute?' asks Robin.

'Yes, of course,' says Charlie, feeling his neck tense up.

'So, a little bird tells me that the board have turned down my transfer request.'

'I'm not afraid to say…yes, they'd be mad to let you go,' says Charlie.

'Well, I hope they're going to put more on the table, or I won't be signing anything.'

'They'll improve it, but you'll have to keep the figure from the other players.'

'Why?'

'Because it's more than they're getting, that's why,' says Charlie, scribbling down the figure on a piece of paper and holding it up to Robin.

Robin looks at the figure and nods. 'It'll do…for now,' says Robin.

Charlie crumples up the piece of paper and throws it into his wastepaper basket.

He reaches across his desk and holds out his hand, and shakes hands with Robin. 'Glad to have you on board again,' says Charlie with a film star grin. 'I'll prepare the papers for you and get you in before your big day,' says Charlie.

'Cheers, Boss,' says Robin. 'See you tomorrow.' Robin walks out of the door, down the corridor, and into the street. He hesitates for a moment. *Where next?*

*

John 'Minty' Murray hands in a written transfer request to Charlie Hurley.

*

Friday 6 August 1976

Robin goes out in Acton with his band of London mates and drinks whatever he's given. He's given coke and snorts it in big lines, keeps him focussed and eager for more piss. He ends up in Soho and fills his boots in the bars and the clubs. Disappears from himself for a while, like. Feels like he's floating outside of himself. Gets to a mate's gaff and sinks into a chair, rolls a spliff, long and bulbous. 'This'll do us, boys,' he says, lighting it up.

He reaches into his pocket, pulls out a packet and takes out his metal pipe and snorts a small line of heroin off a table. Sits and dozes into late morning. The air is stale and stuffy. He opens a window onto a bright day, which stings his eyes. *Time to get my shit together,* he thinks.

*

Saturday 7 August 1976

On the way to the church he takes a couple of speed pills, and after a while he begins to perk up, looks at himself in the driver's mirror. *Eyes like pissholes in the snow*, he thinks.

Robin arrives outside the church; the streets throng with well-wishers and supporters who have skipped the Reading v Charlton Athletic friendly match to see their hero tie the knot. The Southern Television cameras film him. He sits down on a step in his brown velvet suit, lizard-skin patterned shirt and his Cuban heels. Shirt open. Rolls a spliff and looks up at a TV camera and smiles.

Looks at his watch, stands up, and makes his way into the church. The church is packed to the rafters with friends, family, and hangers-on. He greets them and makes his way to his seat. The congregation murmurs in anticipation. Robin's heart begins to flutter.

The organ pipes up with the 'Bridal Chorus'. He stands, takes his place, and watches Liza, veiled, a picture of beauty framed by the light shining in through the open church door. He grins, and she grins back.

She moves up alongside him, and they smile at each other and mumble their way through the service. The congregation sing their hearts out.

They say 'I do' and their union is sealed. Robin reaches in for a kiss and holds his bride tightly. They walk down the aisle and into the street. Robin steadies himself going down the steps, his legs like jelly. They pose for photographs in front of the Southern Television cameras and local press.

Robin leads his bride into the back of a white Rolls Royce and they head for the reception.

*

Watlington House, Reading —

There are speeches and smiles. A crowd of two

hundred. Someone drips some LSD into a bowl of punch. People start to giggle and stare at strange moving patterns. Elderly relatives gambol on the lawns. Wedding presents go missing and punches are thrown, tables and chairs go flying. Liza's parents, Mr and Mrs Deimel, look on with open mouths. Robin and Liza escape.

*

Honeymoon —

They race onto the plane…Robin hides cannabis resin in his mouth…arrives in Amsterdam…checks into their hotel suite…they wander the streets…Robin buys some dope…gets himself high…they go back to their room…under the sheets…they ride on a riverboat…under the Amsterdam sky…look at the ladies in the windows…laugh…smile…walk hand in hand…gaze at each other as if for the first time.

*

Wednesday 11 August 1976

Robin walks into Elm Park for training, his body aching and his mind cloudy. Dark, puffy eyes tell the story.

'Here he is. How was the honeymoon?' asks Eamon.

'I'm still there in spirit,' says Robin, smiling.

'Heavy was it?'

'Fuckin' blindin' from start to finish.'

'You ready to train?'

'If I have to, but I can't say I'm really feeling it today…you know what I mean,' says Robin, looking at the dry turf.

'It's good to have you back anyway, mate,' says Eamon.

'How's it been here?'

'You know…the usual, we've just been getting down

to it, but the contract stuff still lingers in the air like a stale fart,' says Eamon, kicking at the turf and folding his arms.

*

Thursday 12 August 1976

The Professional Footballers' Association passes a special sanction. Players who do not sign new contracts by Friday 13 August 1976 will continue on the same money as their original contracts until July 1977. Those who haven't signed are over a barrel, and they know it.

Charlie Hurley is swamped by players ready to sign on the dotted line.

*

Steve Death refuses to sign a new contract and goes on strike.

*

Saturday 14 August 1976

Elm Park, Reading v Peterborough United, League Cup, first round, first leg —

Robin breathes heavily; he needs to dig deep.

In the thirty-first minute, Minty Murray runs onto a Gary Peters' cross at the near post and throws himself at the ball, connects, and it finds the back of the net. Reading 1 Peterborough United 0. Cheers echo around the ground.

Half-time approaches, Robin is still running hard, fighting Peterborough and pushing his body. He runs with the ball, sees Peters overlap on his right and knocks it through. Peters crosses the ball, and a Peterborough defender intercepts but sends the ball across his own goal, a cardinal sin. Cumming meets it and nods it across to Robin, who races into the area and heads the ball home. Reading 2 Peterborough United 0. Robin raises his arms, sweat dripping down his face. Thanks Gary Peters and

Gordon Cumming. Salutes the fans who wave their scarves.

In the second half, Robin races onto a ball and fires a volley across goal. Clenches his fists and screams in frustration. Eamon Dunphy begins to tire, and the midfield struggle against Peterborough. The ball pings from end to end.

In the fifty-eighth minute, Peterborough race into the area and Peters takes out their ball carrier. The referee points to the spot. The Reading defenders surround the referee but he sends them away. Peterborough score and there is a small cheer from their supporters. Reading 2 Peterborough United 1.

Reading kick off. Robin with the ball at his feet, winds, teases his way through the Peterborough defence, passes one, two, three, and lets a shot go, but it flies just wide of the goal. *Fuck it.* He shakes his head, looks at the ground, then at the sky.

In the sixty-second minute, Charlie Hurley substitutes Eamon Dunphy for Dennis Nelson. Eamon leaves the field with brooding eyes and fire in his belly; he shakes his head and goes down the steps to the dressing room. Kicks his boots off. Seethes.

Reading win a corner and Hiron is pushed at the near post; he appeals, and Robin screams at the referee. Murray is brought down and Reading take a quick free kick. Murray shoots, and the ball deflects to Robin, who puts it away, raises his arms, and screams: 'Yes!' The referee disallows it. 'Are you joking?' asks Robin. The referee ushers Robin away.

In the eighty-second minute, Peterborough win a corner and send the ball in. It's headed out to a Peterborough player and a shot rockets in from twenty yards and ripples the back of the net. Reading 2 Peterborough United 2.

'For fuck's sake,' screams Robin. 'Come on, lads.'

In the eighty-sixth minute, Robin is scythed from behind, but the referee waves for play to continue. 'Sort it out, Ref,' says Robin into the referee's face.

'I beg your pardon?' asks the referee.

'I said sort it out. We'd be winning this if it weren't for you,' he says, spittle flying from his lips. The referee books Robin. His blood boils at the injustice, and he is held back and shepherded away by Cumming.

Peterborough sense Reading's panic and they keep pressing Reading's defensive line. The Reading fans stand with fingers crossed. Hold their breath. Peterborough race forward and get through into the area. A Peterborough player gets one on one with Turner, who tries to snatch the ball from the player's feet, but he can't get it, loses it, and the player looks up and passes it to his teammate, who tucks it away from six yards out. There's a stunned silence from the Reading fans. Reading 2 Peterborough United 3. The Peterborough fans roar.

Robin's head drops, and they're forced to kick off, only for the inevitable final whistle to blow up. Long faces are glum in the summer sun.

'That's a fuckin' kick in the teeth,' says Minty.

'We'll get them back at their place. At least we won't have that cunt,' says Robin, looking at the man in black.

*

Wednesday 18 August 1976
London Road, Peterborough United v Reading, League Cup, first round, second leg —

Clothes off. Reading shirt on. Shorts on…touches

them…wishes them good luck.

'Come on, lads,' screams Robin.

In the first half, the forward line of Murray, Hiron and Robin press on Peterborough. Robin and Minty torment them with runs. Robin dances at his best, dummies, shimmies and makes a nuisance of himself. Peterborough attack, but they bottle it in front of goal. In the twenty-fifth minute, Carmichael passes the ball, and Robin crashes in from behind, studs up, and sends Carmichael sprawling. The referee barks at Robin, telling him to calm down.

'What about them?' asks Robin.

'Don't answer me back. You were out of order there. Calm it down or you're off, got it?'

Robin nods and gives his name, and the referee puts it into his little black book.

Robin is hammered by Lee and Carmichael of Peterborough but doesn't back down.

At half-time, Robin sits sucking on half an orange. Charlie approaches. 'Robin, we need you…you know I don't need to tell you that was bloody reckless.'

'I know, I know…I fuckin' lost it. Those bastards have kicked me to ribbons.'

Charlie drops down to his haunches, level with Robin. 'You know what I always say, Robin…score, it's the only way to get back at them,' says Charlie, patting Robin on the thigh.

The second half kicks off, and Robin and Reading come out with the bit between their teeth. Peters crosses to Hiron, who knocks the ball onto Robin, who shoots wide from eight yards out. He breathes in. *Fuck.* Carmichael and Lee glare at him. At every opportunity, they kick him, and Robin gives it back in spades, kicks them and punches them. Makes them know that they're playing with Robin Friday. He leaves his mark on them.

In the sixty-eighth minute, Cumming and Peters knock a one-two, and Peters pushes through a crisp ball to Hiron, who flicks the ball over his head onto Murray. Murray belts in a shot but the keeper blocks, and the ball falls to Robin, who flicks the ball through the keeper's legs and into the net. Robin throws his arms into the air, mocks his foes with a laugh. Cheers ring out from Reading's travelling fans. Minty, Peters, Cumming and Hiron surround him and ruffle his hair, pat his back. 'Fucking some nutmeg, eh?' says Robin.

'Outrageous,' says Hiron, laughing. Peterborough 0 Reading 1.

Peterborough come in waves to pull one back, but they can't do it. It finishes Peterborough 3 Reading 3 on aggregate. There will be a replay.

*

Thursday 19 August 1976

'Two games, two goals, two bookings, Robin,' says Charlie.

'I know…consistent, aren't I…like you always say.'

'They're out to get you, you know, and it'll keep happening, so you've got to protect yourself. Keep yourself fit, eat properly, and make sure you don't retaliate.'

'We've seen it before, though. I'm not protected by the refs. Players can kick me around the pitch and I can't do nothin' back, but when I do, the inevitable happens, and here I am, again.'

'You've got to manage it, manage yourself, but you're no good to me banned, because if it happens again they'll throw the book at you, and it'll be a three-match ban and a heavy fine,' says Charlie.

'Talking of fines, I owe you a tenner, don't I?'

'Yes, two bookings at a fiver each.'

'I'll give it you tomorrow out of my wages.'

'Fair enough. Just look after yourself. I'm worried about you.'

'Why?'

'Listen, you're a professional footballer, so live like one. This is a small town, and people talk.'

'Gossiping slags is what they are,' says Robin. 'Can I go now?'

'You're a free man.'

Robin leaves, and on his way out he bumps into Eamon. 'All right, Eamon?'

'Yeah, all good, catch up with you in a bit,' he says, heading into Charlie's office.

*

Eamon appears and looks like he's seen a ghost.

'What's up, mate?' asks Robin.

'I've just had a bust-up with Charlie.'

'You what?'

'Yeah, he went for me, and I'm up on a free.'

'A free transfer? Fuck, what did you do?'

'I told him that he should've backed the players in the contract dispute. He grabbed me by the scruff of the neck and had me up the wall and told me he was putting me up for a free transfer. I told him that didn't bother me as he'd probably get sacked before I left anyway.'

'What are you gonna do, mate?'

'I'll start looking at other options, but before then it looks like I'll be rotting in the reserves.'

Robin sighs. ‘Fancy a few pints later, my shout?’

‘Yeah, it’ll help with the fucking shock, man.’

*

Friday 20 August 1976

‘They’ve had the draw for the League Cup, lads,’ says Charlie.

‘Go on then, tell us,’ shouts Robin.

‘If we beat Peterborough, we’ll play Fulham at Craven Cottage,’ says Charlie. ‘But we’ve the small matter of Gillingham tomorrow. We’ve no Robin because of the suspension, so Dennis will take his place. Now go and get yourselves rested.’

*

Saturday 21 August 1976

Reading travel to Gillingham on the bus. Robin lies in bed, thankful of the rest, his legs cut and bruised, his knees sore and aching from the Peterborough games.

Steve Death refuses to get out of bed. He still hasn’t signed a contract. John Turner is injured and can’t play.

‘Where is Deathie?’ asks Charlie. He looks at his watch.

‘We’ve got to go…right now,’ says Maurice.

‘Turner can’t play, he just can’t,’ says Charlie. ‘Someone’ll have to get Deathie; he’s got to play, no choice, and if he fucks about, tell him we’ll fine him.’

A local journalist pulls Death from his bed and drives him to Gillingham. Death plays out of his skin. The match finishes Gillingham 2 Reading 2. Death saves Reading a point.

*

Wednesday 25 August 1976
London Road, Peterborough United v Reading, League Cup, first round replay —

Clothes off. Reading shirt on. Shorts on…touches them…wishes them good luck.

The whistle blows, and Peterborough come straight out of the blocks. A glamour game against Fulham is at stake. Robin gets stuck in with his elbows and Peterborough retaliate. Robin is scythed down and kicked.

In the thirteenth minute, Ray Hiron pulls up, holding his hamstring, and Dennis Nelson replaces him. Charlie has no more substitutes.

Reading look desperate in midfield, and Dave Moreline is moved to the centre of the park to calm things. Still they battle on. Tackles rain in, high, hard and direct. Minty Murray holds his elbow, leaves the field for treatment, and is booked by the referee. The Peterborough defence kick at Reading, they kick at Robin every time he's on the ball, they kick his ankles, kick his knees. They try to stop him in his tracks.

In the thirty-seventh minute, Peterborough score, and it's Peterborough United 1 Reading 0. Reading go in at half-time with cuts and bruises and Maurice gets busy with the first aid.

'This isn't right, Charlie, look at them,' says Maurice. Charlie looks around at the cuts and the bruises, helps Maurice patch them up.

In the second half, the assault continues, and Reading try to fight back. Steve Hetzke is booked for a foul on Ernie Moss. Robin screams. Charlie Hurley yells at the referee. *The injustice.*

Steve Hetzke is given a battering and holds his eye but

limps on. The referee turns a blind eye.

In the eighty-first minute, Reading win a corner. Stuckey sends the ball into the box. Cumming shoots, and a defender blocks the shot. The ball falls, and Minty Murray dashes for it, pushing Gary Peters out of the way, and kicks the ball into the net. He turns and runs, cheering. Peterborough United 1 Reading 1.

The minutes tick towards full-time, and Peterborough United come again, and again, but the final whistle blows. There will be thirty minutes extra time.

Charlie and Maurice leave their bench and walk out onto the pitch. The Reading players sink to the ground. Bruised and battered. Battered and bruised. Cut and sliced. Sliced and cut. Charlie Hurley looks at his men, Maurice Evans sees to the knocks and cuts and tries in vain to patch them up. 'Lads, it's up to you now, you've earnt yourself extra time. Just keep fighting,' says Charlie.

'This referee is a bastard,' says Robin.

Charlie nods. 'Then show him up by putting these lot away.'

The first half of extra time begins. Peterborough advance, and in the sixth minute they score with an overhead kick. Peterborough United 2 Reading 1. The home crowd cheer and Robin looks on in anger.

Robin picks up a ball from Cumming and runs, and he receives a kick to the knee, again. The same knee. He tries to run it off. In the thirteenth minute of extra time, Dave Moreline has the ball at his feet and is hammered in a tackle; he goes over on his ankle, groans in pain and is carried off the pitch. Reading are down to ten men.

The first half of extra time comes to an end. Charlie and Maurice run on with the water and sponges. 'Robin, are you okay to carry on?' asks Charlie.

'Fuck 'em, I can't leave you with nine men,' says Robin, nursing his swollen red knee. His shins are scratched and bloody.

Reading limp out for the second half of extra time, Robin can't run and pushes on the Peterborough backline. Steve Hetzke can't run but tries. Reading fight. Robin fights. In the final minute of extra time, Peterborough win a free kick and Ernie Moss scores. Peterborough United 3 Reading 1. Reading's hopes of making the second round disappear. Robin limps from the pitch. There are false pleasantries between Peterborough and Reading. After three hundred minutes of Peterborough United, Robin and Reading are sick of Peterborough United.

*

Wolverhampton Wanderers phone Charlie Hurley; they want to know all about Robin Friday. They've heard things, some good, some not so good, but they want to know more.

*

Thursday 26 August 1976

The smell of liniment and smoke fills the room —

Jimmy Wallbanks, fag in mouth, rubs Robin's legs, manipulates his knee. 'It's like Battle Hospital in 'ere today, ain't it, Jimmy,' says Robin, looking at a room full of Peterborough's victims. Ray Hiron sits with his leg up, Dave Moreline with his ankle bandaged, Steve Hetzke with a shiner and a dead leg.

'It is, and they'll have to pay me bloody overtime with you lot today. I'm meant to be retired. You'll live though,' says Jimmy, laughing.

‘I’ll be fine, but this lot ain’t looking too good, are they?’

‘Piss off,’ says Moreline with a smile.

‘Peterborough didn’t hold back, did they, and not a single booking either,’ says Jimmy.

‘I reckon the ref was in their back pocket. Otherwise they’d have had at least one booking, surely?’

‘Well, let’s be fair, lad, it’s a miracle they didn’t book you. You weren’t exactly subtle,’ says Jimmy, pushing and pulling Robin’s leg.

‘Serves ’em right, though, eh?’

Charlie Hurley sweeps in. ‘Bloody hell, boys, I’ve never seen it so full in here. How’s it looking, Jimmy?’

‘Robin’s doubtful, so are the others. Maybe Steve will be all right, but that’s it I’m afraid.’

Charlie sighs. ‘At this fucking rate we’ll be playing Shrewsbury with our reserves.’

‘Boss, I’ll be all right, honest,’ says Robin.

‘But your knee?’ says Charlie, pointing.

‘I’ll be okay, trust me. Jimmy’ll give me an injection.’

‘You’re a trooper, kid, a real trooper,’ says Charlie, patting him on the shoulder.

*

Robin takes his own personal painkillers – Diconal, for his knee, and not just for his knee. He feels like he’s got fluffy pink cotton wool around his head and around his knee.

*

Saturday 28 August 1976

Robin travels with the team to Shrewsbury Town. On the bus he’s quiet and hopes his knee will hold out. He pops a couple of Diconal.

Robin takes his place on the pitch and waits for the

whistle. The referee blows and the game starts. He knows that today he'll have to change his game, adapt because of his knee. Robin runs, shouts for the ball, screams for the ball. He looks for teammates and passes perfect balls.

In the fifth minute, Robin traps the ball, and as he goes to turn, he feels his legs go from underneath him. He feels pain sear down the back of his legs and crashes to the floor. He holds his knee and looks up at the referee. The Shrewsbury player's name goes into the book: Atkins. Robin slams his fist into the hard turf, gets to his feet, and tries to walk off the ache. He gets back into the battle. Robin toils up front, lays on passes, passes that should result in goals, but Reading don't take their chances.

In the sixty-sixth minute, Minty Murray leaves the field and is replaced by Eamon Dunphy. The final whistle blows, and it finishes Shrewsbury Town 2 Reading 0.

In the late summer sun, the team bus moves along back to Elm Park, through the highways and byways.

Robin sits on the bus and joins in with the card school, drinks his beer, and starts to feel his knee throb.

Eamon sits next to Robin, the world moving by outside. 'He doesn't know what he's doing, you know,' says Eamon, nodding towards the front of the bus, where Charlie is deep in conversation with Maurice.

'Do any of us?' says Robin, sighing.

'Well, after today, maybe only a few of us do,' says Eamon, looking daggers at the back of Charlie's head.

'Well, I suppose he's brought you on today to shore up the middle of the park, to try and repair burnt bridges…think of it that way.'

'No, for fuck's sake, he's brought me back into the fold because he's fucked, and we're fucked,' says Eamon, with a harsh whisper.

'Well he's desperate, isn't he, we've injuries,' says Robin, laughing.

'You cheeky bastard, but yes, you're right,' says Eamon, laughing and nodding. 'Why the hell do we do this?'

'To play football, man, cos it sure ain't for the fuckin' money or security, is it?'

'Yep, we're only ever a bloody payslip or serious injury away from disaster. Look at me. I'm on the transfer list, on the periphery of the first team…not looking too good, eh?'

'A new club might be a good idea, a new start, that's what I'm starting to think. There's fuck all 'ere, no ambition, and I'd like to win something one day,' says Robin, looking at trees, which blur as the bus speeds along.

'Yes, no fucking ambition, no investment; Reading's arse has fallen out the back of its trousers, and we're the ones tasked to try and pull them up again with this threadbare squad, and, Maurice aside, fuck all leadership off the pitch.' Eamon seethes with bitterness.

'I got something to fix us up for a short while,' says Robin, reaching into his jacket pocket. ''Ere, take one of these…you'll feel much better.' Robin hands a speed pill to Eamon.

'Don't mind if I do, thanks,' he says, popping the pill into his mouth.

'That'll sort us out. Let's get another beer…oh, and no more football talk,' says Robin, with a wry smile.

Then there are giggles, faster talking, the speed making things seems brighter.

*

Robin sits and listens to his records. They stand pristine on a shelf. He takes them out of the sleeve carefully and places them onto his record player, sets the speed to 45 rpm, moves the arm and watches the record drop.

Robin takes the powder and sets it up in the tinfoil, pops a metal pipe into his mouth, flicks the lighter and sucks in the wisps of smoke. Places the tinfoil on the table, puts the pipe next to it. Sits and listens to his records. Sits and listens to Janis Joplin belt her heart out. Robin lies back and closes his eyes and feels like he's floating up out of himself, away from the physical pain, and away from any thoughts of worry. Worry slides away and slips out through the back of his mind.

*

Saturday 4 September 1976

Third Division football arrives at Elm Park. Expectation fills the air, and Walsall are the visitors. A team stocked with former winners: Mick Bates, Alun Evans.

He goes to his usual spot in the dressing room. Clothes off. Reading shirt on. Shorts on…touches them…wishes them good luck.

Reading need something, two games in and no wins. The pressure is on.

In the third minute, Reading win a penalty, and Murray puts the spot kick away, into the back of the net. Reading 1 Walsall 0. Cheers and claps echo around Elm Park.

In the fifth minute, Robin receives a ball and charges forward, and sets up Nelson, who nails the ball at the goal, but the keeper stretches and parries the ball away.

Walsall begin to show their class and start to press on Reading's backline, and in the eighteenth minute, Walsall equalise. Red-and-white scarves wave in the air as the Walsall fans make themselves known. Reading 1 Walsall 1.

Robin tries to get away from the shadow that follows him. A Walsall defender who won't let him out of his sight. Robin's knee gives him gyp, limits his game. Digging deep, he manages to trick his shadow and breaks free from invisible shackles. He moves to the byeline and sends in a cross, which Bruce Stuckey just misses, and with it a chance for Reading to take the lead again.

In the second half, Walsall start to dominate the middle of the park. Eamon and Alun Evans get stuck into each other; they fight for the middle of the park.

In the fifty-fifth minute, Alun Evans and Eamon clash in a tackle, and Eamon sees red. He runs up at Evans and they clash heads. Evans pushes Eamon and punches him. They scuffle. The referee books Evans. Eamon waits for his turn, but the referee doesn't book him. Evans protests and Eamon walks away, knowing he's won this one.

Nelson runs after a loose ball, and the keeper panics and comes off his line and chases Nelson, who knocks the ball to Robin. Robin sweeps the ball around and eyes the goal. From thirty-five yards Robin hits a perfect chip which heads towards the goal, but a Walsall defender with eager hands slaps the ball away. Penalty. Murray steps up and powers the ball straight at the keeper, and the ball ricochets in off the keeper's leg and hits the back of the net. READ–ING, READ–ING, READ–ING are the chants from the crowd. Reading 2 Walsall 1. Death saves shot after shot, and Death saves the day. Death is back, and Robin watches him. Reading win another penalty, but Murray misses.

Walsall control the game but can't catch a break. Reading have all the luck. The game ends Reading 2 Walsall 1. Robin breathes a sigh of relief but knows his team are struggling. Head down, he walks off the pitch and knows that he's struggling too. Frustration sits on his shoulders like a monkey, making minor seem major.

*

Wednesday 8 September 1976
Elm Park, Reading v Wrexham —

He goes to his usual spot in the dressing room. Clothes off. Reading shirt on. Shorts on…touches them…wishes them good luck.

A gang of scouts from Arsenal, Fulham, QPR, Sheffield United, Spurs, and West Ham United watch Robin from the stands.

'I'm fuckin' up for this,' says Robin, pumping his legs.

The game kicks off, and Reading pass and move, taking Wrexham by surprise. The Reading crowd clap and cheer their team on. The smell of pipe smoke fills the evening air. Wrexham can't get into the game, the pace and quick movement forcing them into a reactive panic. The ball pings from Reading player to Reading player.

In the fifteenth minute, Youlden picks up the ball and passes it onto Murray, who flicks it into Robin's path, and from eighteen yards, he kicks it like a mule and sends the volley into the top left-hand corner, leaving the keeper no chance. The crowd scream for their terrace hero. He raises his arms, runs to Minty and thanks him, and gives a thumbs up to Tommy Youlden. Reading 1 Wrexham 0.

In the twenty-fifth minute, Gary Peter's breaks and goes around two Wrexham defenders. Robin screams for a pass. Peters chips the ball, and Robin takes the ball around a Wrexham defender, looks at goal, puts his head down and strikes the ball hard. The ball hits the post. Robin looks on with frustration, but the ball rebounds and Nelson sticks it into the back of the net. Reading 2 Wrexham 0. Robin, Gary and Dennis celebrate with the fans. The fans chant: CHARLIE HURLEY'S BLUE-AND-WHITE ARMY, CHARLIE HURLEY'S BLUE-AND-WHITE ARMY!

With a two-goal lead, Reading begin to relax a little, and with that, Wrexham start to press, and they force corner after corner, forcing Death to make save after save, but Reading hold on. Death is outstanding. He's back and saving Reading. The game finishes Reading 2 Wrexham 0.

Robin beams with confidence, and he goes to the fans and signs autographs.

'You're not leaving are you, Robin?' asks a kid.

'Nah, teams are interested, like, but I'm 'ere ain't I.'

'Yeah, and we don't want you to go, okay!' says another kid, pushing himself through the crowd towards Robin, holding out his programme and a pen.

Robin smiles. 'Cheers, I appreciate it,' he says, signing a programme. He signs and signs. Then, finishing up, he looks at his fans and says, 'Stay cool, and look after yourselves.' He walks away waving. Smiling faces beam back at him.

*

Manchester United are interested in Steve Death. Bristol City are interested in Gary Peters. Wolverhampton Wanderers and West Bromwich Albion and a host of clubs are interested in Robin. Players start to dream of bigger and better things. Robin wants a team in London. He wants to go home.

*

Saturday 11 September 1976

Robin, wearing a leather jacket, walks out onto the Northampton Town pitch for a pre-match amble with Charlie and the team. He pulls on a fag, remembers his debut here. *Ran them ragged I did, we was robbed that day: 3–3.* He looks up and sees the lads standing around inspecting the pitch.

'Look at the state of this,' says Eamon, digging his heel into the dry turf. 'It's like a bloody dust bowl. Look at the cracks…there, there and there.'

Charlie glares at Eamon. 'Never mind that, we've a game to win, and we know what this lot did to us last time, four-bloody-one, but this is a new division, and we're a different team. What we know is this ball is going to bounce high, so let's keep it on the deck like we did against Wrexham. You're good enough to beat anyone in this division.'

In the dressing room there's chatter, laughs, and quiet expectation. Nerves jangle. Robin starts his ritual: clothes off. Reading shirt on. Shorts on…touches them…wishes them good luck.

'Come on, lads, let's fuckin' do this,' he roars. There's a fizz of electricity in the room. Studs click-clack on the floor. Players stretch.

The referee knocks on the door and beckons the Reading team out. Cumming leads them out onto the pitch. Cheers, jeers, whistles and claps come from the fans. Robin feels a shiver run down his spine. He looks across at the Northampton players, recognises some and clenches his teeth.

The first half kicks off, and a ball is sent through to a

Northampton defender who, seeing Robin bearing down on him, clears it in panic, but Robin flies in and sends the defender sprawling into the hard turf. The defender holds his leg and moans. Robin holds out his hands as the ref runs up to him, Robin's face pleading. Robin helps the Northampton defender up, but he pushes Robin's hand away and gets to his feet. 'Sorry, mate,' says Robin. The Northampton defender ignores him and walks away, gingerly.

'That tackle was late. You need to calm down. Another one like that and you're off,' says the ref, taking out his black book.

'It wasn't intentional, honest,' says Robin with his hands on his hips.

'It doesn't have to be, it was reckless,' says the ref. 'Name?'

'Robin Friday.'

The ref peers around and notes Robin's number: nine.

In the eighth minute, Eamon brings down a Northampton striker, and the ref puts his name in the book. Eamon walks away, blood boiling.

Northampton start to apply pressure, they start to test Death in goal, but Death is on point today, and he flies through the air, catching balls left and right. Northampton keep coming, and Reading are penned into their own half, forced to defend.

In the eighteenth minute, Northampton send in a hard driving shot. Death watches it ready to collect, but the ball hits a Northampton player's leg and ricochets in, leaving Death to watch the ball go in. Death kicks the post. The Northampton crowd clap and cheer, waving their claret-and-white scarves. Northampton Town 1 Reading 0.

'Jammy bastards,' says Robin as he walks back to the halfway line for the restart. He's ready to fight.

Northampton come again and again. Death keeping them at bay. Reading forced to wait for a counter-attack.

'Come on lads, we fuckin' need some service,' shouts Robin.

On the stroke of half-time, Robin takes the ball, goes direct and runs at the Northampton defence, who panic. Murray runs, and Robin hears his call and passes the ball inside to him. Murray belts the ball at goal; it's blocked but comes back to him, so he takes another strike and it's blocked again, but this time it falls to Stuckey, who sticks it home. Northampton Town 1 Reading 1. There's jubilation, and the Reading fans wave their blue-and-white scarves. Minty Murray, Stuckey and Robin congratulate each other. The whistle blows for half-time.

Robin makes his way to the dressing room, grabs an orange, sucks on it, and throws it to the floor. Picks up a cup of sweet tea and slurps at it. Sits down on the bench with the other players.

Charlie says, 'Lads, get sat down, come on now. Well, that was a very positive finish to the first half. In midfield we're better than them, so start bossing it, you've got to work your bloody bollocks off. Eamon, start putting your foot on the ball and control it, Robin and Dennis need more service. Let's teach these bastards a lesson. Get out there and put them away!'

'Come on then,' says Robin. They buzz with energy and take it out onto the pitch for the second half.

Reading buzz like bees, and Northampton can't keep up with the pace. In the fifty-second minute, Murray steams down the wing, flies past the full back, and cracks a beauty which goes straight into the back of the net. Northampton Town 1 Reading 2.

'Fuckin' yes, Minty,' says Robin, running up and grabbing Minty around the shoulders. READ–ING, READ–ING, READ–ING.

Dunphy, Cumming, and Stuckey run their socks off, and Northampton are out of the game. Eamon puts a foot on the ball and passes at will, perfect and direct, dream balls. But in the final minutes, Northampton come back fighting, eager to try and get something out of the game. Northampton shoot and Death saves; Northampton come again, and Death saves. Death is having a blinder. The match finishes Northampton 1 Reading 2.

Robin sits in the bath, and they listen to the results coming in on the radio. Reading are in fifth place in Division Three. Robin and the lads chatter and thoughts turn to the night's festivities and the next game: Peterborough United, again.

Robin gets off the bus early, tells the lads to say whatever they need to say to Liza. He takes a pill and goes to The Boar's Head.

Liza waits for him at Elm Park. She watches the players coming off the bus, one by one, but there's no Robin.

'Where's Robin?' she asks Minty Murray.

'I dunno, love, he got off the bus earlier at a service station. He didn't really say where he was going,' says Minty.

'He's pissed off again, the bastard. I'm sick of this,' she says, tears welling up in her eyes.

'He'll turn up, you know what he's like. He just disappears,' says Minty with sympathy in his eyes.

‘It’s what the bastard is doing when he disappears that worries me.’ She shakes her head and walks away.

*

Sunday 12 September 1976

In the early hours —

Robin walks hand in hand with a woman from the dance floor. Disappears into a cupboard. Pulls at clothes and unzips his fly, and there’s heavy breathing. There’s no guilt, not now, that can wait.

He walks home down the Oxford Road, and past Elm Park and back home to his flat. Robin takes his key out, puts it into the lock, and turns it. In he walks, trying to be quiet, trying to steady himself down the hallway. He hears a thump, and a light flicks on in his bedroom, their bedroom.

The door swings open, and Liza stands in her nightdress, arms folded. ‘Where the hell have you been?’

‘I’ve been out, having a few drinks and celebrating a win, like,’ says Robin.

‘Don’t give me your crap. I stood waiting for you. We were meant to go out.’

‘We’ll go out tomorrow, go to the cinema and get some food, honest. Look, I’m sorry…I got carried away.’

She shakes her head. ’Why do you feel it necessary to humiliate me? Why?’

‘I don’t. I’m sorry, Liza, I’m sorry.’ He goes to hold her and she tries to push him away, but he pulls her towards him.

‘You stink,’ she says, looking up at him, squirming in his arms.

‘I’ve ’ad a few, ain’t I,’ says Robin, looking down at her.

'You must think I'm fucking stupid. I can smell perfume, you bastard, you dirty pig. My mother warned me,' says Liza, trying to wriggle out of his arms, finally pushing him away. He falls back, unsteady on his feet.

'Don't be daft, you're overreacting,' says Robin, a glare in his eye.

'You can sleep on the settee. I don't want you near me tonight,' she says.

'Next time I'll go out and have a little fun of my own,' she says.

'You what?'

'You heard. I'll go out and won't come back and see how you bloody like it.'

Robin's face changes from defence to attack, and he frowns with hard eyes. 'Don't you fuckin' dare try and fuckin' wind me up, don't you dare.' Anger swells. 'You can sleep on your fuckin' own for all I care. I've had a few drinks with the lads, that's all. Now fuck off.' He turns and goes to the living room, opens the door and slams it behind him.

Liza thinks better of winding him up when he's like this. Her guts squirm with anger, and she goes back to the bedroom, slams the door.

*

The sun rises. The front door slams shut, waking Robin. He doesn't bother to get up; he knows she's gone to her parents. His head is sore and his body aching. He reaches for his tin of junk, but there's nothing there; the bag is empty. He rolls a spliff and makes a cup of tea. But this won't take the edge off. Guilt comes in sharp spikes with his thoughts from last night, makes him curse out loud.

'Just fuck off,' he repeats, but the thoughts won't go.

As the day progresses, he starts to feel unwell, starts to get junk sick. Needs to get junk, but he knows he needs to pack the shit in, stop it before it becomes a habit. Chipping is one thing, a habit is quite another. *This is not a game any more.*

*

Monday 13 September 1976

Robin lies in bed, sweats buckets, alone. Liza hasn't returned. He craves junk, would do anything for a hit to make him feel well again.

The doorbell rings. Robin looks at his watch and knows who it is. Knows it's Charlie, come to ask where he is, and why he's not at training with the rest of the team. Robin pulls himself up. Looks at himself in Liza's mirror. Sees the dark rings around his eyes, sees his pasty face. His hair a greasy mess. Pulls on a T-shirt and Y-fronts. The doorbell rings again.

He walks down the hallway and sees Charlie through the frosted glass. A tall shadow, waiting.

Robin opens the door. Charlie stands there, and for a moment he freezes as he sees the state of his star striker.

'Robin, you okay? You don't look well at all,' says Charlie, frowning.

'I think I've got the flu, Boss, and my chest is playing up too,' says Robin.

'Right, so you'll not be able to make the trip to Peterborough then?'

'No, I don't think so, Boss, I'm sorry,' he says.

'Okay, we'll miss you, but if you're ill you're ill, so that can't be helped. Just look after yourself, and we'll see you in a few days.'

'Right, yeah, no problem.'

'Take care, Robin,' says Charlie, turning away.

'Yeah, you too. Good luck against Peterborough.'

Robin closes the front door and breathes a heavy sigh of relief, leans back against the wall, his stomach cramping and his legs weak.

Charlie walks down Tilehurst Road, back towards Elm Park. Rubs his chin, and thinks that something isn't quite right with his *man*, Friday.

*

Tuesday 14 September 1976

He lies in bed amongst the sweaty sheets. He smells Liza's scent in the bed, and in the room. Tears well up in his eyes, his heart bruised. His thoughts turn in on him. *You stupid, stupid cunt. What were you thinking? Your second marriage, eh? Five fuckin' minutes you've been married, and you're back to your old ways. Max and Nicola, eh? Shall we go there, you seen your little girl lately? She's growing up without you there, without your help.*

'Fuck off, just fuck off!' he shouts into the empty room.

I need to get out of 'ere, get out of fuckin' Reading, sort myself out – make it right with Liza. A new club back in London and a fresh start. A new beginning.

The doorbell rings, and he ignores it. He doesn't want to speak to anyone today. He wishes he was back in London, and he wishes he didn't have a club flat that's two minutes from Elm Park.

It's all about keeping you like a performing monkey. Don't worry, we'll pay your bills, we'll give you a flat. When we need you, we know where to find you; when you don't turn up, we'll know where you are. Here's a few quid to keep you in food and beer money, not too much because we don't want you to be too independent, we want you to rely on us, depend on us. We want you, and when you're of no further use, we'll show you the door. It's all bullshit!

The drugs and the problems, the problems and the drugs —

The drugs…oh, how he pines for the drugs with every sinew, with every fuckin' pleasure receptor: the highs and the lows, the lows and the highs. He pulls himself into a foetal position, clenches his knees, and rides a rollercoaster of madness.

In the evening, and into the night, he can't turn his mind off and can't get away from himself. He's here, and so are his problems.

He turns on the radio and waits for the football results: Peterborough United 2 Reading 1. Imagines the team bus coming back through the roads and the lanes. The team stopping for food and a quick pint at a pub. He can see it as clear as day. Some of the lads quiet, some loud, angry in defeat, but together. Robin feels a veil of loneliness fall down upon him, as light as a spider's web. Its effects are heavy, brooding, pointing out that he is all alone, here, now, in this world. He turns off the radio, and there's silence, apart from the cars which pass down Tilehurst Road. How he wishes he was in one of those cars taking a journey out of here, but he knows getting away from himself is a different matter.

*

He goes to Liza's parents and begs for her to return. Tells her it'll all be all right, and that he'll speak to Charlie, and that things will change for the better. Liza returns.

*

Thursday 16 September 1976

Robin returns to training. Eamon, Minty and Death welcome him back. Some of the other players look at him with questions in their eyes.

'How're you feeling?' asks Maurice.

'I'm still not one hundred per cent, but it'd be good to be back for Saturday.'

Maurice looks at him and nods.

Robin trains, but he's slower, his touch not great today. He sweats, his hair soaking. He reaches for his inhaler and takes a break, watches the game from the sidelines.

'Robin,' says Charlie.

Robin turns and sees Charlie. 'All right, Boss.'

'I'm okay, Robin. We missed you against Peterborough. You're still not looking too good, kid. Can we have a word in my office after this session?'

'What about?'

'Fitness.'

'Yeah, sure.' A look of puzzlement comes over his face. 'I'll see you in a bit after I've finished 'ere.'

Charlie walks away, and Robin gets back into training. He struggles his way through and is off the pace, his stomach in knots and his legs weak.

*

He knocks on Charlie's door and pops his head into the room.

'Boss…' says Robin.

'Robin, in you come, sit down, please.'

Charlie fiddles with his papers and his pens, makes sure they're neat and tidy.

'I need to talk to you, and this isn't going to be an easy conversation. As you know, I'll always tell you the truth because that works for both of us, and that's what I believe works in general. Look, I want to talk about *you*.'

'What about *me*?'

'You finished last season as bright as can be, no one could touch you. Now, I've watched you closely this season, and your touch is off, you've lost some pace, you pass the ball in the box when before you'd shoot, and score. This is the Third Division, there are fewer long balls, no hit and hope, and there are some really tasty teams. As we've seen, we go two goals up and they come back fighting, they don't roll over like teams did in the Fourth.'

'So you're saying I've lost it?' says Robin, folding his arms.

'I'm saying that you're not playing as well as you did last season. You're not in anywhere near the same condition as you were, and Maurice agrees with me. Look at you, look at this last week,' says Charlie with concern.

'I had a row with Liza, and it sort of got out of hand, but she's back now and it'll be fine.'

'I'm glad to hear that, but there's more to it than that, and you know that too.'

'What do you mean?'

'The *drugs*, Robin,' says Charlie, watching Robin's face.

Robin shifts in his chair and clears his throat, and says, 'What d'you mean, *drugs*?'

'You know what I mean, Robin. I wouldn't be doing my job if I didn't have a fair idea of what my players got up to outside Elm Park.'

Robin blows out his cheeks and sighs. 'I dunno what to say.'

'This is a very small town compared to London, and you're a big fish in a small pond, and people talk, they gossip.'

'Has someone grassed on me?' asks Robin, looking offended.

'People talk, and I know that you're using drugs.'

'It's nothing I can't handle. I've been doing them since I was a kid.'

'You're not a kid any more, are you; you're a professional footballer, your livelihood depends on maintaining a certain level of fitness. You have a commitment to me, this club, not to mention yourself, your wife and family.'

'I'm as good as any of them out there on that pitch, no matter what I'm doing.'

'They're not your measure, you're in a different class. *When. You. Are. Fit.* At the moment you're not, not anywhere near what I expect of you.'

'So, you're saying I'm not the player I was then?'

'Correct, you're not, nowhere near it, and we know why. Four league games and one goal. You came in a few weeks ago demanding more money, so we gave it to you. You went to the newspapers about how this club didn't have any ambition. So, my question now is…where is *your* ambition?'

'I still want to make it, but I know I'm worth more than the poxy money I'm being paid 'ere.'

'No, my question was where is *your* ambition? Because it seems to me that you've lost your focus. I think you're being pulled in the wrong direction.'

'Oh, fuck off, will you, I've had enough,' says Robin, jumping out of his chair and heading for the door. He slams it shut, leaves Elm Park and goes home.

Charlie clenches his teeth and sighs. Robin Friday runs kicking and screaming through his mind. Man Friday is adrift.

*

Friday 17 September 1976

The first team play five-a-side, and Robin chases the ball and puts himself about.

Charlie joins the game, his positional sense still solid, and he has a good touch. Charlie loves to play and wishes he could still do it at a decent level, but the legs are now slower.

Maurice refs the game, and as usual, Robin throws himself about. Robin crashes into Tommy Youlden. Tommy flinches in pain.

'Fucking hell, Robin, what the hell are you doing?'

'You fuckin' what?' asks Robin.

'Calm it down, Robin,' shouts Maurice.

Tommy stares at Robin, doesn't understand him, doesn't know what makes him tick. Robin walks away, ready to start the game again. Ready to get stuck in at all costs. Knows he's fighting for his place in the team.

He picks up the ball, skips past two players, and there in front of him is Charlie. Robin tries to go around him, and Charlie mistimes his tackle and catches Robin on the ankle. Robin thuds into the ground and in one movement is back up on his feet again, fists clenched, and swings a punch at Charlie. The Reading players look on in amazement. Charlie grabs Robin around the neck. 'What the fuck are you doing?'

'You just whacked me on fuckin' purpose,' says Robin.

'Look, I'm sorry, that was wrong of me,' says Charlie,

letting go of Robin. Charlie looks at Robin's eyes, full of the red mist. 'Go and cool yourself off, and I'll see you after training.'

'No, you can fuck off,' says Robin, starting to walk away.

Charlie follows him. 'If you don't turn up to my office after this game, then you won't play again, it's that simple.'

Robin turns and shrugs.

'What the bloody hell is wrong with him?' asks Tommy Youlden.

'I don't know. I just don't know,' says Charlie, brushing himself down.

Robin pulls off his boots, knocks them together and sends chunks of mud around the dressing room. He takes off his training kit and pushes it into his bag. Pulls on his Y-fronts, jeans, T-shirt and Cuban heels and makes his way up to Charlie's office. Waits outside, brooding.

He sees Charlie coming down the corridor, still in his training kit, towel around his shoulders. Charlie nods in acknowledgement. 'Come in and sit down, please.' Robin nods and pulls a mock smile.

Charlie walks around to his chair and falls back into it, sighs, and leans back, looking at Robin.

'I'm going to give you the weekend off, kid,' says Charlie.

Robin's eyebrows rise. 'Why? I wanna play, like. Look, I'm sorry, I was out of order.'

'We were both out of order, but if you react like that against me, your manager, in a five-a-side knockabout, then in the heat of a match with an opponent you are going to end up getting sent off.'

‘I promise I won’t.’

‘After the week we’ve had, I can’t take that risk. You’d have been on the bench anyway.’

Robin looks across at Charlie with crestfallen eyes and nods.

‘All right, I understand.’

‘There’s a reserve game on Wednesday at Cardiff. Play in that and show me that you’re back and that you can hold your temper.’

‘Cardiff? They wanted to sign me last season.’

‘Yes, they did, so what?’

‘You’re not trying to offload me there, are you?’

‘No,’ says Charlie, looking Robin in the eyes.

‘Good, cos I want a London club if I’m going anywhere.’

‘One step at a time, and you need to get your head straight first, Robin, and that’s a fact.’

‘I will.’

‘Then show me, don’t tell me.’

‘Okay, Boss, I’ll show you.’

Charlie rises out of his chair and shakes Robin’s hand. ‘You have a good weekend, and look after yourself,’ says Charlie.

‘Yeah, see you on Tuesday, and good luck against Port Vale tomorrow.’

Robin walks away and closes Charlie’s door behind him. He walks down the corridor and out onto Norfolk Road, passes the Spread Eagle and heads back to his Tilehurst Road flat.

*

Saturday 18 September 1976

Robin and Liza travel to Acton for the weekend. They stay

at Robin's folks and go to Kensington Market. Robin buys a shirt and steals a shirt. They take some speed. They sit with Robin's parents and watch the classified results come in: Reading 1 Port Vale 1. Reading sit in eighth place in Division Three.

*

Wednesday 22 September 1976

Robin sits on the bus on the long journey to Ninian Park. He smokes and fidgets in his seat.

As kick-off approaches, so does dusk, and Ninian Park's stands are empty and full of shadows.

Clothes off. Reading shirt on. Shorts on…touches them…wishes them good luck.

Jimmy Andrews shakes hands with Charlie, then the men retire to their dugouts to watch Cardiff City reserves v Reading reserves. Robin plays up front with Hiron, who returns after injury.

Reading reserves are strong, and Robin and Hiron stand out. This is almost too easy for them. Jimmy Andrews watches Robin Friday and admires his industry, the way he sweeps the ball around players with the outside of his foot. Looks at Robin, all hair and bow-legged, doesn't look like a footballer but is naturally gifted. A real talent. Precious and a rare commodity: a forward who gets back and fights for the ball.

The shouts ring out in the empty stands. Robin sets up a goal. Claps ring out from Reading's dugout. Jimmy Andrews starts to imagine Robin Friday in a Cardiff City jersey. Thinks of him running around, tackling, and scoring goals, and the crowd roaring him on. At half-time, Reading reserves are winning 2–0, and Charlie takes off Robin and Hiron. Charlie wants to save his men for

Saturday.

In the second half, Cardiff reserves come back into the game, no longer at the mercy of Robin's raiding runs. Reading fall into the shadows and Cardiff City score two goals. The game finishes Cardiff City reserves 2 Reading reserves 2.

Robin Friday plays on Jimmy Andrews' mind. *He flickers into motion like on a cine camera, stopping with the ball, pulling it back, and surging past his man, leaving the man with legs tangled, stranded. Robin looking up and passing the ball with the outside of his foot, nonchalantly.* The images won't leave Jimmy Andrews. Jimmy Andrews has questions. *Why is this player not in the First Division?* he wonders.

*

Saturday 25 September 1976
Robin sits in the away dressing room at Portsmouth, taps his feet and can't sit still. Chatters to Eamon.

Clothes off. Reading shirt on. Shorts on…touches them…wishes them good luck.

Charlie Hurley reads out the team: 'Death, Peters, Bennett, Youlden, Henderson, Cumming, Dunphy, Carnaby, Murray, Friday, Hiron. Sub: Hollis.'

Robin starts to feel a buzz of anticipation. There is laughter. The players line up and jog out onto the pitch. They warm up. Robin shoots at Death, and Death stands still, watching balls fly past him. Death will not make a save before a match.

The game kicks off and Reading start well. Portsmouth's troubles in the boardroom are infecting their players on the pitch: players who might not get paid.

In the fourth minute, Hiron runs on the left wing but

twists his knee and hobbles. He's replaced by Hollis. Hiron hobbles off down the touchline to applause from both sets of fans and disappears down the tunnel back to the dressing room. Head down.

'We're not having much bloody luck, are we,' says Charlie to Maurice.

Maurice shakes his head, eyes still on the game.

Robin begins to get into the game, his confidence surging back through his veins. He dances past two players and passes to Cumming on the wing. Robin puts his head down and steams through midfield, his eyes on Cumming. Cumming crosses, and Robin launches himself at the ball. His head powers the ball, but it goes just wide of the goal.

Reading press on Portsmouth, and Death stands in goal untroubled. Dunphy and Cumming control the midfield and pass at will through, up, and over Portsmouth's defence.

In the thirty-fourth minute, Henderson knocks the ball to Cumming on the left wing. Robin shouts for the ball. Cumming passes inside to Robin. Robin passes to Dunphy. Dunphy sees Peters screaming down the right, and he clips an exquisite ball into his path. Peters squares the ball to the far post and Hollis tucks it away into the back of the net. Portsmouth 0 Reading 1. Robin crowds in with the rest of the players, backs patted, hair ruffled. READ–ING, READ–ING, READ–ING. The rest of the eleven thousand strong crowd stand in silence.

Portsmouth come back and strike two shots in quick succession, but Death will not be beaten today.

In the second half, in the forty-sixth minute, Peters is clattered in a tackle. He hobbles back into position.

Cumming and Dunphy look at Charlie on the bench. He

looks at Peters, stands hands on hips shaking his head. Peters is in a bad way. Cumming and Dunphy look and wave their players into position around the pitch. Then they give out their orders. Henderson switches to the right side of the defence. Carnaby goes to right back, Hollis drops into midfield, and Peters is pushed out onto the right wing. Peters hobbles into position.

Cumming and Dunphy are in control, and they command the midfield like generals. Portsmouth have no response and are off the pace.

Murray goes on a raid and leaves the Portsmouth defence in his wake. He sends in a scorcher from thirty yards, and the keeper parries it away like a hot potato, but there is Peters unmarked, and he hammers the ball into the net and falls to the floor as his injured leg gives way. Portsmouth 0 Reading 2. Robin runs over, laughing. 'Come on, mate, up you get.' Robin pulls him up. Peters raises his arms to the Reading fans, who cheer.

'That fucking hurt, mate. I thought my leg was going to buckle,' he says, pointing at his knee.

Portsmouth are washed up. The game finishes Portsmouth 0 Reading 2. Portsmouth are booed off the pitch by their own fans. There are whistles, and they walk down the tunnel, heads down. Robin walks over to the Reading fans and thanks them for their support.

Robin sits in the bath with the other players, and they listen to the results come in on the transistor radio. Enunciated tones read out the scores. Reading now sit in fourth place in Division Three. There are cheers. Robin sinks down into the plunge bath, under the water, his ears picking up the mumbles from above. He comes back up, rubs his hair with soap, and dunks his head under again;

comes back up and wipes his face.

'I think we're not far off being able to walk this league,' says Eamon.

'A couple of extra helping hands, and yes, I think we could,' says Cumming.

'If we stopped getting kicked about and injured,' says Robin.

'That's why those lot should've invested, but no,' says Eamon.

'Look, we've won. Let's leave the other stuff for now,' says Cumming.

Robin stands up out of the bath. 'Let's go and 'ave a few beers. We've earned it, I reckon.'

There are nods of agreement.

*

Saturday 2 October 1976

Swindon come to Elm Park. The buzz of a local derby. Eleven thousand six hundred and seventy fans have come to watch. The rain pisses down but doesn't stop the fans, who taunt each other in the stands.

Robin goes to his usual spot in the dressing room. Clothes off. Reading shirt on. Shorts on…touches them…wishes them good luck.

Robin runs and works hard laying on balls for his teammates. Murray scores two, and Carnaby and Cumming get one apiece. Reading hammer Swindon 4–1, but Robin feels empty, and there seems to be only one thing that will fill the void, an itch that needs scratching.

There's cheer in the dressing room, as Reading now sit in third place in Division Three. There's laughter and chatter, but Robin feels like he's in a bubble, and that he's running out of air. He needs more money, needs another contract, needs another club.

On the radio, the classified results come in, and the players listen. Then there's a sports' bulletin. The newscaster's plummy voice polishes the words: *'Today across the English Football League yellow and red cards replaced cautions for offences on the field of play. Blackburn Rovers' David Wagstaffe was the first player to be shown the red card after thirty-six minutes versus Orient for arguing with the referee. George Best of Fulham received a red card in the game against Southampton at The Dell in the sixty-seventh minute for foul language.'*

Makes a change for somebody to do something before George, thinks Robin.

Robin sits and feels alone, alone in a dressing room full of people and he starts to fidget. He wants away from Elm Park.

*

Robin turns up for training. He runs when he has to. The leaves fall in the streets around Elm Park, and he starts to feel a deep sadness. The season is changing and so is he.

*

Terry Venables phones Charlie Hurley and asks if he'd like to swap Robin Friday for two Crystal Palace players. Charlie informs Terry Venables that he's only interested in cash offers. Crystal Palace don't have the money.

*

Eamon watches his friend, sees the unhappiness in his face.

'I've got a book signing at WH Smith's in town, fancy joining me?'

'Sure, course I will.'

'Good, you might help me sell a few more copies.'

He sees Robin's smile, looks into his eyes and knows he needs to keep his friend busy, involved.

*

Friday 8 October 1976

WH Smith, Reading —

Robin sits with Eamon and they sign books together. Fans gather, eager to meet their heroes.

A local photographer comes and snaps them. Robin reaches out and holds Eamon's hand for good luck. Eamon grins for the camera, Robin doesn't smile, tries to be serious.

The photographer says, 'Have you read it, Robin?'

'Yeah, it's good, very authentic, and tells it how it really is.'

'Do you think Eamon's a good writer then?'

'Yeah, he'd give Kipling a run for his money, I reckon.'

'I hear lots of First Division clubs are interested in you?'

'I'm 'ere for Eamon's book, and we've got Chesterfield tomorrow, and that's the focus, so d'you wanna copy?'

'Sure.'

'There you go then,' says Robin, handing over a pre-signed book and sending him on his way.

*

Saturday 9 October 1976

The Reading bus and fans travel up the M1 motorway looking for victory —

Four thousand and twenty-five have come to the Recreation Ground to watch. Chesterfield sit at the foot of the Third Division. Arthur Cox, Chesterfield's new manager, tells his players they are playing for their futures. His first match in charge. He tells his players that he wants a reaction.

The game kicks off.

Robin toils away, holds the ball up when necessary. He passes inch-perfect balls to his teammates. Chesterfield press and harry the Reading defence, which collapses like wet cardboard. Chesterfield score in the ninth minute. Chesterfield 1 Reading 0.

In the forty-ninth minute, Chesterfield score a second goal. Reading heads drop. The Chesterfield fans feel a victory coming and sing their hearts out. Reading crumple. Robin has to chase back to help out. He picks up balls in the middle of the park and tries to send his team forward. Tries in vain.

Chesterfield score a third and a fourth without reply.

Four-fucking-nil, four to nothing.

'We've got nothing,' says Robin to himself. He trudges off the pitch.

*

Saturday 16 October 1976

Nine thousand four hundred and forty-nine have come to Elm Park, but not all have come to watch. Sheffield Wednesday fans enter the South Bank and fighting breaks out in the crowd. The police wade in to try and stop the scuffles. The atmosphere is poisonous.

Robin goes to his usual spot in the dressing room. Clothes off. Reading shirt on. Shorts on…touches them…wishes them good luck.

The referee appears, whispers to Charlie, and leaves the room.

'It could get hairy out there, there's been crowd

trouble. If it spills onto the pitch I want you all straight off into here, got it?' says Charlie. The players nod.

The bell rings and the players line up, and they run out into jeering, cheering and booing.

The game kicks off and Reading move with the ball, Sheffield Wednesday putting up a stonewall defence. Robin moves with the ball and sends Stuckey away, but the cross comes to nothing. Eamon, Cumming, and Stuckey try to control midfield, but Wednesday press on them. Every time a Reading player picks up a ball, there's a Wednesday player there with a kick or a shove. There are jeers every time Wednesday pick up the ball, boos and whistles when they send Reading players crashing to the deck.

Robin wrestles and battles with Wednesday's number five, Hugh Dowd. Robin pushes him back, elbows him, but still he comes back and won't go away. Robin receives a ball, and before he can turn he's sent crashing into the turf, and Dowd tramples over him.

'Ref!' screams Robin, but the ref isn't interested.

Robin picks up the ball again and is bundled to the floor; Dowd handles the spinning ball and is given a yellow card.

Reading can't break through the Wednesday defence, and try as they might they can't get near the Wednesday goal.

Robin's blood boils in frustration. He goes on a run but is brought down again by Dowd, and Robin bounces up to face his tormentor. Robin spits in his face, and Dowd swings a punch at Robin. The referee calls them over, talks to them, tells them to calm it down.

Moreline goes in for a hard tackle on Wylde and is

given a yellow card for his troubles.

'What the fuck, they've been battering me,' says Robin to Eamon.

'This ref doesn't know what he's doing.'

The half-time whistle blows, and Wednesday and the referee walk off the pitch to boos and jeers. The Reading fans chant: THE REFEREE'S A WANKER! THE REFEREE'S A WANKER!

The Reading players come into the dressing room and sit down, battered and bruised.

'What the fuck are we gonna do, Charlie? Can you go and have a word with the ref?' says Robin.

'You know I can't do that. Their tactics are bloody blatant. They've come here to block us out and nick a goal; you've just got to keep battling. Try to keep your tempers.'

'But Charlie, I'm getting kicked to pieces, and I'm not the only one. If the ref isn't protecting us, then what else can we do?'

'Keep your cool, and do everything you can to stay on that pitch.'

'I won't be able to stay on that pitch because they'll be carrying me off on a fuckin' stretcher if it carries on like this.'

'You're tough enough to put up with their bollocks, just keep a lid on it. Now, come on, lads, get out there and show these lot what we can do.'

'Oh, I will,' says Robin.

The bell rings, and they go back out into the cauldron. Sheffield Wednesday and the ref appear to boos.

The second half begins, and Wednesday start as they began. They soak up the pressure, kick and hit Reading on the break. In the fifty-third minute, Henderson clears from the Reading backline, but only as far as a Wednesday man, who passes the ball into his teammate's path and he sticks the ball past Death. There are cheers from the Wednesday fans and jeers from the Reading fans. Reading 0 Sheffield Wednesday 1.

Reading try to come back, and Stuckey blasts a volley, but it goes just inches wide of the post. Wednesday attack again and hit the post.

Robin tries to go on another run but is brought down. He gets to his feet, hobbles, but won't give in.

Reading push and Wednesday play a back pass to the keeper. Robin chases it through, the keeper collects and is straight onto his feet. He tries to take his goal kick, but Robin jiggles, and dances, and blocks his path. The keeper says, 'Piss off.' Robin spits in his face and headbutts him. The Sheffield fans scream in anger, and Chris Turner, the Wednesday keeper, shakes his head and wipes his face with his shoulder. Looks on in disgust. Robin backs off and lets him take the kick.

'Fucking hell, Maurice, did you see that? I'm taking him off or he'll be sent off,' says Charlie. 'Dennis, get yourself ready.'

Robin is called from the pitch. He claps to the Reading fans and they cheer him off. Wednesday are glad he's gone. He shakes hands with Dennis Nelson and hobbles down the steps and into the Reading dressing room.

He sits in his dirty kit and looks down at his legs, which are full of cuts and bruises, and he knows that, today, his opposite man got the better of him. He sits and reaches into his jacket for his packet of fags. Puts one in his mouth, clicks his lighter and inhales.

The game finishes Reading 0 Sheffield Wednesday 1. Reading sit in ninth position in Division Three.

*

Monday 18 October 1976
Bob Stokoe resigns as manager of Sunderland Football Club, who sit at the very bottom of Division One. The Division Two Champions of 1975/76 and the FA Cup winning miracle of 1973 are soon forgotten as the jeers rang out.

The rumour mill starts, and Charlie Hurley is linked to the job. Sunderland's fans want their hero back at Roker Park. Charlie begins to have thoughts of First Division football.

*

'Boss, can I 'ave a word?' asks Robin.

'Sure, take a seat,' says Charlie, his guts tightening. 'Are you still messing about with drugs?'

'I'm trying to keep a lid on it.'

'What does that mean?'

'It's fine, don't worry.'

Charlie shakes his head, and says, 'You've got to quit or you'll have to go.'

'I want to leave anyway, go to a club in London.'

'I don't think London is the best place for you, I really don't.'

'Why not?'

'It seems that London's where your mates are, and that's not a good mix.'

'You going to Sunderland?'

'No, I've a job to do here, and I'll finish it, but that's not what we're talking about. I'm trying to help you, Robin, help you to understand that if you focus, you can be a great. I'm really worried about you, but I've got a commitment to this football club.'

'You mean saving your own bacon?'

'No, I mean looking after the club and the players, and that includes *you*. Do you know how many times I've had to stick up for you with the other lads? All I know is I'm losing count.'

'I'm sick of it 'ere, sick of it.'

'This club has looked after you. I've looked after you. Can't you see that?'

'I've given this club everything I've got.'

'But it's not just about that. It's about you focussing, turning up to training on time, and doing what you're paid to do. If I let everyone run around doing what they wanted, we'd have chaos.'

'I'm trying, Boss.'

'Then you need to try harder. You've got responsibilities now, and you need to manage them.'

'Okay,' says Robin, and he lifts himself out of the chair, and leaving the room, he turns to Charlie. 'See ya, Boss.'

'See you, Robin.'

Robin walks out of the office and down the corridor. The walls are beginning to close in on him.

*

Robin turns up for training with dark eyes, his football boots slung over his shoulder.

'You're late, that's a fine,' says Charlie, and then he looks at his eyes and sniffs his breath. 'You stink of booze, Robin. Late night was it?'

'I'm okay, I can train.'

'No, you're a risk to my players and a risk to yourself.

Now go home, and I'll see you this afternoon.'

Robin nods and walks away.

The other players continue to train, and Maurice approaches Charlie. 'He's got to go, Charlie. How can we maintain discipline with this lot when he's like this?'

'He wants to go, there's no doubt about it, so I might just let him,' says Charlie, watching Robin disappear down the steps and out of Elm Park.

*

Rat-a-tat-tat —

Robin ambles to the front door and opens it.

'All right, Boss, come in,' says Robin.

Charlie nods, smiles and walks in.

'You wanna cuppa? We was just about to put the kettle on.'

'No, thanks, Robin, I won't be staying long.'

'Oh, okay, what can I do you for then?'

They make their way into the living room, where Liza sits on the settee.

'Oh, hello, Liza, how are you?'

'I'm good thanks, Charlie.'

'Can you give us a minute, Liza.'

'Sure, I've got things to do anyway,' she says, getting up and leaving the room.

'What is it, Boss?'

'You said you're not happy, that you want bigger and better things, right?'

'Yeah.'

'Well, do you want me to talk to the board and get you put on the transfer list?'

Robin frowns and looks Charlie in the eye. 'Yeah, I want to go for more money and get to the First Division.'

'Right, I'll do it,' says Charlie, 'but on one condition.'

'What's that?'

'You've got to turn up for training on time and cut back on your nights out, and the drugs have to go.'

'And what if I say no?'

'Then I'll drop you to the reserves and you'll never play first-team football again.'

'So that's it then? I toe the line and I get to go?'

'You need to realise you've a gift, and that I'm trying to help you out here, trying to help you straighten out.'

'I don't wanna be one of the straights. That's not me, never will be.'

'Look, Robin, play your heart out and calm your extracurricular activities, and hopefully one of the big clubs will come in, but as I've repeated time and time again, you've got to quit the drugs, for your good…and mine. I can't sell you *knowing* that, can *I*?'

'Just talk to the board, get me put on the transfer list, and I'll do the rest.'

'Okay,' says Charlie, reaching out his hand. Robin puts out his hand and they shake on it.

*

Thursday 21 October 1976

The Reading board of directors sit —

The men who decide club business: Waller, Vincent, Davies, Harrison, and Brooks all sit with their papers and their briefcases amongst the smoke, brandy and coffee. Heads nod and eyes peer over eyeglasses, fingers point at figures on balance sheets, and fingers point at league tables.

Charlie comes in clutching his own briefcase, greets the board. There are handshakes and smiles.

'What have you got for us, Charlie? Any news on the transfer front?'

'I'm off on Saturday to Southampton, to look at a couple of players there.'

'You'll miss the Lincoln game then?'

'Yes, Maurice will have it all in hand, don't worry.'

'Right, we've had a couple of shaky results out on the field of late. Do you think we'll be all right?'

'I'm sure we'll be fine, and once I've got a couple more players on board, that'll help steady the ship. We've also been very unlucky with injuries too.'

'Yes, things do seem a little bit more physical in the Third, don't they.'

'They do, but with a lot more skill and technical nous behind it too. These teams are still fighting when they're two-nothing down.'

There are nods from the table.

'Any news on Ian Porterfield from Sunderland?'

'I'm hoping we can get him on loan him for a month. He'll add a bit more class to our attack.'

'Okay, the newspapers are linking you to the Sunderland job, is there any truth there?'

'Frank, I've got a job to do here, and that's my top priority. You have my full commitment,' says Charlie, looking Frank Waller in the eye.

'We're glad to hear it, Charlie, very glad indeed.'

'Now, I've been speaking to Robin Friday this week, and he's requested to go on the transfer list,' says Charlie looking at the board.

'What do you think we should do? There are a lot of teams looking at him,' says Walller.

'He's not happy here and hasn't been happy for a long

time. There's issues with his fitness and he's only scored one goal in eight league games. I think we should put him up for sale… or loan him out.'

'What's he worth…fifty or sixty thousand?'

'Something like that, maybe more if his form picked up a bit, and if we put him in the shop window, at least his performances might improve.'

Frank Waller looks around. 'I think he's lost his way. What do we think, gents?' There are nods.

'Charlie, put him up for sale.'

'I'll get onto it tomorrow.'

*

Saturday 23 October 1976
Away to Lincoln City at Sincil Bank —

'All right, Percy,' says Robin, reaching out and shaking Percy Freeman's hand.

'Good, mate, how are you?'

'I'll tell you after the game when we've beaten you,' says Robin.

'Get out of it…see you out there.'

'You will.'

In the first half, Percy Freeman breaks for Lincoln City, but Moreline is there and brings the big forward hurtling down to the floor. Moreline receives a yellow card from the ref.

In the twelfth minute, Robin sees the ball and watches as the Lincoln City keeper tries to grab it, but Robin charges in and puts the ball into the net. He races away with his hand in the air, and the small band of travelling Reading fans cheer. The referee disallows the goal.

'Why? What was wrong with that, it's a goal!'

'The keeper had his hands on the ball, so I can't allow

it.'

'No, he didn't, it was fifty-fifty.'

'I've spoken to the linesman and that's my decision.'

Robin shakes his head and bites his tongue.

Robin chases the ball, chases lost causes, gets back and tackles, fights for every ball. Tries to conjure something out of nothing.

In the twentieth minute, Percy Freeman flicks on from a corner ball, and a Lincoln City defender smashes the ball into the back of Death's net. Lincoln City 1 Reading 0.

In the twenty-first minute, Dunphy crashes into a tackle and is given a yellow card by the referee. Dunphy shakes his head in frustration.

At half-time, the Reading players sit down. They feel like they're playing twelve men. A disallowed goal and two yellow cards. Robin sits and simmers in frustration, feels like he's doing more than anyone.

In the second half, in the forty-eighth minute, Lincoln break on the wing. The ball is crossed and nodded past Death. Lincoln City 2 Reading 0. The Lincoln fans wave their red-and-white scarves and sing. Some of the Reading players' heads drop, apart from one who roars.

In the fiftieth minute, the Lincoln City keeper kicks a long ball, which bounces and beats Bennett, and then Youlden slips and a Lincoln City forward puts the ball past Death. Lincoln City 3 Reading 0. The home fans' cheers ring out and echo around Sincil Bank.

Reading faces turn sour, and Dunphy breaks and shoots, but the keeper parries it, then the ball falls to Hollis who puts it into the back of the net. Lincoln City 3 Reading 1. A small cheer rises up from the Reading fans.

In the seventieth minute, Hollis limps off and is

replaced by Hetzke. Reading try to come back but they're second best in every tackle and every chase.

Robin fumes, steam rising off his back.

'Bad luck, mate,' says Percy, reaching out his hand.

Robin grips Percy's hand and looks him in the eye. 'You had a good game, but we were shit, just not good enough. That goal of mine could've changed everything though.'

'Maybe, maybe not.'

'There's no maybe about it, Percy.'

They walk down the tunnel, one in victory and one in defeat.

*

Thursday 28 October 1976

Charlie Hurley hasn't slept —

Charlie walks into his press briefing and sits down.

'Good morning, gents,' says Charlie, but his big grin and flashing white teeth can't hide his fears.

He looks up and sees the eager faces, knowing that they know already, knowing that word has got out.

'Robin Friday has been placed on the transfer list at his own request. He's eager to play in a higher division, and the board and I don't want to stand in his way.'

'When was this decision made?' asks Geoff Thompson from the *Chronicle*.

'It was made at a board meeting late last Thursday evening.'

'So other clubs have been made aware of Robin's availability?'

'Yes, I put him on the list last Friday morning.'

'Has anyone come in?'

'No, not yet, but I did approach Peterborough United

last week with a view to exchanging Robin for Peterborough's David Gregory on a loan basis, but Noel Cantwell declined the offer as he's already got two other players out on loan.'

'Peterborough? But they're in Division Three, so why would Robin go there if he's interested in playing in a higher division?'

Charlie feels his face flush and his collar tighten.

The bastards, like bloodhounds on a trail...

He takes a sip of air and says, 'We're looking at all options, and that was just one particular one.'

'Is Robin unhappy?'

'I don't think it's any secret that Robin isn't very happy at the moment, and hopefully his transfer listing will improve things and help him achieve his ambition.'

'Your name has been linked to the Sunderland manager's job. Is that post of interest to you?'

'I have spoken to the board here and assured them that I have a job to do here at Reading and that I won't be going anywhere.'

'Thanks, Charlie, is there any other news on transfers?'

'Er, yes, Tommy Youlden has had his fee cut to fifteen thousand by the Football League Tribunal, and he's now available for that figure. Dennis Nelson has also gone on the transfer list at his own request, as both he and his wife wish to return home to the north of England. Eamon Dunphy is also still on the list. John 'Ian' Porterfield should be joining us on a month's loan from Sunderland. You'll, of course, know him for his famous winning goal in the seventy-three Cup Final.' Charlie smiles.

'Dennis hasn't settled then?'

'It would appear that way.'

'Are there problems with morale here at Reading?'

Weasels, fucking weasels…

'I have a group of very professional players, and they turn up and play for me week in, week out, so I can't fault them for that. Look, this is football, and players come and go.' Charlie purses his lips.

'But don't you think that losing someone like Robin Friday suggests something about the ambition of the club?'

'I'm not sure quite what you're trying to imply, and as I've said, Robin wants to play in a higher division, so we can't stop him.'

'You didn't have to agree to the transfer?'

'I feel like we're going around in circles here, and I'd very much like to talk about Saturday's game against Chester, so if you don't mind, let's get on with that.'

The heads in front of Charlie scribble onto their notepads.

They dig with their questions, they write their stories, and twist the words…

Weasels chasing rabbits down holes…

Weasels cornering rabbits…

Weasels leaving holes with dead rabbits in their mouths.

*

Saturday 30 October 1976

Elm Park —

Robin goes to his usual spot in the dressing room. Clothes off. Reading shirt on. Shorts on…touches them…wishes them good luck.

'Chester today, boys. They've the best away record in this league, so we know they'll not be coming here to defend. From the off let's get at them, get yourself into shooting positions and just have a go. Let's get back to winning ways and put a smile back on the fans' faces.'

Robin knows he's in the shop window, and that somewhere out in those stands there will be scouts watching him.

In the first half, Henderson breaks, passes to Cumming, who passes to Robin at the near post. Robin back-heels the ball at goal, but the keeper dives and pushes it away. The Reading crowd spur Robin on, encouraging his every touch.

Chester attack and move forward. One of their defenders belts the ball, but Death palms it away. Robin puts pressure on the backline and harries Chester's defence. A Chester defender makes a back pass and Robin swoops on it, looks at the keeper and sweeps around him and passes to Hiron, who, with an easy target, hits the ball high and over the top. Robin shakes his head.

In the twenty-second minute, Hiron passes to Dunphy, who passes to Murray. Murray shoots, but the keeper pushes the ball away, and a Chester defender puts the ball out for a corner. Reading crowd the area and press.

Dunphy steps up and sends in his corner kick. Hiron jumps high and heads on to Robin, who nods the ball home. He turns and runs to the crowd, flanked by Eamon, Hiron, and Murray. His arms wide, he blows kisses to the Reading fans, who cheer and wave their scarves, enjoying their Man Friday, knowing they might not have him for much longer. Reading 1 Chester 0.

In the second half, Chester come out of the blocks fighting and push Reading's backline. Death makes save after save.

Reading attack. Robin races into the box but is sent crashing to the floor by a Chester defender. He screams for a penalty, but nothing is given. He hits the floor at the injustice. The Reading crowd whistle and boo.

In the eighty-third minute, Minty Murray speeds down the left wing. He passes inside to Hiron. Hiron shoots, and the ball starts to go wide, but there's Cumming to nod the ball in. Reading 2 Chester 0. The fans sing: READ–ING, READ–ING, READ–ING. Dunphy pulls up with an injury and is replaced by Nelson.

In the final minute, Robin goes on a run and shoots, missing by inches. He throws his head back in frustration. The game finishes Reading 2 Chester 0.

Robin claps the fans, walks to the South Bank and signs autographs for eager young fans. They beg him not to leave. 'Robin…Robin…Robin,' they cry, just for a look from him, or a wink, or a smile. 'You're why we come here,' says one young fan. 'You make our Saturdays, and you're our Friday too.' Robin's heart aches.

*

Monday 1 November 1976

John 'Ian' Porterfield joins from Sunderland. He scored the winner against Leeds United in the 1973 FA Cup Final, his only goal in the FA Cup that season, and Sunderland's only goal in the FA Cup Final. He hasn't played for ten months after an injury to his skull in a car accident. Ian Porterfield is eager to play again, but Ian Porterfield's heart lies in Sunderland.

*

'I've some news,' says Liza.

'Yeah?'

'I think I'm pregnant.'

‘Bloody hell, girl.’ He holds her tight and smiles.

There’s not enough to live on as it is. Robin Friday needs more money.

*

Wednesday 3 November 1976
Robin goes to his usual spot in the dressing room. Clothes off. Reading shirt on. Shorts on…touches them…wishes them good luck.

‘Right, Brighton today, lads; they’re top of the league. They’ve beaten Walsall by seven goals to nil. They’ve beaten York City by seven goals to two, but they were at home, and today they’re here at Elm Park, where you’ll go at them, and go at them. Don’t let them rest. Defenders, keep your line, because you’ll have to have eyes in the back of your head.’

‘Another tactical masterclass,’ whispers Eamon to Robin.

Robin turns to him with a wry smile, and says, ‘I don’t care. I’ll beat them on my own.’

Twelve thousand and ninety-seven fans have come to Elm Park with expectations.

The first half kicks off, and Brighton set out their stall from the off; they start to carve lines through the Reading defence.

In the fourth minute, a Brighton midfielder breaks, moves one way, then the other. Death stands stranded, and the Brighton midfielder lets go with a fierce left-foot shot. Reading 0 Brighton & Hove Albion 1.

‘For fuck’s sake, Maurice, what the hell were we doing at the back?’

Maurice shakes his head, doesn’t answer.

Brighton run lines, open channels, turn Reading’s

defence inside and out. Eyes wide at every Brighton move.

In the eighteenth minute, Robin speeds down the right wing. He comes inside and shoots, but the ball is bundled away for a corner. Dunphy swings in the corner and Hiron heads it on, and there's a goalmouth scramble and Minty pops the ball home. He runs and the Reading fans roar; he's surrounded by Robin and the rest of the Reading players. Reading 1 Brighton & Hove Albion 1.

The ball travels back and forth, end to end, at a frenetic pace. Robin makes a nuisance of himself, presses on Brighton's defence. Dunphy sends in an inswinging corner, and Robin launches at the ball but sends it high and over the crossbar.

The referee looks down at his watch, and as the seconds tick down to half-time, Brighton break. A Brighton forward leaves Youlden for dead, and then shoots, and Death dives, but the ball screams past him. He watches it, sees his empty net, sees the ball, sees the line, and watches the ball strike the post and come back to him, and he holds it in his arms, pulls it to his chest, welcomes its return. Reading fans blow their cheeks out in relief. The referee blows for half-time.

'Come on, lads, you can do this. You keep making chances, just bloody put them away, and for God's sake, tighten up at the back,' says Charlie.

The second half kicks off, and in the forty-seventh minute, Murray races away down the right wing and crosses. Robin heads the ball down to Hiron, who passes it back out wide to Porterfield on the left. Porterfield crosses to Dunphy, who shoots, first time, but a defender clears the ball off the line.

'How the fuck did they save that, Maurice?' says

Charlie, holding his head.

Robin makes runs down the right wing, and Porterfield runs down the left wing, stretching Brighton. Cumming and Dunphy shout their orders and shape their team.

In the sixtieth minute, Robin sees a defender with the ball. He swoops down and reaches in and sweeps the ball away with a sliding tackle, and he scoops the ball and races away and sends a through ball to Murray. The keeper narrows his angle and the ball falls to Hiron, who stalls and then shoots, but the ball is cleared and falls to Porterfield, who shoots too high.

In the sixty-fifth minute, Brighton break away, and Henderson is turned inside out by a Brighton midfielder, and then a belting shot sees Death watch the ball go into the net. Reading 1 Brighton & Hove Albion 2. The Brighton fans cheer on their table toppers.

Dunphy sends in a free kick, and Hiron outjumps his marker and heads the ball onto Robin, who freezes and watches the ball fly past him, his movement towards it too late. He grits his teeth in anger, holds up his hands to his teammates and shakes his head.

Robin ghosts past two Brighton defenders and passes through to Murray, who races onto the ball, shoots, but sends the ball wide. Robin throws up his hands in frustration.

In the seventy-eighth minute, Hetzke powers through and goes around three Brighton players, and Friday collects the ball from him. Friday passes it through to Dunphy, who strikes it, but the ball is blocked by the keeper and it falls to Hiron, who shoots from close range and scores. Reading 2 Brighton & Hove Albion 2. The roars ring out from the stands. Reading are back in it.

In the seventy-ninth minute, a long ball goes in towards the Reading defence. Cumming heads it out, but it falls to a Brighton defender, who, from twenty-five yards, sends the ball flying into the back of the Reading net. There's a raucous cheer as most of Elm Park stands in shock. Reading 2 Brighton & Hove Albion 3.

Charlie sits on the bench, head in hands. Maurice sits with his arms folded.

Robin and Reading try to make their way back in, but Brighton shut up shop. The final whistle blows, and it finishes Reading 2 Brighton & Hove Albion 3.

In the dressing room, Robin kicks the physio table in anger. Charlie Hurley walks in. The dressing room simmers with rage.

*

Friday 5 November 1976
Adwest Training Ground —

Charlie stands with his players, his face ashen. 'Brighton didn't beat us on Wednesday night, we handed them the game. Three defensive errors cost us, and we've got to clean up our act, got to. I'm sick we lost the game. The best team in the Third Division and you were all over them at times. In the last two games we've produced as many chances as we have all season. I think some of you have been coasting, happy to pull a wage whatever the result. Well I'm bloody not, and if you're not up to it, you'll be dropped to the reserves.'

Faces look back, and there are murmurs of discontent. Charlie stares at them, shakes his head. 'Maurice will talk to you about tomorrow,' says Charlie, walking away. Maurice looks on with surprise.

'Right, Palace tomorrow and another tough one, but if

we play like we did on Wednesday night, minus our defensive errors, then I think we can nick it. We'll work on our defensive set-up today.' Heads nod and the mood lightens.

*

Saturday 6 November 1976

In the dressing room at Selhurst Park, the room hums with excitement. Clothes off. Reading shirt on. Shorts on…touches them…wishes them good luck. He is home in London, and plenty of friends and family will be watching from the stands.

He lights up a fag and smokes it to calm his nerves, sits in his kit and boots. He takes a swig of hot tea. 'Come on, boys, let's put on a fuckin' show.' He jumps up and down, picks up the ball and bounces it off the floor. Its pinging echoes around the dressing room like a pulse.

The referee opens the door and calls them out. They line up and jog down the corridor and up the steps. Palace fans hang over the walls, waving scarves in their faces and booing them. Robin runs out onto the pitch and stretches. A voice hums over the tannoy, and the smell of Bovril and hot pies hangs in the air. Fifteen thousand three hundred and twenty-two voices whistle and shout.

Crystal Palace put the pressure on Reading from the off, and every time they move forward the crowd roars and gets behind them. Reading's defence stays strong, and Dunphy chases down every loose ball and scrambles into every tackle.

In the thirty-fifth minute, Porterfield takes the ball down the left wing and then passes to Murray. Murray looks up and sends in a deep cross, which sails over everyone in the box. Hiron collects the ball on the right wing, moves in, takes his time, and floats a ball across, which Robin sees, and he outjumps his marker and the keeper, and nods the ball into the net from a tight angle. Crystal Palace 0 Reading 1. There's a roar from the Reading contingent, and Robin wheels away, arms aloft. The Crystal Palace keeper sits on his backside, his head shaking; his defenders look on in disbelief. Robin's smile beams. He's doing it in London, and he hopes Terry Venables is watching, and anyone else who's interested.

Crystal Palace try to get back, try to get something, and their players run lines, try to turn Reading but they can't. Each and every Reading player is at their best, showing what they can do.

In the last twenty minutes, every Palace attack is met with huge cheers of encouragement, willing their team to score. Palace and their wall of noise come again and again.

In the eighty-fourth minute, Crystal Palace win a corner, and the ball is sent in low and it skids through a melee of players. Death watches as it falls to a Palace striker, and from six yards out he thumps the ball into the back of the net. Crystal Palace 1 Reading 1. A roar reverberates around Selhurst Park, and Robin stands hands on hips shaking his head. He looks at Eamon, who looks back with bitter disappointment.

In the final minutes Reading try to get the win, but it's gone. The final whistle blows: Crystal Palace 1 Reading 1. Robin waves to the Reading fans and knows that today he's had a great game. Palace fans run onto the pitch to meet their heroes, and Robin and the rest of the Reading team make their way back to the dressing room.

They soak in the bath and wait for the results to come in, and Reading now sit in thirteenth place. Thoughts turn to the next game, up at Mansfield Town.

Robin goes out to quench his thirst.

*

Sunday 7 November 1976

He wakes up in a strange bed, to a female scent he doesn't recognise, and opens his eyes, but he can only make out shadows in a dark room, and he looks beside him, sees a figure snug asleep under the blanket, gently snoring. He tries to recall last night. *Booze…lines of coke sniffed off backs of hands, off toilet cisterns, and then more booze…and in the early hours he dropped some pink Diconal tablets, which sent him into a stupor and finally to sleep.*

He moves and tries to look at his watch, and sees that it's a quarter past four on Sunday afternoon. Twenty-four hours ago he was on that pitch playing to the crowd, in his element. He holds his head, rubs his temples, and feels an overwhelming sense of anxiety. He thinks of Liza and feels sick to the bone. The highs and lows.

He slips on his clothes and leaves without saying goodbye, and he finds the nearest Tube station and decides to head back to Acton, and from there he will concoct his story and make his way back to Reading.

*

Monday 8 November 1976

The Reading team bus waits as players sit eager to get on the road for the match at Mansfield, to get the job done, but there's no Robin Friday. Charlie looks at his watch, and Maurice looks at Charlie. 'I'll go round and get him,' says Maurice.

Maurice rings the bell. Robin picks up his boots and slams the door and walks up the drive. 'Quick,' says

Robin.

'What?'

The front door swings open, and Liza comes screaming out of the door. 'You bastard, I'm sick of this, sick of it!' She shakes her fists in a rage.

'Need I ask, Robin?'

'No, don't, I've fucked up again.'

They speed up their pace and get back to the bus.

'Sorry, Charlie, sorry lads,' says Robin getting onto the bus.

Charlie looks at him and looks at the dark rings around his eyes.

'I'm glad you could make it, Robin. Now go and sit down and let's get on our bloody way.'

Robin heads to the back of the bus, and as he looks out of the back window, he sees Liza standing there still shouting at him, red-faced, eyes wild.

'Fucking hell, mate, have you been a bad boy again?' asks Minty.

'Fuck off,' says Robin, sitting down and taking out a fag.

Robin sits and fidgets on the bus and keeps himself to himself.

They arrive at Mansfield's Field Mill ground, in the dark, and in the cold.

Robin's guts turn over, his mind fuzzy, thinking laboured, his body still aching from the weekend. The players start to get ready in the dressing room. It's quieter than usual – the atmosphere flat.

Charlie claps his hands. 'A hard game tonight, make no mistake about it. This is the opposite of the glitz and glamour of Saturday, but we've a job to do. Play like you did on Saturday and we'll have no problems. Let's not sit back, but go at them; they won't expect that.'

The game kicks off, and six thousand seven hundred and ninety-three fans watch on, in the cold, under the floodlights.

Reading find it hard to get into second gear, and Mansfield are first to every ball. Robin has a shadow. Every move he makes his shadow moves with him. Stocky and unforgiving. There are kicks, and there are elbows, and Robin gives it back.

In the eleventh minute, a Mansfield striker is held back, and a penalty is given. The ball is put on the spot and sent crashing into the net. Mansfield Town 1 Reading 0. The crowd roar on. Amber-and-blue scarves wave into the night.

Three minutes later, the same player pounces onto the ball, and it's Randall's second. Mansfield Town 2 Reading 0. The Mansfield crowd cheer, sensing easy meat.

Robin feels a rout coming on and is eager to fight back and lose his shadow. In the seventeenth minute, Hetzke passes a gilt-edged ball through to Robin. Robin runs onto it and steams towards goal, and as he moves, so do two defenders, who cut in on him. One goes to body check him and the other rugby tackles Robin's legs. Robin crashes to the ground and looks up for a foul. He turns and sees the Mansfield player getting to his knees, holding his shoulder, face pale. He is carried off the pitch, his shoulder dislocated.

Reading start to hold off the Mansfield attacks, but nothing is happening in midfield and Robin can't get away from the Mansfield centre backs. They kick and crash into him.

At half-time, Charlie stands, arms folded. He looks around the dressing room and says, 'That is the worst half of football I think I've ever had the displeasure of fucking watching. How is this the team that played on Saturday? Defenders, you're not picking up your men, and we're giving away stupid fouls. Our midfield is overrun. We're second to everything. Robin, that Foster has got you in his back pocket, you look like you're running in bloody treacle. Those of you on the transfer list, do you realise there's a lot of managers and scouts watching tonight?'

Robin and the other players look up at him and stare.

'And on your performance tonight, nobody will fucking sign any of you. Now get out there and put up a bloody fight.'

The second half kicks off and it's more of the same. Robin's energy begins to fade. He's chased down and shackled by Mansfield's defence, by Foster and by MacKenzie.

In the fifty-ninth minute, Moreline throws a last-ditch tackle and brings down a Mansfield player. Another penalty. Randall steps up and tucks it away: a hat-trick. Singing and chanting ring out from the stands. Mansfield Town 3 Reading 0.

Robin feels the last of his energy start to disappear, and he starts to flag, his breathing heavy and his legs gone, battered and bruised. He's angry at Mansfield and angry at himself.

'That's it, he's not even in it,' says Charlie to Maurice.

Robin is substituted, and he limps off the pitch, head down. As he walks off, scouts, coaches, and managers leave too; they've seen enough. He walks down the steps into the tunnel and down the corridor and into the dressing room.

Stripping off, he throws his muddy kit to the floor and pulls on his clothes, anger flooding through his body. He kicks the bench and slings his kit bag over his shoulder and heads to the Mansfield dressing room.

Looking around, he sees that no one is about, and he heads to the team bath, hot water gushing in, ready to greet the victors. Robin drops his kit bag, unzips his jeans and pulls them down. He sits on the red quarry-tiled wall of the bath, leans forward, and heaves from his bowels, sending a steaming turd plopping into the hot bathwater behind him, and he feels the relief. *Bathe in that, you cunts!* Robin grabs a Mansfield towel and wipes his arse, throws it to the floor and pulls up his jeans. He heads down the corridor and out of the ground, and into the Mansfield night.

*

Robin goes back to London and locks himself away, doesn't show up for training. Nobody knows where he is. He needs to get away from the pain. He sorts out a fix and sprinkles the powder into some tinfoil. Heating the tinfoil, he inhales the smoky vapour and finds peace.

'Hey, man, how's it hangin'?' says Janis.

'I'm okay now that I'm with you.'

Janis chuckles, strokes her hair, and says, 'You high?'

'I'm going up past the rooftops and into the sky,' says Robin, grinning.

'That's my man.'

'Sometimes I don't wanna come down.'

'Crazy ain't it. Just relax and go with the flow.'

*

Tuesday 9 November 1976
Steve Hetzke walks into Charlie Hurley's office and hands in a written transfer request. Tommy Youlden, Steve Death, Mick Hollis, John Murray, Eamon Dunphy, Dennis Nelson, Robin Friday, and now another wants away from Elm Park. Robin Friday is on the missing list. Charlie has a headache and can't get rid of it.

*

Adwest Training Ground —

'Where's Robin?' asks Tommy Youlden.

'He's not well,' says Charlie.

'What's up with him?'

'Never mind, let's just get on with our preparations for Saturday.'

*

Saturday 13 November 1976
A cold, winter's afternoon at Elm Park, and there's no Robin Friday. Six thousand six hundred and twelve fans stand in groups to fight the cold.

Preston North End have come to attack, have come to embarrass and rub Reading's noses in it. They chase and harry and cut through Reading. Charlie Hurley shouts from the bench, tries to encourage his team. Charlie rubs his neck, rubs his chin, and shakes his head. Preston score once and score again. Reading 0 Preston North End 2. It looks like Preston can score at will. Reading are under siege.

As the whistle blows for half-time, the boos ring out. Charlie is up off the bench and down the steps and into the dressing room. He waits like a coiled spring.

The players filter in, and Charlie stands, his face red, his eyes hard. The players take their tea and sit down.

‘What the fucking hell was that? Have we even got a fucking defence? You’re all a bloody disgrace! Professionals…there’s fuck all professional about any of you. I don’t want anything more to do with any of you. I’m sick of it, pig fucking sick of it. Now fuck off and get back out there.’ Charlie slams the door and goes down the corridor, up the steps and back onto the bench. He ignores the shouts and the jeers. Has thoughts of running off down the corridor, out the doors, and driving away in his car.

Reading tighten up in the second half, but the damage is already done. The game finishes Reading 0 Preston North End 2. Boos echo out around Elm Park.

*

Tuesday 16 November 1976

Robin returns to training at Elm Park. His eyes dark and his chest still full of phlegm.

Charlie takes Robin to one side. ‘What happened at Mansfield, we forget about it, right?’

‘Yeah, I’m feelin’ a bit better now, like. I was just fuckin’ sick of being kicked around the park.’

‘I know, but you stepped over the line.’

‘Yeah, I know, I don’t feel great about it. It was a heat of the moment thing, like.’

‘Let’s get you stretched off and ready for Wealdstone on Saturday.’

‘Thanks, Boss.’

‘Don’t mention it.’

*

Thursday 18 November 1976

At the Thursday morning press briefing, Charlie walks in with a clipboard, holds it to his chest. He sits down to face the questions. *The prying fucking questions…*

'Morning, Charlie,' asks Geoff Thompson from the *Chronicle*. 'Why have seven players asked for transfers so far this season?'

'Well, that's a lovely question to start with, isn't it, Geoff, thank you. I've said it before, football clubs are busy places, and players come and go, it's part of the game.'

'But if we look, five of them requested their moves in the summer, before a ball had even been kicked: Friday, Death, Youlden, Hollis, and Murray. Why is that?'

'That's a private matter between those individuals and me, and they've all signed their contracts now, if I'm not mistaken?'

'Well, okay, since then and after contracts were signed, Nelson and Hetzke have requested a move…why?'

'Right, Friday wants to play at a higher level, and as a club, we won't stand in his way. Hetzke has requested one, and this will be discussed at the next board meeting. Dennis Nelson hasn't settled in Reading and would like to move back up north.'

Charlie feels his collar tightening, his anger rising.

'Now, that's seven requests, and not to mention Eamon Dunphy, who the club put up for a free transfer a week after he signed his contract, so that's eight out of a squad of seventeen professionals, so there must be more to this, surely…wouldn't you agree?'

Eamon-fucking-Dunphy and his pen, and his words, and his big bloody gob…

'I'm not going to answer that, Geoff. You must think I'm daft. You're here to report on this club and support this club, so please do that instead of trying to dig up bloody dirt,' says Charlie, staring at the reporter.

‘Do you think the players might be trying to undermine you?’

Charlie Hurley doesn’t answer, picks up his clipboard, and walks out of the room.

*

Friday 19 November 1976
Charlie picks up the *Reading Chronicle.* He sees the headline: *WHAT’S WRONG AT ELM PARK?*

He sits down at his desk and reads it: *players transfer-listed...players undermining Hurley’s authority...Dunphy added to the transfer list after comments he made after the Peterborough match...*

He screws the newspaper up and hurls it to the floor. He picks up the telephone and phones the *Chronicle.* Wishes the dial moved fucking faster.

The phone rings out. ‘Hello, the *Chronicle*, Sports.’

‘Thompson, is that you?’

‘Yes, Geoff Thompson here, how can I help?’

‘Yes, you certainly can help me by not stepping foot in Elm Park again. I’ve just had the misfortune to read your tripe, and as of today, you will not be allowed access to Elm Park or to any of my players. Got it?’

‘Who is this?’

‘Charlie-*fucking*-Hurley.’ He slams down the phone and rubs his face.

*

Saturday 20 November 1976
The magic of the FA Cup returns to Elm Park. Reading entertain Southern League side Wealdstone in the first round. Five thousand seven hundred and ninety-one fans descend on Elm Park, eager to see a few goals.

He goes to his usual spot in the dressing room. Clothes

off. Reading shirt on. Shorts on…touches them…wishes them good luck.

Robin gees himself up, says to Death and the defence, 'Watch George Duck, he's a top striker. Put the shackles on him or he'll do you.'

The referee blows his whistle and the game kicks off. Reading put pressure on from the off, and Gary Peters makes a run and sends in a centre ball, which Robin heads on towards goal, but the ball goes over the crossbar.

Reading win a corner and it's sent in high. Hiron heads the ball down to Robin, who shoots hard and low, but the keeper makes a tremendous save. As the half-time whistle sounds, it's Reading 0 Wealdstone 0. Reading are in control, but only a goal away from disaster.

In the second half, Death pumps the ball up long and high. Robin and Minty race through and past the Wealdstone defence, who are caught off guard. Murray belts the ball, but it goes over the crossbar.

In the sixtieth minute, a Wealdstone defender struggles to control the ball, and Robin pounces and heads the ball at goal. Another Wealdstone defender sprints and saves the ball off the line, but he freezes, and instead of getting rid of the ball, he can only watch as Minty crashes in and forces the ball over the line. Reading 1 Wealdstone 0. There are cheers of relief from the Reading fans. Minty and Robin grab each other and celebrate with the fans.

In the sixty-third minute, Robin charges towards the area but is hacked from behind and falls to the floor. The Wealdstone player is shown a yellow card and his name goes into the book: Watson.

A few minutes later, Robin receives a ball and is sent slamming into the hard turf. The referee holds up a yellow card and the player's name goes into the book: Fursden. Then Fursden crashes into Hiron, and he receives a red card and an early bath.

A minute later, Carnaby runs onto a ball and is bent in half by a thigh-high tackle, and the red card is shown again: Arnold, who joins Fursden for an early bath. Wealdstone are down to nine men.

In the eighty-third minute, Painter comes on for his debut and replaces Hiron.

Robin goes in and steals the ball from a Wealdstone defender with a sliding tacking and pops the ball inside to Murray, who, instead of shooting, passes to Painter, who with his first touch hits the ball wide of the goal. Painter looks to the sky, knowing he should have scored.

Wealdstone cannot do anything with nine men, and Reading hold them off. It finishes Reading 1 Wealdstone 0. Reading are into the draw for the second round of the FA Cup. Robin shakes hands with the Wealdstone players and goes to the stands to meet his fans and sign a few autographs.

*

Robin goes to meets his dealer and can't get what he needs. He starts to shake, starts to feel like he's got the flu. *Clucking hell.* Needs a fix to feel okay, to make the pain go away and feel well again.

*

Thursday 25 November 1976

Robin walks into Elm Park in his Afghan coat, his mud-encrusted boots slung over his shoulder.

'Robin, how are you?' asks Charlie, looking at the black rings around his eyes and the pale face.

'I'm still not great, but I'll try and do some training,'

says Robin with a nasal voice, his chest full of phlegm.

'Go and get yourself changed, and we'll see how you get on.'

'Okay, Boss.'

Charlie looks at his *man,* Friday, and knows the signs and sees the excess on Robin's face and deep in his eyes. Charlie is starting to lose *his* man and is fighting to keep him onside. Charlie thinks of the board, thinks of his players, and thinks of Robin, and is torn up, but he knows at some point he's got to offload the one element he can't control. Charlie looks up at the grey skies and looks for chinks of sunlight, but there are none.

He announces his squad for Tranmere: Death, Peters, Moreline, Bennett, Henderson, Nelson, Carnaby, Stuckey, Porterfield, Murray, Williams, Friday and Painter. Charlie knows Robin is doubtful but would rather keep his player where he can see him.

*

Friday 26 November 1976

The Reading bus heaves its way through the heavy wind and rain towards Birkenhead —

Forty minutes before kick-off, Charlie Hurley sits on a table in the away dressing room at Prenton Park; his players look up from the benches. 'The team will be: Death, Peters, Henderson, Bennett, Moreline, Stuckey, Carnaby, Porterfield, Murray, Nelson, Hiron, and on the bench, Williams.'

Charlie looks at his players, looks at Robin, and sees his face with sad eyes, crestfallen. Tonight, Robin won't play but will watch Reading play Tranmere Rovers in the wind, and in the rain.

Robin's mind flickers back to his goal of the season at

Elm Park against Tranmere: the key to promotion and the glory. This memory of a brighter evening stirs his melancholy.

Robin takes his place on the bench and watches as the rain pours. A paltry crowd of two thousand five hundred and twenty-five watch from the stands, their voices carried on the wind.

The whistle blows and Tranmere attack and force a save from Death. Tranmere storm through the mud and hustle and bustle the Reading defence.

In the twenty-sixth minute, Tranmere break, and the ball is struck into the far corner. Tranmere Rovers 1 Reading 0. There are cheers. Charlie shouts from the bench.

In the fortieth minute, Dennis Nelson is brought down in the mud by a Tranmere defender. He comes up snarling at his attacker. The referee awards a free kick. The free kick is sent towards Nelson, who feels a push in his back as the ball travels over. Nelson lashes out, swinging his arms around and knocking back his marker. Nelson shouts into the face of the defender and then headbutts him. The crowd yell: 'Get him off!' The defender holds his face. The referee runs over and holds up the red card. Nelson is off. He drops his head and walks off the pitch to boos. 'I don't fucking believe it. I really don't fucking believe it,' says Charlie, shaking his head in anger.

Robin watches, knowing how Dennis Nelson feels, knowing he's been singled out for special treatment. To wind a man up, to pull and push and elbow and kick him until he explodes.

In the second half, and in the forty-seventh minute, Tranmere make a raid on the Reading goal and win a free kick. The kick comes in and loops over Death, who stands in the thick mud and watches as a Tranmere forward nods the ball into the back of the net.

'There's not a man fucking near him,' says Charlie. Maurice shakes his head. Robin sits with his arms folded, cold, staring into the distance. Tranmere Rovers 2 Reading 0.

In the sixty-seventh minute, Stuckey receives a pass from Hiron and charges past two Tranmere players, then passes to Peters, who goes around two men and chips the ball with his left foot into the top left-hand corner. There's a cheer from the small band of Reading fans. Tranmere Rovers 2 Reading 1.

'That's more fuckin' like it,' says Robin. Charlie claps his hands. 'Come on, lads, now keep that going.'

A minute later, Tranmere charge into the Reading area and a player is brought down by Carnaby. 'Penalty,' says the referee. Charlie looks away. Tranmere's Moore steps up, shoots, and Death saves, then Tranmere shoot from the rebound, but Death saves that too. Charlie punches the air in relief.

The rain continues to hammer down, and with it come Tranmere. Reading try hard to compete, but with ten men they fall short. The match finishes Tranmere Rovers 2 Reading 1.

The players walk in, soaked to the skin, heads down. They bathe, they dry, and get back on the bus.

The bus pulls out of Birkenhead and makes its way back down south, through the wind and the rain, and at three o'clock in the morning the bus pulls into Elm Park. Robin says his goodbyes and heads home.

*

Tuesday 30 November 1976
Ian Porterfield returns to Sunderland, his month loan at an end. He goes back with a few games under his belt and a few tales to tell his pals.

*

Saturday 4 December 1976
Frost makes the Elm Park mud as hard as concrete, and the Reading v York City fixture is postponed.

*

Tuesday 7 December 1976
Robin plays against Arsenal reserves, along with Hollis, Murray, and Youlden. Charlie is eager to test their fitness. Robin looks at the empty stands of Highbury and works hard, keen to get himself back into the team and in front of a crowd again. Minty scores, but it finishes Arsenal reserves 3 Reading reserves 1.

Charlie watches on and is happy with what he's seen of his men and is glad that Robin Friday seems to be back up for it.

*

Saturday 11 December 1976
Charlie walks out onto the ground at Wycombe, stamps his heel into the icy ground; it doesn't budge. 'Jesus, Maurice, they'll break their bloody necks. How's this game still on?'

'I don't know, but it is.'

Charlie and Maurice head back to the dressing room. 'Lads, have a look at the pitch. You may want to change your boots or studs,'

'Or put some fuckin' ice skates on,' says Robin, laughing.

The players rush out of the dressing room, inspect the

pitch, try on different boots and try and run. The stands are empty, save for a couple of people shovelling grit and scattering it onto the stands.

'For fuck's sake,' says Minty, 'have you seen that dip in the pitch.'

'Seen it, mate? I've fuckin' played on it, but never like this. Eleven foot it slopes they reckon,' says Robin.

'This is madness, a sloping pitch covered in ice,' says Minty.

'Yep, the magic of the FA Cup, right 'ere.'

The players go back into the dressing room; a throng of excitement builds and there are laughs and giggles.

Clothes off. Reading shirt on. Shorts on…touches them…wishes them good luck.

The ground is full, with seven thousand seven hundred in the crowd, huddled together in thick coats, hats and scarves. The smell of Bovril fills the air.

The first half kicks off, and Robin laughs at the adversity of the icy conditions. He isn't scared of slipping or sliding on the ground.

In the fifth minute, Bennett sends a free kick into Wycombe's area. The ball bounces loose and Robin is there. He chests the ball down and past a Wycombe defender and smashes the ball in from six yards. He runs away, arms outstretched, and the travelling fans cheer, the goal warming them up. Wycombe Wanderers 0 Reading 1.

Two minutes later, Robin chases a defender, the defender passes the ball, but Robin has already committed and crashes into his man, sending him sprawling into the icy ground. The referee calls Robin over and shows him a yellow card. Robin apologises to his man, helps him up from the ground.

At every chance Robin chases the ball, chases lost causes, eager to get the ball, to win at every opportunity. He flicks the ball about, caresses it with the outside of his boot, and turns defenders inside out, beats players twice, just for the fun of it.

In the thirty-second minute, Murray lets go with a powerful shot, but the keeper palms it away. Robin charges in and bears down on a defender, who panics, and Robin belts the ball home. He runs away, his right arm aloft, his fist clenched. The Reading fans jump about, knowing they may well be going into the third round of the FA Cup. Wycombe Wanderers 0 Reading 2.

For the rest of the first half, Reading dominate, and Robin dominates the non-league side.

In the second half, Wycombe try to come back, and they force Death to make save after save.

In the sixty-eighth minute, Wycombe attack, and there's a loose ball in the Reading box. Death looks on, wrong-footed, as Pearson strikes a half-volley into the back of the net. A deafening cheer rings out from the stands as Pearson peels away, arms raised. Wycombe Wanderers 1 Reading 2.

Wycombe Wanderers try their luck, desperate for an equaliser, and they push Reading back. Robin and Reading are forced to defend. The clock ticks down and the Wycombe fans will their team on.

In the final minute, Wycombe push all their players up, and they run and harry the Reading defence. The ball falls to Pearson, Reading fans hold their breath, and he shoots, and the ball flies towards the goal, and Death looks on, Robin looks on, but the ball strikes the post and deflects out for a goal kick. Reading breathe a sigh of relief.

The match finishes Wycombe Wanderers 1 Reading 2. Reading are into the third round of the FA Cup.

Robin leaves the pitch with a grin and wishes he'd got a hat-trick, knows he could've done, but this'll do. A female fan grabs his attention as he leaves the pitch, her eyes brown and her skin olive. Robin goes out for the night and doesn't go home.

*

Monday 13 December 1976
In the Elm Park dressing room, the players, Charlie, and Maurice gather around a transistor radio. There's no Robin Friday. There's a chatter of excitement as some players cross their fingers and hope for a First Division club.

'*Fulham at home will play...Swindon Town...Halifax Town at home will play...Luton Town.*'

'No United or Liverpool yet,' says Painter.

'*Shhhh*!'

'*Hereford United will play...Reading...*'

'Oh, for fuck's sake, what a poor draw,' says Charlie.

The other draws are made but no one is really listening, and nobody really cares, the chance of a dream draw against Liverpool or Leeds United has gone for another season.

*

Jimmy Andrews calls Charlie Hurley and asks if Robin Friday is still available for transfer. Charlie confirms that he is.

*

Thursday 16 December 1976
Richie Bowman, midfielder, signs from Second Division Charlton, for a fee reported to be just under £10,000.

*

Friday 17 December 1976
Robin and Reading travel to Grimsby. Their train is late leaving Reading. Charlie checks his watch. 'We'll never make it.'

The players run down the steps into the Tube station, and there are delays.

'We've got to get to King's Cross. We need taxis, follow me,' says Charlie.

The players, with their kits, run back up the steps to the taxi rank, and there stands a queue a hundred yards long.

'All we need now is the "Benny Hill Theme" tune,' shouts Robin. Charlie runs to the front of the queue, uses his charm, and procures the first three black cabs.

The team squeeze into the back of the cabs, and as they turn the corner, they run into heavy traffic. Charlie looks at his watch again. 'We'll never make the train to Doncaster. It leaves in two bloody minutes, for Christ's sake.'

The players laugh and joke and as they pass Madame Tussauds. 'We've another couple of miles yet,' says Robin.

'Tell me something I don't know,' says Charlie, red in the face.

'This is what we get for going to khazi country,' says Robin. Charlie shakes his head.

The black cabs pull into King's Cross Station and the doors swing open and the players run out, and Charlie runs around paying the fares. They look up at the board and see their train is still in; they run along and down the stairs to the platform.

'Is this the train for Doncaster?' asks Charlie.

'Yeah, we thought the bleedin' Queen was coming. Luckily the Tube inspector rang ahead for you,' says the

British Rail guard.

'Thank you, thank you. No good for my blood pressure this.'

The players sit on the train and tuck into the food and make their way to Doncaster, and onto their connection to Cleethorpes.

On Friday night, in the hotel, there's a stillness, and Robin's thoughts turn to tomorrow's game.

*

Saturday 18 December 1976

At Blundell Park, a freezing wind blows in from the North Sea, and seagulls mock from overhead. Three thousand and eighty fans have come to watch Grimsby Town v Reading.

Clothes off. Reading shirt on. Shorts on…touches them…wishes them good luck.

The crowd cheer and clap as the teams run out onto the pitch. The whistle blows and the game begins in the wind and the cold. Grimsby start the brighter and push Reading to defend.

In the fifteenth minute, a loose ball in the Reading area is slammed past Death, and it's Grimsby Town 1 Reading 0. The fans roar from the stands.

Grimsby come again, and again, attack after attack, cutting through Reading's midfield. Robin gets back to help out his teammates. Reading hang on and Death saves their skin, again and again.

In the twenty-eighth minute, Murray picks up a ball inside the Reading half and makes a run, then he passes to Hiron on the right wing. Hiron switches the ball back to Murray who, in full stride, knocks the ball in from thirty yards; it curls in the air and lands in the back of the net.

Grimsby Town 1 Reading 1. A small band of Reading fans cheer into the wind.

At half-time, Robin sips on the sweet tea, and Charlie rallies his troops. 'Come on, lads, you can do this. Throw the kitchen sink at them and shoot on sight.'

The second half kicks off. Reading and Grimsby push and pull at each other, trying to break the deadlock and get ahead.

In the sixty-eighth minute, Grimsby flick the ball into the area, and it goes to a Grimsby midfielder who cracks the ball home. The fans roar and seagulls screech from the roofs of the stands. Grimsby Town 2 Reading 1.

The game kicks off and Reading are awake again, eager to get back into it. Robin shouts encouragement and chases down defenders and midfielders.

Murray makes a run and sees Bowman, unmarked, and slots a pass to him. Bowman rushes his shot and hits the ball wide.

Robin runs with the ball on the outside of his boot down the right and sends a pass over to the left wing for Carnaby, who cuts in but shoots wide.

Robin picks up the ball from midfield and knocks it on to Stuckey, who sends in a centre. Hiron throws himself at the ball, but his header is wide.

Robin rallies the troops and runs from deep, cuts through the defence and sends Murray clear with a perfect pass. Murray looks up and belts the ball…over the crossbar. Robin falls to his knees and holds his head and knows Murray should've scored.

The Reading revival ends, and as much as Reading try, they can't get back into it, and it finishes Grimsby Town 2 Reading 1.

Robin goes to the fans who've made the journey and signs autographs.

In the dressing room there's quiet. 'It's a long way to come for a bloody defeat,' says Minty.

'You should've scored that sitter then, shouldn't ya,' says Robin, laughing. Robin pulls on his clothes and heads to the players' lounge.

*

Monday 27 December 1976

Robin walks into the Elm Park dressing room —

'Nice of you to join us, Robin. I was just saying to the lads that we've not had a league victory since the thirtieth of October – two months without a win. Today we face Peterborough. We've played them four times this season and only won once. Let's put them away today. I don't need to remind any of you of the kicking they gave us in those matches. Just go at them, they're struggling, and after being thumped four-nothing by non-league Northwich Victoria in the cup, they'll be feeling very sorry for themselves, so they'll be eager to get back to winning ways. Now, let's give our fans a bit of festive cheer, lads.'

He goes to his usual spot in the dressing room. Clothes off. Reading shirt on. Shorts on…touches them…wishes them good luck.

Robin runs into the Elm Park cheers to the sound of Belgian pop. Seven thousand two hundred and sixty-four. The whistle blows and the first half kicks off.

In the seventeenth minute, Robin makes a run but is sent crashing into the mud by a Peterborough defender. The referee awards a free kick from twenty-five yards out. Stuckey plays it square to Carnaby, who sends it on to Murray, who smashes a shot which goes in off the inside of the post. Reading 1 Peterborough United 0. Robin runs to Minty and congratulates him, they wave to the crowd, and Reading's cheers sound out around Elm Park.

In the second half, a ball comes over and Robin makes a run, keeps his eye on the ball and heads it goalbound, but the keeper palms it away and into the path of Murray, who shoots, but the keeper somehow manages to stop it and brings it under control.

Peterborough keep coming, trying to grab an equaliser. In the eighty-sixth minute, a Peterborough defender lets go with a fierce shot from twenty yards. Robin holds his breath, and the whole of Elm Park hold theirs. As the ball looks to be going in, Death flings himself, cat-like, and pushes the ball away, and for the final minutes Reading form a ten-man defence. The final whistle blows: Reading 1 Peterborough United 0.

*

Tuesday 28 December 1976

Charlie sits in his office, and the phone rings —

'Yes, Charlie Hurley.'

'Ah, Charlie, good morning. It's Jimmy Andrews from Cardiff, how are you?'

'Ah, not too bad after a good result yesterday, and you?'

'Aye, I saw, and we had a good win against Hereford. I can give you a bit of intel on them before your cup game if you like?'

'Yes, that'd be appreciated, Jimmy. Have you had any more thoughts about Robin Friday?'

There's a pause at the other end of the line.

'Yes, we've a few tricky games coming up, and Derek Showers limped off yesterday, so, yes, I think we'd like to sort something out, but I'll have to talk to the board about finances as things are a little tight here. You're playing tomorrow?'

'Yes, Oxford, away.'

'Right, I'll drive down and take a look.'

'No, problem, I'll let him know you're coming down,' says Charlie, rubbing his neck.

'Okay, thanks, Charlie. I'll see you at tomorrow's game.'

'Okay, goodbye, Jimmy.'

Both men put the phone down, thinking of the deal, and thinking of that man, Friday.

*

Wednesday 29 December 1976
The Reading fans hear a rumour that Robin Friday may be off to Cardiff City —

The Reading team bus moves through the snow, which keeps coming down, and pop music plays on the radio. The heater keeps the bus warm. There's a smell of cigarettes, and the sound of laughter rings out.

At the Manor Ground, Oxford, they arrive and go into the car park, the snow still coming down. Charlie exits the bus and disappears into reception, and after a couple of minutes he pops his head out and waves the lads off the bus.

Robin goes down the corridors and into the away dressing room, finds a spot and sits down.

Clothes off. Reading shirt on. Shorts on…touches them…wishes them good luck.

'Now lads, it's going to be horrible out there. Don't try and flick it about, just go direct and hit long balls over to Minty, Robin and Ray. Keep it really simple out there, no fancy stuff.'

The referee calls them out, and the players get into line and run out onto the pitch in the freezing cold, the snow still coming down. The referee places a bright orange ball down on the spot. Five thousand three hundred and forty-nine fans stand in the snow and the sleet, hands numb, Bovril the order of the night. Jimmy Andrews has come to watch Robin Friday, come to make his mind up about signing him, here in the freezing cold and snow.

'Get ready for Bambi on ice,' says Robin, winking at Minty.

The first half begins, and Oxford United and Reading go at each other with long balls. Oxford start to put the pressure on, and Reading defend with every man.

A long ball comes over, and Robin plays a clever flick onto Hiron, but his header comes to nothing.

The half-time whistle blows, and the players rush off the pitch, eager for their hot sugary tea.

In the second half, the game slows as the snow sweeps down across the pitch, and then in the final minutes, both teams try to go for the win.

In the eighty-eighth minute, there's a scramble on the edge of the Reading area and Bennett is pushed. An Oxford player sends in a cross, which is met by a stinging Oxford shot, but Death saves and slams the ball away. It falls to Oxford again, and the ball is struck hard and low. Bowman saves it off the line, but the ball falls to Oxford yet again, and this time they don't miss. Oxford United 1 Reading 0. The Oxford crowd cheer, while the Reading crowd stand frozen in silence.

In the dying seconds, Reading attack and a cross is sent in, which Hiron heads at goal, but the ball is saved off the line. The final whistle blows and Robin and the players wave at the fans and run off the pitch, eager to get out of the weather.

Robin throws his clothes on and heads to the players' lounge. He orders a lager and downs it, orders another and swigs it back. He sits at the bar and has another.

'Where's Robin?' asks Charlie.

'He's gone up to the players' lounge,' says Maurice.

'Right, get up there before Jimmy Andrews claps eyes on him. You know what Robin's like, he'll be throwing them down,' says Charlie.

Maurice runs up the stairs and stops at the players' lounge door, peeps around, and sees Robin at the bar, laughing and joking with Minty. He rushes in. 'How many pints have you had?'

'Three, why? You buyin'?'

'No, I'm not. Jimmy Andrews is here from Cardiff,' says Maurice with raised eyebrows.

'Is he buyin'?'

'He wants to buy you. Now calm it down, Robin,' says Maurice.

'He can buy me if he gets me another pint,' says Robin, laughing.

Charlie walks in with Jimmy Andrews, and Maurice stands in front of Robin, tries to shield him. The other players hover around the bar.

'Robin, can we have a moment,' says Charlie.

Robin peeps out from behind Maurice and moves forward, hand out, and shakes Jimmy Andrews' hand.

'A good game, Robin. I'm a big fan of yours,' says Jimmy.

'Cheers, would've been nice to come away from 'ere

with a result, but as Charlie says, you can't always have everythin', can you.'

'No, you can't, but it's the trying that counts, eh?'

'Sure is.'

'Look, I'd very much like you to join us at Cardiff – what about it?' say Jimmy, offering his hand.

'I'm sure we can sort something out,' says Robin, shaking hands with Jimmy.

'Now, Jimmy, let's get back to the boardroom. We can carry on our chat there,' says Charlie, escorting Jimmy away.

Maurice stands in no man's land as Robin makes his way back to the bar and pushes through the crowd.

'Minty, your round.'

'Yeah, sure…so you off to Cardiff then?'

'Between you and me, I don't really fancy it, mate, but then it's not really up to me, is it.'

*

Thursday 30 December 1976

Charlie Hurley sits in his office, the radiator on full. The phone rings, and he knows who it is. He clears his throat.

'Charlie Hurley,'

'Good morning, Charlie, it's Jimmy. I've spoken to the board, and we'd like to sign Friday.'

'Okay, and what's the offer?'

'Twenty-eight thousand pounds.'

Charlie pauses. 'That's a fair way off the valuation, Jimmy,' says Charlie, trying his hand.

'That's all we can manage, and all the board have authorised. It really is the most we can do,' says the canny Scot.

Charlie writes '28k' on his desk notepad. Thinks of the

man he signed for £750 from Hayes. Thinks of the man he's got now. Charlie circles the '28k' on his notepad. 'Okay, it's a deal, but what about his wages?'

'We can do two hundred and fifty pounds including bonuses, and of course a signing on fee for him at the usual five per cent plus a little extra.'

'That'll do it, so when do you want him?'

'Can you get him here this afternoon?'

'I'll get onto it,' says Charlie. 'He should be in for training in about half an hour.'

Charlie hopes his man turns up today.

*

Charlie's Office —

Charlie sits, then stands. Looks at his paperwork, looks at his telephone. Shuffles the paper into a neater pile. Looks at the photo of his wife and daughters. Thinks about the incoming storm. Charlie closes the window.

There's a knock at the door. Charlie knows who's on the other side. He knows. He knows too well. He clears his throat.

'Yes, come in,' says Charlie.

The door swings open with Robin attached to it.

'Mornin', Boss, you wanted to see me?' A half-smile flickers on Robin's face as he rubs his chin.

'Yes, yes, I did. Please, take a seat.'

Robin pulls the chair out and drops into it. Charlie wishes he'd left the window open just a fraction.

'So, what's the griff then?'

'Jimmy Andrews has made an offer for your services this morning.'

As the words fall out of Charlie's mouth, Robin leans back in his chair, arms crossed, casting a glance. 'I've thought about it and I'm not going to fuckin' Cardiff; it's miles out the way. I want a club in London, not somewhere even bloody further away from London. Anyway, they're Second Division. I want to be in the First. In fact, they could be back in the bloody Third again next season.'

'That's why they want you; they need goals and your fighting spirit.'

'I'm not fuckin' going. I'd rather stay 'ere, Boss.'

'Look, they're offering you up to two hundred and fifty quid a week, Robin, and of course you'll get a signing on fee too. It's all far more than we can offer you here.'

Robin eyeballs the ceiling and then brings calmer eyes back to Charlie.

'That all? I'm not doin' it. It's not a big enough club, and it's not in London either.'

'Steady now, kid, take some time to think about it. It's a good offer. I'd recommend it. A good signing on fee too.'

'No.'

'Look at me when I signed for Sunderland. I didn't even know where it was, and it turned out to be a smashing move. Very unexpected. This is a great opportunity for you, and think of the money. The chance to play in Europe too.'

'I don't need to think about it. I'm not going.'

'Well, you see…er…Mr Waller, the chairman, wants to sell you.'

'What the fuck has it got to do with Waller.'

'As I've told you before, it's his club, Robin.'

'But he's not the cunt that will have to move to Cardiff, is he? Also, he don't fuckin' own me.'

‘We’re both employed by Mr Waller. We are his employees. When I signed you from Hayes, he paid for you.’

‘So, I’m like a fuckin’ slave then, to be bought and sold. Go ’ere, go there, even if I don’t want to?’

‘Look, it’s the modern game. We’re getting off the point here. I’d like you to sign for Cardiff. It’s a good move. You’ve just got to…well, look at it from a different angle. An opportunity to test yourself at a higher level.’

There’s a rattle and tinkle outside the door. A knock follows. A tray of cups and saucers and some large teapots appear on a stainless-steel trolley pushed by an old lady with a white-and-blue uniform. The smell of fresh tea fills the room.

‘Dolly, how are you?’

‘Oh, I can’t complain, Mr Hurley, thank you. Tea?’

‘Yes, just one sugar please.’

‘Cutting back, are we?’

Robin mutters under his breath: ‘On his team, yeah.’

‘Yes, looking after the choppers,’ says Charlie, bearing an excellent set of teeth for a centre half. Dolly pours the tea and hands Charlie a blue-and-white china cup and saucer with two Rich Tea biscuits on the side.

‘Thanks, Dolly.’ Charlie nods. Dolly smiles. The interlude halts the verbal volley between the two men.

‘Robin, cup and saucer or mug?’ says Dolly.

‘Well, a mug would seem very appropriate right now. Yep, a mug, please, love.’

Charlie coughs and makes for his teacup, but it can’t contain the storm.

‘Sugar?’ says Dolly.

‘Yes, two please, although we know I’m sweet

enough,' says Robin, winking at Dolly.

'You'll make me blush.'

Dolly pours the tea into the mug and pulls out a separate plate for Robin and puts a generous helping of biscuits onto a plate for him.

'You're breaking up something' good 'ere, Boss.'

'Robin.'

Charlie does a small shake of his head at Robin while trying not to draw the attention of Dolly.

'What's this? You leaving us, dear?'

'Yep, they wanna sell me to Cardiff.'

'No!' says Dolly, raising her eyebrows.

'Yep, trying to send me packin'.'

Charlie leaps to his feet, and with a forced smile he ushers Dolly out of his office. He then slowly walks back to his chair behind his desk, not looking at Robin until he sits down.

'Come on, Robin, you know the score.'

'I dunno what you mean, Boss.' Robin reaches for his hot tea and takes a swig.

'Come on, you know that I know what's happening to you outside this club; we've discussed it countless times. This is a small town, and people have seen things. You're not exactly subtle, Robin. It won't be long before other clubs find out, and then no one'll be interested in signing you. You need to get away from here and make a fresh start. You need to get away from London too.'

'Look, I'll pack it all in. I'll stop all the shit.'

'Frank Waller wants to sell you.'

'What about you? Do you want to sell me an' all?'

'You've been brilliant for us, helped us up into the Third Division, but you're different now on that pitch –

you know that. End of last season you were as bright as a button, but since you've come back you've not been the same. You're head and shoulders above these lads you're playing against, but you can't turn it on like you used to. This isn't easy for me to sit here and do this like this. The times I've had the other lads in here moaning about you not training and I've let it slide. I can't defend you any more because you're not doing it on the pitch, and I know you've been messing about with drugs. In my position, I just can't have that. It's my job on the line here too, and I won't lie, Robin, so just accept the offer, and then no one loses out.'

'And what if I refuse to go?'

'Then, as I've said before, I drop you to the reserves until your contract runs out, and we both know you're too good for that. I can't make it any clearer than that, but if I were you, I'd sign for Cardiff. Sort yourself out and prove me wrong.'

Robin sits fiddling with something on his left cowboy boot. He brings his eyes back to Charlie. 'Right, I'll go.'

'It's not easy, I know, but you've overcome all sorts. It could be worse. You could be me managing a team near the bottom of the Third Division.'

Robin slurps down the last of the tea and picks up the biscuits, shoves one in his mouth and the rest into his jacket pocket. He stands up and holds out his hand.

'Goodbye, Charlie.' They shake hands.

'Thanks, and goodbye, kid. Good luck. He's expecting you in Cardiff this afternoon.'

Robin looks at his watch. Charlie hands Robin a slip of paper with Jimmy Andrews' phone number on. Robin turns and heads for the door, then turns around and says,

‘No hard feelings, Boss. I know the score.’

The door closes and Robin is gone. Charlie strokes his face and breathes a sigh, and knows that once this news breaks he’s in for a world of shit from the supporters and local press. There’s no Happy New Year here, and the Christmas cheer is gone. The turkey is stripped and its carcass cold – it sits stinking in the dustbin.

*

Charlie calls Jimmy Andrews —

‘Hello, Jimmy, Charlie here. Robin’s on his way, should be with you this afternoon.’

‘Great news. Can you offer any advice to help things run smoothly?’ says Jimmy, staring down at the doodles he’s creating in his notebook.

‘*Mmm…*It’s better for Robin if he’s away from London, and I think he’d agree with that too. If I were you, I’d get him digs up in Cardiff sooner rather than later. Get him settled. Somewhere away from distraction is best.’

‘I think you’re right, and you know him better than anyone. We’ll arrange for him to come up and look at some places after he signs.’

‘Okay, Jimmy, and good luck,’ says Charlie, tapping his finger on the fixture list.

‘Aye, thanks, Charlie. Bye for now.’

‘Goodbye, Jimmy.’

The phones are placed in their holders, and the men continue to tend to their teams.

*

Tilehurst Road —

He puts on his brown velvet suit and brown-and-beige striped shirt, and puts his fags in his top pocket. He reaches over to Liza. ‘Right, I’m off, girl,’ he says, swooping down to kiss her. She holds him tight. He pulls on his Afghan coat. Then he's out the door and off to Reading train station. He ignores the ticket office. Robin goes to the machine and puts in a penny for a platform ticket. The machine whirrs and punches out an orange ticket. He pops it in his pocket and heads to the platform for the Cardiff train. He finds a seat and waits; the platform is quiet. He fidgets on his seat, and he reaches into his jacket and finds his John Player Special fags. He pulls one out and places it between his lips – tastes the dry tobacco. He sparks it up. The cigarette soothes him, brings him back. He checks his watch on his wrist and waits for the train that will take him away from Elm Park to Ninian Park. The train pulls in, and he boards it and sits down. He picks up a newspaper and whiles away his journey.

The train pulls into Cardiff Central and halts with a gentle bump. Robin rocks out of his seat and heads through the door, minding the gap and stepping onto the platform. He ambles up the platform, hands in pockets. Spotting the exit, he sees no ticket inspectors and relaxes. He lights up a fag and heads outside. As he rounds the corner, he sees two ticket inspectors clipping tickets, and behind them is a burly copper: a member of the British Transport Police. *Shit.*

He can't turn back without causing suspicion, so he decides to bluff it out and strides past the three men. One inspector holds a hand out and asks for Robin's ticket, so Robin reaches into his pocket for the platform ticket and hands it over while walking away.

'Excuse me, sir!'

Robin stops and turns around. 'Yeah?'

'This isn't a valid ticket; have you got your ticket?' says the inspector.

'No.'

'Well, why not?'

'I got to the station late and realized I'd forgotten my wallet, so I just grabbed a platform ticket.'

'Look, we're cracking down on this sort of thing, you know. This is a serious offence, and with it comes a serious fine,' says the copper.

'Look, mate,' says Robin rubbing his chin. 'I'm 'ere to sign for Cardiff City today, and they'll pay for my ticket.'

The policeman looks Robin up and down, watches him draw on his fag, looks at his Cuban heels and Afghan coat.

'Right, you're coming with me.'

Robin walks after the copper and the other ticket inspector, and they head towards the British Transport Police office.

A clerk sits behind the desk and looks over his glasses. 'What've we got here then?'

'Non-payment of a ticket,' says the copper.

'The ticket'll be paid for by Cardiff City, as I said,' says Robin, eyeing both men.

'How are we going to solve this?'

'Ring Cardiff, they're expecting me.'

The arresting copper interjects. 'This gentleman says he's here to sign for Cardiff City today.'

'And I'm the Prince of Wales,' says the clerk, laughing.

'Look, I'm not joking. My name is Robin Friday, and I've left Reading, and I'm signing for Cardiff today.'

'All right then, which position?'

'Centre forward.'

'Last game?'

'We played Oxford United last night, and we lost one-nil.'

'Reading's manager?'

'Charlie Hurley.'

The clerk picks up his paper and looks at last night's football results. Raises his eyebrows.

'Look, this isn't solving anything. He could just be a fan. Besides, if you're a footballer why haven't you got any money?' asks the arresting copper.

'I forgot me wallet. Now, can you get on the phone and call Jimmy Andrews at Cardiff City for me?'

The copper looks at the man in front of the desk. They look at each other. The arresting officer nods at the clerk.

The clerk reaches back into his dog-eared phone directory, thumbs through it and finds Cardiff City's number. He picks up the receiver and dials.

'Hello, yes, this is the British Transport Police at Cardiff Central. We've just apprehended a gentleman for travelling on a train without a ticket, and he hasn't got any money to pay for one. He claims that he's signing for you today and that you're going to pay for his journey?'

The clerk looks at Robin and nods.

'Yes, that's him. Can you come down here and sort this out?'

The clerk looks down and stares at the phone, nodding.

'No, I'm afraid we can't release him until the ticket is paid for, it's an offence…Look, I can understand that, but I'm bound by the laws and byelaws of our country, you must understand that. If I make an exception for one person, then I have to make an exception for everyone.'

Nodding.

'Right, okay, we'll detain Mr Friday until you arrive.

Goodbye.'

The clerk puts the phone back on the receiver and folds his arms. 'Right, we've got to write you up, so you'll just have to wait until Mr Andrews arrives.'

'This is a joke. It's Cardiff City for Christ sake – they can afford it.'

'Again, sir, as I've just said to Mr Andrews, I can't make any exceptions. If you'd just taken the responsibility of paying for your ticket, then we wouldn't be going through all this palaver right now.'

'Cardiff said they were going to pay for the ticket, and I've no wallet. I thought it'd be all right. What a welcome, eh?'

'It's nothing personal, but the law is the law. What would we have if we had no laws?'

'Freedom?'

'No…anarchy, Mr Friday, anarchy.'

'Well, it don't seem to be workin' too well, does it? Have you read the papers lately?'

'Yes, but that's a separate issue, we need the laws to protect us.'

'So what am I being nicked for then?'

'For travelling without a ticket.'

'So who's that protecting?'

'If everyone went about not paying, we'd have no British Rail.'

Robin thinks about it, then nods. 'Fair enough, any chance of a cuppa? It's bleedin' Baltic in 'ere.'

'Of course, Mr Friday, anything else?'

'I wouldn't mind that orange of yours?'

The clerk looks at Robin, fixes him with a stern stare, then smiles. 'There's no side to you is there?'

'If you don't ask, you don't get.'

The clerk and Robin chat about football to pass the time over their cups of tea. After Robin is tired of the chat, he fiddles with a fag packet and strikes up a smoke. He looks up at the yellowing clock on the wall and watches the seconds tick away.

The door opens and Jimmy Andrews walks in.

'All right, Jimmy,' says Robin, looking sorry for himself.

'Right, Robin, let's get this sorted, shall we,' says Jimmy, with a hopeful smile on his face as he heads to the clerk. 'Afternoon, sir, can we get this fare sorted?'

'Yes, of course,' says the clerk, picking up the paper bill and presenting it to Jimmy.

'Right then, here you go,' says Jimmy, reaching into his pocket to count out his notes and change. 'Can I have a receipt, please?'

'You certainly can,' says the clerk, scribbling out a note, which he tears off from a book that has crisp blue carbon copy paper underneath – he removes the blue paper and below is a copy of the receipt. 'There you go, Mr Andrews.'

'Right, let's get you to Ninian Park,' says Jimmy, holding the door for Robin.

'See you around,' says Robin, winking at the clerk. 'But not too soon.'

'Likewise, Mr Friday, and good luck.'

The station is busy as travellers go about their journeys, heading here and there, oblivious of Cardiff's new centre forward walking in their midst. Robin braces himself as he walks out into the cold.

Jimmy turns to him and says, 'Right, let's get back to

the ground and give you a more positive welcome to Cardiff. That's if you still want to sign for us?'

'Of course, I'm looking forward to it, and thanks for sorting out the ticket. It's always a bit tight after Christmas – I owe you one.'

'Look, don't worry about it. It's not like you've been arrested for murder.'

'No, not yet,' says Robin, laughing.

'You can just repay me by helping us beat Fulham at the weekend,' he says, letting Robin into his car. They travel the short distance to Ninian Park.

Robin sees the big blue corrugated shed that is Cardiff City's ground. The car pulls into the car park, and Robin follows Jimmy into reception.

'We'll not keep you long, Robin. I'll give you a tour of the ground, and then we can do the paperwork. Doc Hamilton wants to give you the once over to check your fitness.'

'No problem, Jimmy.'

Robin walks with Jimmy around the ground. It has seen better days but is much bigger than Elm Park. Doc Hamilton gives Robin a quick check over and a clean bill of health. They head to Jimmy's office.

'Right, take a seat, Robin.'

Robin pulls out the chair and falls into it. Jimmy hands the contract to Robin and says, 'Here you go, have a read of this, and when you're happy, sign here and here, and do the same on the other one, please. I'm just going to disappear for five minutes as I've got to go and see the physio, okay?'

'Okay,' says Robin, with one eye on his new contract.

He scans over the paper, waiting to get to the important

part. He checks the money, and that's okay: £250 a week including bonuses and a good signing on fee.

He signs his name four times and dates the documents. He's now a Cardiff City player. First game up is Fulham, against George Best and Bobby Moore. He feels a glow.

'We've sorted a hotel for the night, and we'll show you a house you might be interested in tomorrow.'

Robin nods, but with a squint in his eye. *I ain't movin' 'ere.*

PART TWO
CARDIFF CITY
SEASON 1976/77

Friday 31 December 1976
In the morning —

Robin walks through the gates of Ninian Park. He spots Jimmy Andrews, and another man stood next to Jimmy. The man, mid-fifties, round, wears a beige macintosh and a tweed cap. The man raises his hand and waves at Robin with a reassuring smile. Jimmy waves too.

Robin ambles up to the pair of them.

'Glad to see you, Robin,' says Jimmy, shaking Robin's hand. 'And may I introduce Harry, Harry Parsons. He's a coach, kit man, fixer – a man for all seasons.'

Harry grips Robin's hand and secures it with a second hand; Robin feels his warmth. 'Welcome to the club, Robin, very pleased to meet you, and looking forward to seeing you play in that famous blue jersey.'

'Yeah, likewise, Harry,' says Robin, smiling.

'Harry's going to take you out to a place we've found to rent in Saint Athan. The club will foot some of the initial rent for you, and we'll sort the deposit too,' says Jimmy. 'We'd like to get you settled down as soon as possible.'

Robin hears those last words: settled down as soon as possible; settled down as soon as possible; settled down as soon as possible – they echo through his mind and loop through each other like chains. He knows where they've come from. He's heard them before, many times, over and over again. The words grate against his mind, against his body; they rub like shackles around his soul.

'I'm sure you do,' says Robin, rubbing his chin and looking at Jimmy. 'But where's Saint Athan? Never 'eard of it.'

Harry answers, 'Oh, it's just outside Cardiff, a bus ride away, a lovely little village, it is. It'll be great for you and the wife, and some of the other players live out there too.'

For Robin, it sounds quaint, and the sort of place he'd like to go on holiday for a week, but not to live.

Jimmy is eager. 'So, I'll let you two get to know each other, and have a nice outing, and I hope you like the house.'

'Yep,' says Robin.

Harry gets into the car and lets Robin into the passenger seat. The car pulls out of the car park and heads away from Ninian Park. The car rumbles along, and they wind through the streets of Cardiff.

'There's a lot to do here, Robin, and we've a good bunch of lads. Where are you from?'

'Grew up in London.'

'Which part?'

'Acton, you?' asks Robin, looking out the window at the fields of frosted grass.

'Here, Grangetown, right by the river Taff,' says Harry with pride.

'You worked for 'em for long?'

'Started as a scout in sixty-six, and I've been many things. Tinker, tailor, soldier…'

Robin looks at Harry, his eyes on the road. 'A fair ol' stint then.' Robin looks out of the window and sees signs for Rhoose airport. Where they're going doesn't seem anywhere near Ninian Park. Harry drives steady, like the man he is.

'Almost here now, Robin, not far at all,' he says, eyes still fixed on the road.

'Okay, cool.'

The car pulls into a road and pulls onto a drive outside of a white bungalow with a porch and a blue door.

'Here we are then, Robin.'

'I thought only pensioners lived in bungalows?'

'No, not always. Look, I'll open it up for you and you can have a walk around and see what you think, okay?'

'Yep, fine by me,' says Robin, stepping out of the car.

Harry walks Robin up the garden path and into the porch. He fumbles with the keys and opens the door.

'After you,' he says to Robin.

Robin walks into what appears to be a reception area, with pine boards covering the walls.

'Just lock up when you're done,' says Harry, handing Robin the keys. 'No rush, and I hope you like it.'

'Yep, see you in a bit.'

Robin looks around the rooms; they're comfortable but bland. He heads into the lounge, closes the door behind him. He looks at the fireplace, containing logs waiting to be lit and traces of ash from old fires. He looks out into the garden and looks at the rolling hills behind. He feels a hundred miles from Cardiff, and a thousand miles from anywhere he'd want to be – there's no life here. The sky is grey. There's no fucking way he will move in here. He sits down on the settee and listens to the silence. He decides to inject a little life into the situation. He reaches into his Afghan coat and pulls out a small packet of white powder; he takes a pinch between his thumb and forefinger and sniffs it up into his left nostril. He hears the voices a little less and his thoughts are crystal. There is no fucking way he will move into this coffin, no way he'll bring Liza here.

What were they thinking? Who the fuck do they think I am? Miles from life, and life is for living. Plenty of time to be boring, plenty...

Robin gets up from the settee. Leaves the lounge and heads for the kitchen. There's a sideboard, and it glistens with silverware. Robin laughs and reaches into his pocket and pulls out his John Player Special cigarettes; he pulls out his lighter and strikes it up. He rocks back and forth on his Cuban heels looking at the silver. The smoke peppers his mouth and he feels a dryness. Robin walks to the fridge and pulls out a bottle of milk. He takes a sniff and then takes a swig. He feels the goodness and wipes his mouth, puts the milk bottle back in the fridge with a clink and closes the fridge door.

He walks towards the sideboard and looks at the silver. He swipes a butter dish and puts it in his pocket, a cream jug, and a trinket box, which he stuffs into separate inside pockets, and takes a last drag on his fag and puts it out in a small silver dish. He then picks up the dish and finds the bin, and drops the cigarette butt into the bin. Robin wipes the dish on his coat and puts it in another pocket. He opens the door and heads into the reception area and opens the front door. Looking back, grinning, he closes the door behind him and pulls it to.

He sees Harry Parsons with his head in a newspaper sitting in his blue car, waiting. Robin opens the passenger door and swings into the passenger seat.

'Any good, Robin?'

'No, not for me, Harry, it's just too out the way. I'll get to know Cardiff first before I make any decisions, like.'

'Okay, son, whatever works for you, but a few of the other lads live locally, so you'd get lifts, I'm sure.'

'I'm a London boy, Harry – nothin' but sheep for neighbours 'ere,' he says, pointing with his thumb out the window.

The journey home is faster. Robin's talk is quick, machine-gun like. He tells tales of the games he's played and his hopes for the future. Orange streetlights light the way back into Cardiff, the way back to life. They pass orange buses along the road, commuters stare out of the windows, glum. Harry talks about the set-up at Cardiff, what's what, who's who, and that he'll always be there to help Robin out. Robin feels inside his pocket and touches the silver, feels the hard metal, but the metal isn't hard enough to stop the guilt.

'Where d'you want dropping, son?'

'Train station, please.'

'Okay, off home?'

'Yeah, Reading, got some loose ends to tie up before tomorrow's game.'

Harry wishes Robin a safe journey.

*

In the evening —
The Boar's Head pub, Reading —

Robin slurps at his pint and leaps up onto the table. He starts to dance as the alcohol buzz lights up his system. Tomorrow he'll face George Best and Bobby Moore. But tonight is New Year's Eve and he must have a drink. Robin dances and laughs amongst the locals.

A new start, a new club, a new league, a new country. Far away from the bright lights of London, but like a moth he will return, eager to dance around its tempting light.

He drains the last dregs from his pint glass and heads to the bar, where Dick Smith, the landlord, is busy serving the locals and keeping an eye out for any bother. Robin puts his empty glass on the bar. 'Lager, please,' says Robin, wiping his mouth with his sleeve.

Dick says, 'You've got George Best facing you tomorrow, so if I were you I'd make this your last one.'

'That's why I'm 'ere. I've got to level the playing field. George'll be more pissed…' – Robin looks down at his watch: 8:45pm – '…than me by now,' says Robin, laughing.

'That might be true, but he's no example for you,' says Dick, looking at Robin.

There's a nod from Robin, and he says, 'You're right, Dick. I mean, what's he ever done in football? You know, he's got more medals than fuckin' Prince Charlie, and as for money, well it grows out his ears. Just give me a six-pack of Colt Forty-Five lager and I'll be off.'

Dick reaches down and takes the six-pack and hands it over to Robin. He puts two one-pound notes on the bar and bids farewell to Dick. He heads to his posse and tells them he's off. Good luck, they say; you make your own luck, he says. Off to Liza, and off to have a few quiet ones.

*

Saturday 1 January 1977

Robin wakes from his slumber and looks at Liza, who is still sleeping. He gets up carefully from the bed and moves on silent feet towards the window. He brushes a hand at the curtain and peers out into the dark; his eyes scan the orange streetlights which show up the snowflakes which are joining a light quilt of snow on the ground. He wills the snow to stop and lets his forehead and nose rest against the glass. A cloud of condensation appears, and he draws a smiley face in it. He climbs back into bed, looks at the alarm clock: it's half past four in the morning. He's got three and a half hours more kip before he has to get up. Three and a half more hours for the snow to stop.

DRING-DRING-DRING-DRING-DRING-DRING – The alarm wrenches him out of his sleep. He pushes out his hand with closed eyes; seeing with his hands, he finds the clock and stops the alarm. Leaping from the bed, he goes straight to the window. The snow is lighter, but a thin white quilt of it still lies on the ground.

'Snow,' he says.

'Good morning to you as well,' says Liza.

'Sorry, love, mornin',' says Robin, as he reaches across the bed to kiss her.

RING-RING-RING-RING-RING-RING-RING – The phone rings and Robin sprints out of the bedroom. 'Yes,' he answers.

'All right, Robin.'

'All right, Dad.'

'D'you reckon the game'll be on then?'

'Dunno, I'll just make my way to Cardiff and see what the griff is.'

'Okay. I hope it stops for you. Just have a safe trip, and your mum and me will see you after the game. Good luck.'

'Cheers, Dad, have a safe one yourself, catch you later.'

He jumps on the train at Reading and buys a ticket this time. He sits in his seat next to his sports bag. The train rumbles along until it pulls into Cardiff Central. Robin gets off the train and heads for Ninian Park. He swings into reception and announces his arrival. Jimmy Andrews appears. 'Happy New Year. Was the journey okay? No problems this time?'

'Happy New Year, yeah, yeah, all fine, no coppers today!' says Robin, grinning.

'Now come and meet the lads, follow me,' says Jimmy, heading off through a door and down a blue-painted corridor.

Jimmy opens the dressing room door, and Robin's nose is filled with the smell of liniment and cologne.

'Gents, can I have your attention' – Jimmy waits – 'this is our new recruit, Robin Friday.'

'Happy New Year, lads,' says Robin.

'Happy New Year,' they all chorus back with wide eyes.

'This is our captain, Doug Livermore.'

'All right, Robin, I'll introduce the boys.'

Robin is led around the dressing room and introduced to Ron Healey, Phil Dwyer, Clive Charles, John Buchanan, Paul Went, Albert Larmour, Steve Grapes, Tony Evans, Peter 'Leo' Sayer, and Brian Attley. He shakes their hands.

Robin heads to an empty clothes peg and claims it. Clothes off. Cardiff shirt on. Shorts on. Straps up his ankles. Left sock on. Right sock on. Left boot on. Right boot on. No shin pads. The lads rub on the liniment. Robin shakes his legs; they are strong. He is strong. He goes to every player in the dressing room, touches them, each and every one, and wishes them good luck.

Jimmy stands holding a ball. 'Right, lads, pop on some tracksuits and let's go and get ourselves warmed up.'

Robin walks with the others along the corridor and down the tunnel onto the Ninian Park turf; the stands are empty. The team start off with a slow jog around the pitch, and then Jimmy calls them to the centre spot. He runs through tactics and what he expects. Robin doesn't listen. He looks around, familiarising himself with his new surroundings.

The players get into two groups and knock balls to one another, back and forth. People start to trickle into the stands. Robin rubs his hands together to keep them warm. A messenger runs out onto the pitch to tell Jimmy that Fulham have arrived. London has come to Cardiff. There's a buzz amongst the players.

John Buchanan approaches Robin. 'You up for this?' says Buchanan in a Highland Scottish lilt.

'I'm well up for it, can't fuckin' wait,' says Robin, bouncing on his toes.

'I just hope you play better than the last time we met and I scored two goals against you.'

'Piss off, you were lucky, mate.'

'All skill, Robin, all skill.'

'Let's see how you get on against George Best then.'

'Aye, he'll take some stopping, but hopefully he'll have

enjoyed last night a bit too much. Anyway, pal, let's see how you get on against Bobby Moore.'

'Who?' says Robin laughing, and he shows John Buchanan his tracksuit pocket. 'That's where Bobby'll be today.'

The players move down the tunnel, and there's a hustle and bustle as the Fulham players come down the corridor in their suits and big overcoats. There are handshakes and smiles. The Fulham lads talk of the double tyre blowout on their team bus on the motorway and having to hitch a ride on a Fulham fans' bus.

Robin looks at George Best. *He remembers sitting at the dinner table in Acton, with the back page of the Sunday papers spread out, showing George skipping through hapless defenders. Creating a likeness of the player with careful pencil strokes, drawing from the image.*

Robin feels a new hope, that this is the right move for him, that there is a method in this madness that is football. The Cardiff players head into the dressing room and move to their spots. Jimmy fills out the team sheet and takes it to the referee; he returns with the Fulham team sheet. 'Lads, there's been a few changes to the Fulham team.' He pins the sheet up on the wall. 'Bestie isn't playing today, he'll be watching.'

Disappointment fills Robin's stomach: George Best has slipped through the net again. He'll have to make do with the accolade of playing against England's World Cup winning captain, Bobby Moore; for Robin, it's second to Best. He relishes the idea though of playing in front of his hero, being watched by someone he's watched and admired for years.

Still swallowing the news, he turns to Buchanan. 'You

should be all right then, Buchy.'

'I'd a rather he played though.'

'Me too,' says Robin.

Jimmy calls the players together. 'A few out for Fulham today, but let's not be complacent. We need the two points here today. Let's give these fans a good show. They'll be disappointed Bestie isn't playing, but hopefully his absence helps our cause.' He draws the players' attention to a blackboard and talks to each player about their positions and movements, and scrawls circles and arrows on the board. Robin nods as Jimmy talks to him. *Didn't he talk about this earlier out in the centre circle?* Robin doesn't hear him as he starts to listen to the movements outside the door, down the corridor and onto the pitch – his mind wanders: *Bobby Moore, big smile, red-shirted, and held upon the shoulders of fellow players to a sea of fans: the Jules Rimet Trophy tight in his hand.* Today there will be no respect for Bobby Moore's reputation, no thoughts of yesteryear, no allowances for age.

They are called out onto the pitch and 'Men of Harlech' blares out over the tannoy as the players run out. Robin thinks *Zulu* and looks out at the crowd of blue. Twenty thousand two hundred and sixty-eight fans have come to watch.

From the kick-off, Robin makes himself known, marks his territory. He kicks through Fulham keeper Richard Teale and sends him crashing to the floor. Players surround him but he pushes through. He sends John Lacy and Bobby Moore into rages with his hard tackling and sharp elbows. There's a corner, and he notices Bobby Moore breathing down his neck. Robin turns. 'All right,

Bobby,' he says, and grabs at Moore's crotch. Enraged and protective of his single crown jewel, his private secret, Bobby Moore screams at Robin and chases after him as the corner swings in.

In the thirteenth minute, Steve Grapes mishits a shot which balloons in the air; it falls to Buchanan who stabs it home. Cardiff City 1 Fulham 0. The players celebrate with the cheering fans.

In the forty-second minute, Buchanan sends in a centre ball to Robin, who skips past Bobby Moore and hits the ball hard past the struggling keeper. Goal! He raises his arms out and greets his new crowd and blows them kisses. The terraces roar with approval. His name is called out over the tannoy and there's another cheer. At half-time it's Cardiff City 2 Fulham 0. Robin walks off the pitch and smiles at the fans.

In the dressing room, Robin sips at the sweet tea. Jimmy pats him on the shoulder and says, 'Good work, Robin, you've got them on the run, keep it up.' Robin nods.

The referee calls them out and the players line up and head back out to the cheering fans.

The second half starts with frantic energy. Robin keeps linking up well with Tony Evans, and they run rings around the Fulham defence, who still seem full of their Christmas turkey. In the sixty-fifth minute, Robin breaks onto a scrambled pass from Evans and breaks the Fulham line, and from sixteen yards he belts his shot into the back of the net as the helpless Bobby Moore looks on. Robin runs with his arms outstretched and the fans run down the terrace steps. Wide-eyed kids punch the air. The other Cardiff players run up to celebrate with him. *Fuckin' magic!*

Fulham kick off and they are soon dispossessed; the ball makes its way through the Cardiff midfield and it's given to Robin. He ghosts past Bobby Moore and heads for goal. He nutmegs John Lacy, and as Robin moves past him, Lacy dives at Robin's legs and rugby tackles him to the ground – there will be no hat-trick today. Robin turns snarling and kicking at Lacy, who covers his face. The referee steps in to stop the fracas.

The referee blows his whistle and the players clap the home fans. Robin raises his arms and claps high into the air. He blows kisses. Steam rises in wisps from his long hair and shoulders, and he greets the other players. They congratulate him. Robin feels ten feet tall. *Fulham, I've shit 'em*, he thinks.

Bobby Moore approaches. 'Good game,' he says, his hand outstretched.

'Likewise,' says Robin, taking Bobby's hand.

Robin is called over by a crowd of fans. He signs autographs and queues form, and he keeps signing.

Jimmy calls to Robin, calls him to the dressing room, but Robin is too busy chatting with fans and signing autographs. He tells the fans that he'd better get changed. He turns and waves at the crowd, and a little kid shouts, 'Who needs Bestie!' Robin laughs, waves, and heads down the tunnel.

The dressing room is full of chatter and strong smiles mixed with pride. The smell of liniment, wet turf, and copper fill the dressing room, and cologne breaks through in patches.

'What a debut, son. It looked like you and Tony had been playing together all season. Marvellous.'

‘I’m delighted, absolutely delighted, but I couldn’t ’a’ done it without the rest of ’em out there, and Tony in particular. Feels good to be ’ere.’

‘And we’re delighted too, and very glad you’re here.’

Robin showers and does small talk, but he wants to get into the players’ lounge. He sees his mum and dad. ‘Cracking game, son,’ says his dad.

‘Cheers!’ He nips a quick kiss on his mum’s cheek and says he’s heading straight for the bar, where George Best is perched.

‘Good game out there today,’ says George, smiling at Robin.

‘Thanks, man, I really appreciate it,’ says Robin. ‘I heard about the blowout, must have shaken you a bit, like.’

‘No, I’m used to blowouts,’ says George, with a wry smile.

Robin laughs. ‘See ya, George, stay lucky.’

George raises his glass.

Robin heads back to his parents, who are talking to Jimmy.

‘Talk of the devil,’ says Mr Friday.

‘Yes, here he is, the man of the moment,’ says Jimmy. ‘They’re not trying to tap you up, are they?’

‘No, not yet,’ says Robin, grinning.

‘We was just talking to Mr Andrews here about you moving up here,’ says Robin’s mum.

‘Yes, I’m gonna have a look at some more houses in the next couple of weeks,’ says Robin.

‘You’ll love it up here, sea breeze and plenty of countryside nearby,’ says Jimmy.

‘I can stay south for a while, so there’s no rush, like.’

‘We’d prefer to get you settled in, Robin, get your feet

under the table, so to speak.'

'Yep, we'll sort all that out,' says Robin, scratching his neck.

'What are your plans this evening?'

'I'm gonna head back to London, and I should probably catch up with the missus.'

Robin's dad chuckles. 'Always getting yourself in the dog 'ouse. You'll never change, will you, son.'

Robin catches his dad's eye and gives him a stare.

'Anyway, lovely talking to you, Mr and Mrs Friday,' says Jimmy.

'Call us Alf and Sheila, great to meet you, and thanks for this free booze,' says Robin's dad.

Robin waits for Jimmy to be out of earshot and turns straight to his dad. 'What's with the "You'll never change"? That's my new gaffer,' says Robin, jerking his thumb in Jimmy's direction. 'Let's not set his beady eyes on me just yet. I can do that all on my own.'

'All right, son, look, sorry, wasn't thinking.'

'Right, let's get ourselves to the station, shall we, before you do any more damage,' says Robin, laughing.

Robin says his goodbyes and leaves with his parents and heads back to London.

*

He meets up with his brother Tony at Old Actonians' sports club. Holds court. Tells them about his goals. Tells them about Bobby Moore. Goes out in London, quenches his thirst, dances into the night, watches white lines disappear from the tops of toilet cisterns. Blows himself up. Laughs. Falls about. Fights.

*

Sitting at his desk, Harry Parsons picks up his cup of hot tea and takes a sip. He sits and thinks about his list of jobs today. Always busy, and always making lists of lists: players, kit, boots, supplies, coaching equipment. All in a day's work, the love of work and his beloved Cardiff City, who sit near the bottom of Division Two. Harry will do everything he can to help Jimmy get through this sticky patch. If Robin Friday continues to play like he did against Fulham, then there will be no need to worry.

The phone rings. 'Harry, we've got a problem,' says Jimmy.

'Jimmy, what is it?'

'You went with Robin to Saint Athan, to look at that bungalow?'

'Yes, you saw me take him.'

'Yes, but…erm, did you notice anything when you went into the house, anything strange?'

'No, no, it was all right when I looked. What's happened?'

'So, you or Robin didn't leave any doors open then, didn't forget to close any windows?'

'Look, what's this about, Jimmy?' asks Harry, frowning and tapping his desk.

'I've just received a phone call from the irate owner of the bungalow saying that some of his silver has gone missing from the house, and if we don't get it back to him he's going to press charges. The godsend is they haven't spoken to the press.'

'You've got to be kidding.'

'I wish I was, Harry, but I'm afraid it's true.'

'There must be some kind of mistake. I mean, he couldn't, could he? He wouldn't, surely?'

‘I don’t know, but did you notice anything suspicious, anything at all?’

‘I let Robin into the bungalow to look around by himself, so I’ll have to talk to him.’

‘Get hold of him, and quick.’

‘I will, I’ll get onto Robin now to see what on earth’s going on.’ Harry puts down the phone, wipes his brow with his handkerchief. He takes a deep breath and looks into his address book and finds Robin’s phone number.

He puts his index finger into the hole above the number and dials, pulls at another number, and another…

He hears clicking on the line, then the phone rings and rings, until…

‘Yeah.’

‘Is that you, Robin?’

‘Yeah, who’s this?’

‘Harry, Harry Parsons. I just wanted a quick word about our little trip out to the…er…that bungalow, Robin.’

‘Go on then, Harry.’

‘There’s a bit of a problem you see.’ Harry twirls his finger in the looping telephone wire; he places his feet over imaginary eggshells. ‘Well, I was just wondering if, when you went into the bungalow, if…you know…you left a window or a door accidentally open. These things happen, don’t they?’

Robin laughs into the phone. ‘They didn’t like my practical joke then?’

‘Practical joke?’

‘Yeah, I was just pissing about, like – I was gonna return ’em, honest.’

‘Oh, dear God, Robin, well the owners haven’t seen the funny side. They’ve said they’ll press charges if we don’t get the silver back.'

'Silver, no, I didn't take any silver,' says Robin, enjoying himself.

'So, so what did you take?'

Robin looks around his living room. 'I took some porcelain,' he says, smiling.

'So, you didn't take the silver?'

'Course I bleedin' did, Harry, just messin' with you.'

'I'm not enjoying this. Is there porcelain as well then?'

'No, I made that bit up. Look, I'll bring it straight back, promise. I was just playin' about, and things sort of got out of hand, like.'

'Look, don't worry, just bring the stuff back and I'll smooth things over with the owner. I'll speak to Jimmy too, okay.'

'Yep, I'll bring 'em back, Harry.'

'Okay, Robin, see you soon.'

'Yep, catch you later,' says Robin, putting the phone down. He sits in his armchair and relights a spliff. He looks out the window and pulls on the spliff, taking in its smoky scent of tobacco and cannabis. He fidgets in his seat, puts on a record, anything to blot out the thoughts: *Harry didn't deserve that, nor did Jimmy. What will they think? Robin sees himself back in the kitchen, looking at the sideboard with all the silver. He tells himself to just leave it, no point. Just leave it, but it's done. Argh, fuck it, play well next game and it'll all be forgotten. He sits and fidgets, uneasy. Time to get out back on it, time to obliterate the memory. Robin pops a couple of Diconal.*

*

Jimmy Andrews begins to think he may have signed the Artful Dodger.

*

Robin goes through his paces in training at Jubilee Park, a council owned park; days melt into each other.

*

Saturday 8 January 1977

Cardiff City entertain Tottenham Hotspur in the third round of the FA Cup. Cup-tied Robin watches from the stands, watches with envy for not being allowed to play in such a game, for the rules don't allow it. Peter 'Leo' Sayer bangs one in. The crowd roar the roof off. Cardiff City 1 Tottenham Hotspur 0. Spurs can't find a way through. The final whistle blows and Cardiff will go into the velvet bag for the fourth round draw. Robin heads down to the dressing room to congratulate the lads.

'Well fuckin' done, boys,' says Robin with a smile.

'Cheers, Robin' says Phil Dwyer.

'Have you seen Archie?' asks Robin.

'Who?' asks David Giles.

'Jimmy.'

'Why'd you call him Archie?' asks Giles.

'You know Archie Andrews, the ventriloquist's dummy,' says Robin, laughing.

Giles laughs, and says, 'I think Mr Andrews is with the directors.'

'Cheers, Gilo, I need to borrow a couple of quid off him.'

*

Saturday 15 January 1977

Robin travels to Bristol Rovers brimming with confidence.

Nine thousand two hundred and seventy-two watch from the stands at Bristol Stadium.

He chases, battles, and smashes into the Bristol Rovers'

defensive line. He laughs at them, pulls at their shirts. They remember him from Hayes from back in '72. He beat them then and feels he can beat them again.

Everything moves in cycles, he thinks, *everything repeats itself.*

He scores from twenty yards, but the referee disallows it. Robin roars at the referee in disbelief. As busy as Robin is, he can't finish off Rovers. Bristol Rovers 1 Cardiff City 1. Today, there is no repeat, no victory.

On the way back to Cardiff on the bus, Robin sits, fidgets, stands up in the aisle, tells his jokes. The Cardiff players look at him, sitting in their club blazers and ties, trying to figure him out: Afghan coat, open-collared shirt, jeans, white plastic bag with his boots in. Some of them think he might be a gypsy.

*

Wednesday 19 January 1977
Ninian Park, Cardiff City v Stourbridge, Welsh Cup, fourth round —

Stourbridge, an English team who play in the English Southern League, have come to Ninian Park to play on Welsh soil in a Welsh competition. One thousand seven hundred and eighty-two fans stand in the cold evening air.

He goes to his usual spot in the dressing room. Clothes off. Cardiff shirt on. Shorts on…touches them…wishes them good luck.

The whistle blows.

Cardiff keep the ball and move forward as a unit. The ball is out on the right wing, and Robin screams for a pass and runs forward towards goal. He watches the ball come over, and Robin shoots and the ball flies into the back of the net. Robin punches the air. A linesman's flag goes up.

Cheers and shouts ring out. The referee disallows the goal for offside. Robin shakes his head in disagreement.

Stourbridge play with all their heart and go toe to toe with Cardiff. Then, as Stourbridge's amateur legs start to tire, so Cardiff begin to gain the upper hand.

In the seventy-fifth minute, Cardiff cross into the box. Stourbridge hesitate, and Phil Dwyer crashes into the area and sends home a low shot from eight yards out. Cardiff City 1 Stourbridge 0. There are cheers.

In the eighty-seventh minute, David Giles thumps a twenty-five-yard shot which hits a Stourbridge defender and rebounds into the goal: Cardiff City 2 Stourbridge 0. The whistle blows for full-time and Robin waves to the fans. Cardiff are into the next round of the cup.

*

Saturday 22 January 1977

Robin wakes, bleary-eyed, his body full of poison. He looks at his watch and sees that he won't make the train.

'What the fuck am I gonna do?' he says, thinking out loud. 'I've gotta get there.'

He phones Pat the taxi. 'Pat, I'm stuck. I've missed my train to Cardiff. Any chance you could give us a lift?'

'Course I can, mate, give us five.' Robin pulls his jeans and T-shirt on, denim jacket and cowboy boots. He grabs a cup of tea.

'Look, Liza, can you phone up the club, just let 'em know I'm on my way.'

'Sure, course.'

Pat appears.

'Cheers, geezer, you're a fuckin' life saver.'

'No problem, mate.'

Robin climbs into the Ford Cortina.

The Cortina weaves in and out of the traffic speeding towards Cardiff.

Just outside Cardiff, Robin grabs a bag of chips with plenty of salt and vinegar.

Robin picks at his chips and makes his way towards the ground; he looks at his watch: 2.36pm. He moves towards the ground, still grabbing greasy handfuls of chips and stuffing them into his mouth. The car stops, he thanks Pat, and Robin opens the door and jumps out.

He runs down Sloper Road and into Ninian Park, shouting at fans to move out of his way. He runs through the car park, into reception, down the corridor, and into the dressing room.

He walks in with a bag of chips in one hand and his kit bag hanging on his arm.

'Anyone for a chip?'

There are laughs, looks of bewilderment: 'Just in time.' 'Better late than never.' 'Thank God for that.' 'Where have you been?'

Jimmy Andrews' face is a storm. 'What time do you call this? And get rid of those,' he says, pointing at the chips. 'And get yourself kitted up.'

'Sorry, I missed the train.'

'I know, your wife phoned. It's not good enough, not for me, not for Cardiff – you'll be fined for this! Now hurry up.'

'I'm 'ere now, aren't I? It wasn't my fault.'

'You miss a train, it's your fault. I don't want excuses.'

'But…'

'But, nothing,' says Jimmy with a glare in his eyes.

'There's still twenty minutes until kick-off. I've only got to put my bleedin' kit on.'

Jimmy ignores Robin.

He goes to his usual spot in the dressing room. Clothes off. Cardiff shirt on. Shorts on…touches them…wishes them good luck.

The players line up and head out into the crowd. Eleven thousand one hundred and fifty-three fans have come to watch Cardiff City v Charlton Athletic.

Robin lines up one of their defenders and puts a dig into the back of his ribs. The player retaliates and Robin acts like butter wouldn't melt. Robin continues to harry Charlton's defensive line.

In the twentieth minute, Robin jumps up for a corner ball and sees a flash of red shirt fly at his face, feels a sharp, sickening pain in his cheek. He turns, half blind in the melee and kicks out at the nearest Charlton player. The referee blows up. The trainers run on.

'Stand still,' says Harry Parsons looking at Robin's swollen cheek. Harry presses and feels a hole. 'That hurt?'

Robin winces. 'Yeah, it fuckin' does, Harry.'

'Just watch yourself and watch Les Berry's elbow,' says Harry rubbing the sponge over the side of Robin's head and cheek. Harry drops the sponge back into his blue bucket and runs off the pitch.

The referee calls Robin over. The Charlton trainer runs on to assist Bob Curtis of Charlton, who's on the floor holding his ankle.

'Ref, have you seen this?' says Robin, pointing to the large swelling on his left cheek.

'You retaliated. If there's a problem you let me know.'

'I am, look,' he says.

'I'm afraid I didn't see that. The only thing I saw was you kicking out at a player.'

Robin stands hands on hips, his cheek swollen and throbbing, and watches as the referee shows him the yellow card.

Robin fights on for the rest of the game, always mindful of his cheekbone. He feels sick to the core, sees the hard lump sitting in front of his left eye. Breathes hard when play stops.

At half-time Charlton lead by one goal to nil. Robin trudges off the pitch into the tunnel holding his cheek, protecting his cheek.

'Robin, you okay?' asks Jimmy.

'No, I'm in fuckin' agony. Look at this.' He shows Jimmy and presses his fingers into a hole where part of his cheekbone is dented.

'Jesus Christ, Robin. I'll get Doc Hamilton to have a look.'

Robin sits and sips his tea, the left half of his face throbbing, his face pale.

Doc Hamilton comes and takes a look, examines him, prods at Robin.

'Look, I'm okay, really.'

'Are you sure you can continue?'

'Yeah, I'll just cover my face up whenever I'm near them dirty bastards.'

'Just keep doing what you're doing, Robin, and we'll get back into this,' says Jimmy.

Robin goes out for the second half, covers his cheek, and tries to hide his pain. In the fifty-sixth minute, Paul Went sends a volley crashing into the back of the net. Cardiff City 1 Charlton Athletic 1. Cardiff and Charlton continue to go at each other but neither can break the deadlock. The final whistle blows.

Robin doesn't go to the players' lounge. He sits holding his cheek in the dressing room. He starts to feel sick, weak; he takes a puff on his inhaler.

'We'll have to take him to hospital,' says Doc Hamilton to Jimmy, who looks on concerned.

Robin is helped up off the bench, his body aching and his face contorted with discomfort. He walks towards a mirror on the wall.

'Fuckin' hell, I look like Quasimodo – look at the state of me. And I'm the silly cunt that got booked,' says Robin into the mirror.

Tony Evans comes into the dressing room and looks at Robin.

'You okay, mate?'

'Nah, I'm fucked.'

'Your mum and dad are upstairs, what do you want to do?'

'I don't want them to worry. Just let 'em know I've gone to hospital to get my cheek checked out. Play it down though, will you?'

'Course I will,' says Tony, squeezing Robin's shoulder. 'I'll go and sort it now. Good luck.'

'Come on then, let's get you to hospital,' says Doc Hamilton.

Robin walks out of Ninian Park into Doc Hamilton's car and is driven to St David's Hospital.

He sits Robin down and heads to the nurse at reception.

Robin touches his face, feels the hole, and wonders if he'll be disfigured by this – knows he's lucky to have his front teeth as it is. Robin sits down and sees the other faces looking at him, people holding their arms, stomachs. He looks at them, and they look away; they don't want to hold his gaze. He peers at them from his peripheral vision, sees them looking, and when he clocks them, they look elsewhere. He likes this game – likes that they think he's been in a scrap. Smiles to himself. The hospital admit him for observations.

*

Sunday 23 January 1977
His mum and dad visit in the morning. He asks for morphine to stop the pain. Enjoys the morphine, watches the walls bend and flow. His mum shows him the Cardiff match programme, opens it at the right page and points to the 'Letter of the Week'. He reads it and she watches his eyes as he smiles:

> *From Peter Welch*
> *I was totally delighted when manager Jimmy Andrews signed Robin Friday. I had seen him play for his former club, Reading, and came home telling friends I would love to see him playing in City's forward line. I rate him in the same class as Trevor Francis, Paul Mariner and Duncan McKenzie.*
>
> *He has the skill, flair and knack of being in the right place at the right time to score brilliant goals. City supporters are fortunate to see such a fine player. Alongside Tony Evans, Robin will add extra excitement to City's goalscoring exploits – and I'm sure that crowds will pack Ninian Park to see them in action.*
>
> *Replies manager Andrews: I see the signing in just the same light as you, Peter, and many other supporters. Only recently, I said that Robin's*

entertaining play will regularly add 3,000–4,000 supporters to our gates. I have no doubt that his partnership with Tony Evans will be brilliantly effective.

'A good write-up, isn't it,' says his mum.

'Yeah, that was before the little bastard fined me for turning up late.'

'I'm sure it'll all blow over, son.'

*

Monday 24 January 1977
Robin is transferred to the University of Wales Hospital, Cardiff, they prod and they poke but decide not to operate. His cheek is still sore; they give him two boxes of prescription painkillers.

The doctors tell him he'll be okay in a couple of weeks. Robin goes to Ninian Park and the press photograph him holding the number '2' while holding his damaged cheek. Two weeks without football.

*

He lies in bed, the light filtering through his eyelids, sees faces like photographs, sees the future – tosses and turns under the sheets.

*

Early February 1977
Robin walks into Elm Park, walks towards Charlie's office, knocks and waits.

'Just a minute,' answers Charlie, shuffles his papers, takes a swig of his tea. 'Come in.'

'Afternoon, Boss.'

'Well I never, Mr Friday, how the devil are you?'

'I'm getting by, Charlie, getting by.'

'Sit down, kid. So you've made a pretty good start to life in Cardiff. Jimmy phoned me after the Fulham match. He was over the moon.'

'I don't like it there, it don't feel right. I don't think it's gonna work out. I was late for the Charlton game but got there before kick-off and he bloody fined me, even after ending up in fuckin' hospital.'

'You're a tough nut, you can take a knock.'

'But I don't wanna play for him. He's a right little shit.'

'You're going to have to play for him, you signed a contract.'

'Can't I come back here and play for you?'

'We'd never afford you now. We've money troubles here as it is. We couldn't pay Cardiff, and we certainly couldn't pay you what you're on at Cardiff.'

'I'm stuck then.'

'I'm afraid that's football. How are things otherwise?'

'I'm back and forth to Cardiff. Liza's due in a few months, so we need to get settled.'

'Robin, if I were you, I'd get yourself moved up to Cardiff pronto.'

The words grate across Robin's skin.

'I wish it was as simple as that.'

'Dig in, kid, it's early days at Cardiff. Just knuckle down and show them what you can do.'

'I'll try.'

'You look after yourself, and maybe we'll see you on the road.'

'Sure, take care.'

Robin turns and walks down the corridor, out the door, and onto Norfolk Road. He leaves Elm Park behind him. He pops into the Spread Eagle for a pint, tells everyone that Cardiff is great and that he's glad he signed – it's all working out fine…just fine.

*

He can't play, so what else is there to do? He reads the papers, keeps up with the news. Drinks when he can. Takes the prescribed painkillers and some of his own too.

*

Saturday 5 February 1977
Cardiff City travel away to play Blackburn Rovers without Robin Friday. Blackburn Rovers 2 Cardiff City 1.

*

Monday 7 February 1977
Robin appears at Ninian Park clad in a denim jacket, T-shirt and jeans, and carrying a white plastic bag.

'How are you, Robin, ready to get back into it?' says Phil Dwyer.

'Yeah, much better, cheers.'

'Have you got your training kit?'

'Yeah, here,' says Robin, holding up his white plastic bag.

Dwyer raises his eyebrows. 'It's good to have you back.'

Robin gets himself changed and takes a Bustaid pill.

They go through the motions: doggies, drills, sprints. Then they play five-a-side; he chases the ball down, makes a nuisance of himself, feels the boost of the Bustaid. His face is angry, angry through injury, and he can't wait to get out there again onto the pitch. He can't wait to get paid too.

*

Training happens. Jimmy Andrews watches Robin pull up with his hands on his hips, breathing heavily. He picks him for a reserve game to test his fitness.

*

Wednesday 9 February 1977

Robin walks out onto the pitch. Ninian Park is empty and quiet. He looks around and sees the empty stands. The last time he was here it was all hustle and bustle. He's back and eager to get himself into the first team for Saturday, keen to prove a point.

Cardiff are poor, and by half-time it's Cardiff City reserves 0 Orient reserves 2. Robin tells his teammates what he thinks. He doesn't hold back and makes them understand what he expects in the second half. In the fifty-fourth minute, Robin puts in a wonderful pass for Ray Bishop, who pulls a goal back. Robin fights to get back into it, fights for his team, but it ends Cardiff City 1 Orient 2. He ambles back to the dressing room, gets changed, and makes his way back to his hotel room. Twiddles his thumbs and sits and waits for tomorrow.

*

Saturday 12 February 1977

The crowds pour into Ninian Park, ready for the visit of Oldham Athletic, twelve thousand seven hundred and eight of them.

He goes to his usual spot in the dressing room. Clothes off. Cardiff shirt on. Shorts on…touches them…wishes them good luck. Robin jumps about the dressing room, builds himself up into a rage, can't sit still, doesn't stop talking. His mind speeding, his body too.

The usual team talk and tactics: you do this, you do that.

Robin just wants to get back out in front of the crowd, to entertain them.

They walk through the mouth of the tunnel side by side with Oldham Athletic. Robin glares at his opposite number. His opposite number stares back. Robin puts his arm around him and whispers into his ear, 'Don't worry, darlin', I'll look after you.'

The Oldham player looks at Robin, up and down, and frowns and quickens his steps out onto the pitch, away from the disturbing encounter.

The game kicks off and Cardiff attack; the ball goes out wide and is crossed in high. As the ball comes in Robin jumps up and knocks the ball down with his hand. The ref blows up. 'Handball, free kick.' And again, and again. In the twelfth minute, Oldham Athletic score. Cardiff City 0 Oldham Athletic 1. Cardiff try to nick a goal but can't. The whistle blows for half-time.

Robin heads down the tunnel into the dressing room.

'What are you playing at, Robin?' asks Jimmy.

'What d'you mean?'

'We're one-nil down and you're handling balls like you're in the Harlem-bloody-Globetrotters. Why?'

'Because it's the only way I can fuckin' get to the crosses.'

'I'm not having this conversation. Don't do it again, understand?'

Robin nods.

Jimmy Andrews asks for quiet. 'We should be beating this lot, they're nothing. Now get out there and get some pride back!'

The second half kicks off. It's tight, cagey, Oldham trying to keep their lead and hoping to nick one on the counter-attack.

In the sixty-third minute, Robin snatches onto an uncleared corner and hammers home a shot to equalise. Cardiff City 1 Oldham Athletic 1. The crowd cheer and Robin runs towards them arms outstretched, jumping in the air. A hero returned. Friday and Evans make runs through the Oldham defensive lines. In the seventieth minute, Evans pops the ball into the back of the net. The Cardiff fans cheer. Cardiff City 2 Oldham Athletic 1. Oldham come back again, trying to snatch a point. Then, in the eighty-eighth minute, 'Leo' Sayer passes to Robin, who sees Sayer's run and whips the ball back to him. Sayer drives the ball home. Cardiff fans cheer and enjoy the last few minutes, knowing they can't be beaten today. Cardiff City 3 Oldham Athletic 1.

The dressing room mood is buoyant. Robin gets himself a pint, does small talk, then makes his excuses and heads back to London on the train. On the train, he pops a couple of pink Diconal pills and feels his scalp tingle, soothing him. Tonight he'll celebrate.

*

Wednesday 16 February 1977

Farrar Road, Bangor City v Cardiff City, Welsh Cup quarter final —

A crowd of almost five thousand people pack into the small ground.

Clothes off. Cardiff shirt on. Shorts on…touches them…wishes them good luck.

The first half is a stalemate; Cardiff's opponents revel in the home atmosphere. All the pressure is on Cardiff's shoulders.

In the forty-seventh minute, Robin stands on the edge of the Bangor penalty area, a defender blocking his way.

He sees David Giles running in and knocks a pass through the defender's legs. Giles picks up the pass and shoots, but the keeper manages to push the ball out. It falls to Giles again but he doesn't miss this time. Bangor City 0 Cardiff City 1. There's a roar from the crowd. Robin runs back to the halfway line punching the air, a big grin on his face.

In the sixty-sixth minute, Tony Evans sees Robin surging forward. Sends a pass into his path. The keeper runs at Robin, trying to put him off. Robin shoots, but the ball hits the post and bounces into touch. Robin bares his teeth and shakes his head.

In the seventy-second minute, Robin picks up a loose ball and runs into the penalty area. The keeper comes out, Robin tries to sweep the ball around him, but the keeper brings Robin crashing to the floor. *Cunt.* The referee blows his whistle and points to the spot. Penalty.

Steve Grapes puts the ball down. He shoots, but the keeper blocks the ball. The ball bounces back to Grapes, who puts it away. Bangor City 0 Cardiff City 2.

The final whistle blows and Cardiff City are into the semi-finals of the Welsh Cup. The Cardiff fans sing their hearts out. Robin smiles and waves to the fans.

The Cardiff City bus whirrs its way towards a hotel in Bangor…Robin leans his head against the glass, watching headlights come and go. Then he overhears someone talking about him, cocks his ear, listens.

'…Well, he needs to sort himself out, what are we paying him for? He gets it all his own way, disappears off to London every weekend, won't move to Cardiff. Then there's the ill-discipline on the pitch…'

Robin turns, looking at where the voice is coming from, sees Clive Griffiths, a member of the board.

Griffiths, as if feeling Robin's stare, looks down the bus. Their eyes meet. Griffiths holds the stare, shakes his head and folds his arms.

Robin tears himself out of his seat. 'You don't know what you're fuckin' talkin' about, mate.'

'You're out of order, and I'm not your mate,' says Griffiths, shifting in his seat.

'You think you can slag me off in earshot, you cunt,' says Robin, pointing at Griffiths.

'Listen, we're paying your wages.' He turns, looking at the other board members, who look elsewhere.

'You know fuck all about football, but the problem is you think you do – you couldn't run a brothel and you're not fuckin' payin' me enough anyway!'

'Sit down and try and hold your drink instead of having a go at me,' says Griffiths, sneering at Robin.

A switch in Robin's head clicks and the red mist rises; he reaches into his plastic bag, pulling out a half-empty bottle of Cinzano Bianco.

'Right, you cunt, now I'm holdin' my drink, do you want some, eh?' says Robin, brandishing the bottle with menace.

Robin shakes the bottle, staring down the bus at Griffiths, who presses his back against his seat. Griffiths looks around, players' eyes staring back at him, caught in the wild moment – no movement. 'W-Well, isn't someone going to do something?' Griffiths stammers.

'Too right I fuckin' will,' says Robin, taking a couple of steps up the aisle. 'I'll fuckin' brain you,' says Robin, shaking his Cinzano Bianco bottle. 'I'll use this!' he says, pointing at the bottle. The players look on. The directors sit in their seats. Wenty and Dwyer rush out of their seats and block the aisle.

Jimmy stands up. 'Stop this now! Robin, sit down. Mr Griffiths, kindly leave the players to me.'

Griffiths thinks about opening his mouth but replies with a nod and sits back down. Jimmy ushers Robin back to his seat, using the bulk of Wenty and Dwyer to persuade him.

'Budge up, mate,' says Wenty, moving into the seat next to Robin. Jimmy looks around the bus, nods and goes back to his seat, sitting down with a sigh.

'Not a fuckin' clue, has he. Bottle? I'll put a cloth in it and light the arsehole up,' whispers Robin to Wenty.

Wenty smirks, looking at his pal, and whispers, 'Would you have hit him with it?'

Robin shakes his head. 'Nah, course not, but I don't think he'll bother me again though, d'you?'

'I think we can safely say he won't, mate.'

'Do you want one of these?' says Robin, holding out a couple of pills.

'No, you're all right, mate.'

'Fair enough, more for me,' says Robin, throwing them into his mouth and taking a swig out of his bottle.

Robin leans his head against the cold glass window, breathing in and out. Thinks of Liza. Thinks of London. Thinks of his mum and dad. Wonders what his brother Tony is up to. The bus is quiet for the rest of the journey. Robin starts to liven up as they reach the hotel, his speech machine-gun like.

*

Robin sits on the edge of the hotel bed. He holds his head in his hands and last night's antics come flooding back: *hotel bar…a sea of drink…sinking away from himself...snarling...shouting...a broken bottle...threats made...Griffiths' eyes white and wild...more money demanded...a room full of directors and teammates with open mouths. Fuck.*

He pulls on his clothes. Leaves the hotel and thumbs a lift back to London.

*

Robin returns to Cardiff. He smiles, says he's sorry, and shakes hands. Training happens and he's given plenty of space. Wary eyes watch on.

*

Saturday 19 February 1977
The away dressing room at Meadow Lane, the home of Notts County —

Robin pulls off his muddy shirt and walks to his peg. Heavy boots click-clack on the concrete. Jimmy Andrews slams the dressing room door.

'You threw it away, lads, threw it away,' says Jimmy, rubbing his neck. 'Sayer, you should've had a goal. Friday put it on a plate for you and you pass it to their goalkeeper, McManus.'

Peter Sayer looks up and nods.

'If you want to succeed at this level, lad, you've got to be more clinical,' says Jimmy.

'Leave off, he's had a go. No one likes losing, least of all me. It was like a fuckin' ice rink in that mud today,' says Robin.

'Well, they managed to score, didn't they. One-nil, and if we'd have taken our chances, we could've had three or four.'

Robin stares back and throws his muddy shirt to the floor. 'It's the defence you should be talking to.'

‘Don’t tell me how to do my job,’ says Jimmy.

‘Over to you then, Archie,’ says Robin, pulling off his muddy shorts. ‘I’m off for a fuckin’ shower.’

*

Saturday 26 February 1977
Ninian Park, FA Cup fifth round —

Cup-tied, Robin watches as Cardiff City entertain Everton. He watches fans climb up onto a corrugated iron roof above the stands. He wishes he could be out there playing. Cardiff put up a brave fight but their cup run finishes: Cardiff City 1 Everton 2.

*

Robin hears on the grapevine that Charlie Hurley has walked out on Reading. Losing 3–0 to Bury at half-time and bottom of the Third Division, he decided enough was enough. Maurice Evans takes over the reins.

*

Monday 28 February 1977
After a good cup run the Cardiff City board offer Jimmy Andrews a five-year contract. Jimmy Andrews considers it.

*

Wednesday 2 March 1977
Orient arrive at Ninian Park. They sit twenty-first in the league table. Cardiff City sit in fifteenth place. Nine thousand eight hundred and fifty-seven fans make up the crowd.

He goes to his usual spot in the dressing room. Clothes off. Cardiff shirt on. Shorts on…touches them…wishes them good luck.

The game kicks off.

In the first minute, Cardiff move the ball out to the

wing. It swings in and Robin launches himself at the ball with a bicycle kick, firing the ball just wide of the Orient goal.

In the twenty-fifth minute, Derek Possee chases down Cardiff's Brian Attley and nicks the ball away; he turns and runs and passes to Laurie Cunningham, who scores from twelve yards out. There's a crackle of applause and cheers from the Orient faithful. Cardiff City 0 Orient 1.

Robin tries to get his side back in it. He chases the ball down and works hard off the ball, but there's little support from his teammates. It finishes Cardiff City 0 Orient 1.

*

Saturday 5 March 1977
Nine thousand four hundred and seventy-nine make up the numbers at The Den, Cold Blow Lane, London.

Clothes off. Cardiff shirt on. Shorts on…touches them…wishes them good luck.

The Millwall fans sing: WHEN I WAS YOUNG AND JUST A BOY, I ASKED MY MUVVER WHAT WILL IT BE? WILL IT BE ARSENAL? WILL IT BE SPURS? HERE'S WHAT SHE SAID TO ME: MILL–WALL, MILL–WALL, MILL–WALL, MILL–WALL, MILL–WALL!

In the twenty-seventh minute, Steve Grapes passes to Tony Evans, who puts the ball away, and it's Millwall 0 Cardiff City 1.

In the fiftieth minute, Clive Charles chips in a cross to Phil Dwyer, who steams after the ball, but Dwyer cracks heads with Goddard, the Millwall keeper. Both men fall to the floor, unconscious. The trainers run on. Robin watches on, and then he hears shouting from the stands. He looks up and sees a group of Millwall fans in surgical masks.

Then another group of Millwall fans run towards the Cardiff City supporters. The police struggle to keep things under control.

Dwyer gets to his feet and gives the thumbs up, but the Millwall keeper is groggy with concussion and leaves the field. Dave Donaldson, Millwall's full back, goes in goal. A Millwall fan vaults a wall and punches Dwyer. There are cheers. Dwyer grapples with him, and the police pull the Millwall fan away, handcuff him, and lead him away.

Robin makes clever runs but doesn't get a clear chance at a goal.

In the seventy-eighth minute, John Buchanan threads a through ball for Evans, who runs onto it and shoots. Millwall 0 Cardiff City 2.

Robin claps the Cardiff City fans and goes down the tunnel. He changes and heads straight out into London. He meets up with his mates and stays up until the late hours.

*

He wakes up, coughing, in a stranger's living room in London. Empty cans of lager fill a table, and an overflowing ashtray sits on a coffee table. There's tinfoil, syringes, and half-empty packets of gear.

*

Tuesday 8 March 1977

Robin travels with Cardiff to Bramall Lane, the home of Sheffield United —

Robin sits in the dressing room, pulls on his boots. Then with a bandage he binds a small wooden box, containing his inhaler, to the inside of his wrist. He feels uneasy in his skin, his stomach cramps up, but the show must go on.

Twelve thousand nine hundred and seven fans watch

under the glowing floodlights and under a large waning moon.

Robin charges at the Sheffield United defence and puts them under pressure. Robin smacks players around the head with his wooden box. *Pop*. Tony Evans and Robin keep pushing at their backline, but Sheffield's defence is like steel.

There's a corner to Cardiff and as the ball floats over…*pop*. The ball goes into touch. A Sheffield United player holds his head. Alan Woodward approaches Robin. 'What the hell are you doing to my players?'

'Fuck off,' says Robin. He glares at Woodward. Woodward shakes his head and walks away.

Robin runs and runs, but his stomach and chest start to burn. A searing pain pierces his stomach. He struggles to breathe and takes his inhaler out of its box and pulls on it and breathes in…takes another pull and breathes in.

It's 0–0 and Cardiff City are still in it. In the thirty-eighth minute, Robin pulls up clutching his stomach. He leaves the pitch.

'What's up?' asks Harry Parsons.

'It's my stomach, Harry, it don't feel right,' says Robin, grimacing.

His chest starts to tighten.

He sits on the bench, takes a breather. Takes his inhaler. He grips his stomach. He feels a cramping urge to shit and runs off down the tunnel. He shits and feels a sense of relief, a lightness. He goes back out onto the pitch. For a few minutes, he tries to get something out of the game. The half-time whistle goes.

'Right, let's get you down to the dressing room…you feeling better?' asks Jimmy.

'Better after that shit. I'll just get some water on board and I should be okay.'

In the dressing room, Robin sits on the bench and drinks water. He starts to feel sick but keeps it down. Everyone asks him how he is. 'I'm all right, I'll be back out there second half,' he says.

Jimmy looks on with concern: 'Are you sure you'll be okay?'

'I wanna go back out there,' says Robin, staring at Jimmy.

Jimmy wants him back out there, knows he needs him back out there. He needs a fighter.

Robin goes out for the second half, but each run he makes, each step he takes, pulls on his stomach, makes his breathing uneasy. For five minutes he tries, but he bends over double. *Fuck.* He looks at the bench, shakes his head and grimaces. He signals for a substitution. Robin leaves the field and John Buchanan replaces him. Robin goes to the bench and watches. He sits with his arms folded across his stomach, trying somehow to hold back the pain.

He watches as Sheffield United start to apply the pressure to Cardiff's defence. In the fifty-fifth minute, Sheffield United score, and they look like a different team. Three minutes later, they score again. Cardiff fold. In the eighty-seventh minute, Sheffield score. Sheffield United 3 Cardiff City 0. Robin is sick to the core.

Robin sits on the team bus, quiet. His stomach is still cramping and his face pale. He feels inside his jacket pocket, touches his tin of works and knows that soon this will all stop.

Wanting off the bus, he jumps up from his seat and makes his way down the aisle towards the driver, saying quick goodbyes as he goes, leaving confused frowns behind him.

Robin taps Jimmy on the shoulder and wakes him from his slumber. 'I'm off, see ya soon.'

'Okay, Robin,' says Jimmy, closing his eyes again.

'Drop us here, mate,' says Robin to the driver.

The driver looks around, looks at Robin's dark eyes. 'Are you sure?'

'Yeah, just here is fine, I'm meeting someone.'

'Righty-o,' says the driver, slowing down the bus and pressing on the brakes, which hiss as the doors open.

He goes down the bus steps, turns and waves as the bus doors shut, and it whirrs away up the road.

Robin looks at his new surroundings under the moonlight, the fields and the trees. He breathes in the fresh country air and heads into a field to find a quiet corner. He finds a way over a stile and heads to an old oak tree. Sitting down, leaning against the tree, he reaches inside his jacket for his box of tricks. He slides off the left half of his jacket, draping it over his shoulder, and taps against the crook of his elbow.

He pulls on a rubber cord and plumps up his vein. He threads the needle into it, pulls back and watches the blood create a tiny mushroom cloud in the vial. He pushes and the solution enters him, becomes part of him. Is. Now. Him.

Floating in nothingness, lying on a blanket of pink cotton wool. He sees a grin.

'Hey, man, whatcha doin?' asks a familiar voice.

'Just, er, you know, being here, Janis...you?'

'Always here, just rockin' and a-rollin', diggin it, you know.'

'What else is there to do?'

'Exactly, my man, exactly,' says Janis over her round pink sunglasses.

'There are storms brewin', and I've got to meet them head-on.'

'I'm always here, man, you know, when you need a little headspace,' she says, lying back on pink pillows.

'Thank you,' says Robin, laughing and feeling a tickle in his stomach.

*

Robin doesn't train on Wednesday or Thursday. He keeps taking his personal medicine and starts to feel a little better.

*

Saturday 12 March 1977

Table-topping Chelsea come to Ninian Park. Twenty-thousand one hundred and ninety-four fans fill the stands. The Chelsea who released him. Peter Bonetti will tend goal today, Bonetti of the 1967 Cockney Cup Final, where Robin watched with the rest of the Chelsea youth team.

Robin passes a late fitness test. He goes to his usual spot in the dressing room. Clothes off. Cardiff shirt on. Shorts on…touches them…wishes them good luck.

The whistle blows.

Robin tries to fight his way into the game. He knows that he's far from fit but pushes himself. In the fifth minute, Robin holds up the ball and sees Tony Evans speeding through, and he sends through a perfect ball as Evans bursts into the area, but a Chelsea defender slides in and stops the attack.

In the nineteenth minute, Steve Grapes chips a through ball to Robin, who throws himself at the ball and sends his header just wide of the far post. Chelsea are on another level, and Cardiff City work to hold off their energetic attacks. Robin and Evans keep making runs at the Chelsea defence.

David Giles receives a pass and sees Robin running screaming into the box. He puts a looping ball high into the area. Robin sees the ball, sees Bonetti, and charges him. Bonetti watches the ball, catches it and sidesteps Robin. The Chelsea fans clap. Robin glares at Bonetti…then winks.

In the second half, Cardiff go at Chelsea with venom. Robin sweeps the ball around two Chelsea players, breaks through and shoots but sends the ball wide of the posts. *Fuck!* Cardiff start to gain the upper hand, with Tony Evans and David Giles opening up Chelsea. In the fifty-seventh minute, Grapes sends a free kick into the box. Evans smashes a header but Bonetti, cat-like, palms the ball clear for a corner. Chelsea smile and feel like they can't be beaten today.

In the seventieth minute, Britton catches Albert Larmour in possession and belts the ball past Ron Healey. Cardiff City 0 Chelsea 1. The Chelsea fans roar and scream from the terraces. Cardiff heads drop.

In the seventy-ninth minute, 'Butch' Wilkins pounces on 'Leo' Sayer, steals the ball, runs and sends the ball to Kenny Swain, who sidesteps Phil Dwyer and from twelve yards sends the ball fizzing past Healey. Cardiff City 0 Chelsea 2. Robin shakes his head, burns in anger.

In the eighty-third minute, Grapes knocks a ball into the mixer and Dwyer heads the ball into the turf. It ricochets and sends Bonetti and the ball into the back of the net. Dwyer grabs the ball from Bonetti and runs back to the halfway line. Cardiff cheers ring out around Ninian Park. Cardiff City 1 Chelsea 2. There is hope. Robin and Evans make a nuisance of themselves and try to level the score.

In the ninetieth minute, Gary Stanley breaks for Chelsea and sends in a cross which loops and beats Healey and ends up in the back of the net. Chelsea cheer, knowing they've done it. Cardiff City 1 Chelsea 3. The whistle blows and it's over. Robin trudges off the pitch, head down.

Robin sits in the dressing room, pulls off his sweaty kit. Showers. He puts his clothes on and pulls on his Afghan coat and heads up into the players' lounge. As he enters the room, everyone looks around, and eyebrows rise.

'Good to see you both,' says Robin to his mum and dad.

He kisses his mum and pats his dad on the shoulder. They smile.

'You did all right out there, son, but Chelsea look like champions,' says his dad.

'Yeah, they played well 'specially Bonetti. I should've scored; I'm still not a hundred per cent,' says Robin.

'What's up?'

Robin shrugs his shoulders, and says, 'It's a problem with my chest and stomach. Dunno what to do, but I need it to clear up soon.'

'You need to rest up or get yourself to the quack,' says his dad, looking at Robin with concern.

*

Robin goes back to London, takes lines. Sees his reflection in tinfoil. Breathes in clouds of white smoke. Crushes Diconal into pink dust and sets out his works.

*

Tuesday 15 March 1977
Robin trains and still feels a tightness in his chest. He holds back in training, tries to keep himself together.

*

Wednesday 16 March 1977
Robin is coughing and hacking, thinks of the game later today: the Welsh Cup semi-final. Wishes he could make it but knows he can't.

Robin picks up the phone and turns the dial. The phone rings.

'Jimmy, it's Robin. I'm sorry but I'm gonna have to cry off today. These chest and stomach problems are still giving me a load of gyp. I don't want to let you down on the park again.'

Jimmy pauses, and says, 'We'll miss you today, but try and get yourself fit for next weekend.'

'Yep, my doc has given me some stronger inhalers, so hopefully it'll do the trick. I'm going to take it easy at home.'

'Okay, you do that, Robin,' says Jimmy.

'Good luck, I'll be thinking about the lads against Bridgend.'

'Thanks, Robin.'

*

Robin misses training and goes back to London. Locks himself away. Sweats buckets and shakes. *Fights the demons day and night. Longs to catch up with Janis.*

*

Tuesday 22 March 1977
Robin turns up at Ninian Park. He has a smile, and his chest is clear and his cramps gone. He sees Jimmy

Andrews.

'All right, Jimmy, how'd we do against Bridgend?'

'We beat them two-one, but it wasn't the most convincing performance. More to the point, how are you?'

'I'm much better and looking forward to Plymouth on Saturday.'

'I'm glad to hear it. We'll put you through your paces this morning and see how you get on.'

'Sure thing.'

*

Saturday 26 March 1977
Ninian Park, Cardiff—

Nine thousand five hundred and eighty-seven have come to Ninian Park to watch Cardiff City v Plymouth Argyle.

He goes to his usual spot in the dressing room. Clothes off. Cardiff shirt on. Shorts on…touches them…wishes them good luck.

Robin feels looser in himself, his legs stronger again. Cardiff move the ball down the wing and Robin surges forward towards goal. A cross comes in and Robin throws himself at the ball with his eyes on goal. He smashes his head into the ball but the keeper stretches and pushes it away. Robin threads clever through balls for his teammates, but nothing comes of it.

In the eighty-sixth minute, a ball pings into the Cardiff City box, there is a melee of confusion and a Plymouth foot stabs the ball home. Cardiff City 0 Plymouth Argyle 1. Robin shakes his head. Jimmy Andrews holds his head. The final whistle blows and Cardiff City sit fourth from bottom in Division Two. The dressing room is full of regret; it fills with brooding anger.

Robin pulls on his clothes and ambles out into the night, gets the train back to London. Sits and sips at a bottle of Cinzano Bianco.

*

Saturday 2 April 1977
Bloomfield Road, Blackpool —

Cardiff City hold out against Blackpool, who are pushing for promotion. Both teams look to be sharing the points. A crowd of seven thousand three hundred and fifty-one watch on.

In the eighty-sixth minute, Cardiff clear a ball, but it falls to a Blackpool defender who hits the ball from twenty yards and the ball sails into the Cardiff City net. Blackpool 1 Cardiff City 0. There are roars from the Blackpool fans, who wave their tangerine scarves. Robin looks on. Shakes his head. He battles with the rest of the Cardiff side to get one back, but Blackpool are too strong.

Robin leaves the pitch with his head down, goes down the tunnel and into the dressing room. The scores from the other games filter through. Burnley have lost against Nottingham Forest, so Cardiff stay out of the relegation places by the skin of their teeth.

*

Wednesday 6 April 1977
Robin arrives at Hereford United's Edgar Street with the team and the club directors —

Cardiff are ushered to the away dressing room. The players put their kit bags down and start to change. Clothes off. Cardiff shirt on. Shorts on…touches them…wishes them good luck. Jimmy Andrews chats with Harry Parsons, thinks and thinks about today's match.

'Gather round, gentleman, this is a vital game for us

today. I make no bones about it – we cannot afford to lose. Hereford have only won one of their last nineteen fixtures, but they'll want nothing more than to drag us into the mire with them. Don't let me down, but most of all don't let yourselves down.'

Robin listens, shakes his legs and moves his arms as Jimmy goes on, talks in riddles about tactics. Jimmy talks to each man, one to one. He approaches Robin.

'Keep your work rate up, Robin, and don't let them get to you.'

Robin nods, clenching his teeth.

They head out onto the pitch. Robin hears the whistles and the cheers, smells the damp turf. The game starts, and it's a physical encounter. Both teams fighting for survival. Robin hustles and bustles with Hereford's number seven, Sheedy. Testing for weakness. With one eye on the referee, Robin puts a sharp elbow into his man, livens the lad up. Sheedy rears up at Robin. Robin looks into his eyes and smiles and spits into his face. The spit dribbles down the kid's face and he wipes it away in disgust with his shirtsleeve. The kid is white-hot with anger, his eyes locked on Robin.

'You dirty bastard.'

Robin stares at the kid, looks right into him. 'Watch yourself, I'll be waiting for you.'

In the thirty-fourth minute, Robin sees the kid break, and true to his word, Robin smashes into him and brings him down.

'Told yer, didn't I, and I'll break your fuckin' legs next time.'

The kid gets himself up and ignores Robin, looks straight through him. The referee beckons Robin towards him. Robin walks over with his hands on his hips.

'You need to calm yourself down next time or you're off.' The referee flashes the yellow card at Robin. Robin walks away.

Hereford take the free kick and the ball is intercepted, and Robin takes a pass and runs. He feels someone closing in, then feels his legs go from under him as he sees the ground careering up at him and he thuds into the ground.

'How'd you like that then?'

Robin laughs and looks up at the kid, admires his spirit.

'Your turn now,' says Robin, watching the incoming referee. The referee holds up the yellow card to the kid, who shrugs in acceptance. Puts his name into the book: Kevin Sheedy. In the thirty-third minute, Hereford score, 1–0 – the crowd roar. John Buchanan is shown a yellow card for a foul.

The referee blows up for half-time. The Cardiff players trudge down the tunnel into the away dressing room. Jimmy is already there with Harry and coach, Alan Sealey. Jimmy Andrews has his arms folded, glum.

'I told you they'd put up a fight. Right now we're heading into the bottom three, and you know what that means, right? Relegation, then we're right up the creek without a paddle.'

There are nods from the players.

'They were lucky with the goal, we're still in this,' says Phil Dwyer.

'We need to stay alert and keep our discipline when that ball goes dead. And on the subject of discipline, two bookings already. Robin, John we don't need it – you've got to keep your cool, because second half they're going to be trying to wind both of you up. Now get out there and turn this around, lads.'

The studs click-clack on the concrete down the corridor and through the tunnel, then they stop as the players stride onto the pitch

The second half kicks off, and for twenty minutes, Cardiff try to pull a goal back. In the sixty-seventh minute, Hereford score again. Hereford United 2 Cardiff City 0. The Hereford fans cheer. A fire burns inside Robin; he checks himself, talks himself down.

In the sixty-eighth minute, Cardiff win a free kick on the edge of the Hereford box. The ball is placed down and a Hereford player kicks the ball away. Robin watches the referee, watches the ball run away. Robin stares at the referee, runs towards the referee.

'Are you not gonna book him for that? Sort 'em out, Ref!'

The referee looks at Robin and pulls out his red card.

'What the fuck is that for?' says Robin, holding his head with both hands.

'Arguing with me, now go.'

'Are you fuckin' jokin' me!'

The Cardiff players rally in support, but the referee ushers them away.

There are cheers, jeers and boos from the Hereford fans, jubilant that they are 2–0 up and that Cardiff are down to ten men.

Robin walks off the pitch, head down. Shakes his head. Walks down the tunnel into the dressing room. He sits, dejected, elbows on his knees, head in his hands. He takes out a fag and lights it, pulls on it and then reaches into his bag and takes a swig of the Cinzano Bianco before hiding it back inside his towel. He hears the noise from above, the boos, the cheers. He wishes he was still out there – knows he should still be out there. He waits. He hears the rumble of feet above, hears the click-clack of studs down the corridor and the voices. The door opens and the lads trudge in. Robin looks up. 'What was the final score?'

'Two all,' says Phil Dwyer, 'Sayer got both.'

'Great stuff.' Robin feels a weight lift from his shoulders, feels a flutter.

The players all come in, and Robin waits. 'Lads, I'm really sorry about my sending off, but I swear I didn't do nothin'.'

'Are you sure?' asks Jimmy.

'Jimmy, all Robin said was "sort them out, Ref" says Doug Livermore.

'Right, we'll have to appeal it,' says Jimmy.

Jimmy claps his hands and the players look up. 'All I can say is, well done lads, to come back from two-nil down, with only ten men, shows great fighting spirit, something we've been missing of late. Hopefully we've turned a corner.'

Robin listens to the talk, feels the guilt pang up inside him – *only ten men, only ten men.*

On the way back they stop at a pub. Robin loves free piss and fills his boots. They take cans of lager onto the coach and he drinks – livens up but reins it in – *only ten men, only ten men.* He knows he'll be banned, knows he's in the doghouse.

*

Robin checks into a hotel room. Calls Liza to check she's okay. He undresses and turns on the side lamp and lies on the bed. Looks at the cuts on his shins. Shuts his eyes and tries to drift off to sleep. Sees white shapes morphing into scenes. People appear, dreamlike, he falls deeper…

*

He runs, trains, and takes the train to and from London and Reading. Back and forth, back and forth.

*

Friday 8 April 1977

Jimmy Andrews tells Robin he's dropping him to the bench. Robin shakes his head, feels the anger rise. 'Your call,' says Robin.

Fire and brimstone in his belly —

I'll show you —

Cunt. Cunt. Cunt.

*

Saturday 9 April 1977

Cardiff City v Wolverhampton Wanderers —

He goes to his usual spot in the dressing room. Clothes off. Cardiff shirt on. Shorts on…touches them…wishes them good luck.

Robin sits on the bench and looks at the crowds around Ninian Park, all fifteen thousand four hundred and forty-five of them. He sits on the bench watching and waiting. Looks at Jimmy Andrews fidgeting on the bench in the dugout. Robin sits, arms folded, legs outstretched, watching Cardiff City fighting against the onslaught from league leaders Wolverhampton Wanderers. At half-time it's 0–0.

In the second half, he wills for Wolves to score and teach Jimmy a lesson for making him sit on the bench. In the fiftieth minute, Wolves go one-nil up. Still no signal from Jimmy.

'Come on, let me out there, Archie, or we're gonna get done.'

'Not yet,' says, Jimmy, keeping his eyes on the action.

In the sixty-eighth minute, Wolves go 2–0 up. Robin sits and grins inside, but shakes his head in disgust.

'Right, get yourself warmed up, Robin. I'm putting you in midfield.'

'Sure.'

Robin jogs up and down the touchline and revs himself up. The crowd shout and wave at him, and he smiles back and waves. The Wolves fans sing: 'GYPO, GYPO, GYPO, WHERE'S YOUR CARAVAN?' Robin looks at them and laughs. *Cunts.*

Doug Livermore, the captain, comes off and Robin makes his way onto the pitch. There's applause and cries of: 'COME ON, FRIDAY!'

Robin makes himself known, and Cardiff begin to chase down Wolves. Robin jumps for every ball and smashes into the opposition. He stands next to a Wolves player, looks around for the referee, looks at the linesman. He knocks his head into the Wolves' player's face. Robin ambles away. The Wolves' player holds his face in shock. Shouts in outrage.

Cardiff are eager to get on with the game, but Wolves try to slow it down. Robin continues to put himself about.

There's a corner, and as the ball comes over Robin throws himself at it, heading over the keeper's outstretched arms and over the line, but a defender knocks it onto the far post, and 'Leo' Sayer nips in to put it away. Cardiff City 1 Wolves 2. The Cardiff crowd cheer, arms aloft. Robin grabs the ball out of the back of the net and runs back to the halfway line.

The clock continues to run down, and Cardiff pile on the pressure. In the ninetieth minute, Cardiff win a corner.

The ball sails over and Robin outjumps the opposition and sends the ball over to Wenty who belts it into the net. Robin runs up to Wenty and wraps his arms around him. The players run to the crowd, who run down the terraces to meet their heroes. Cardiff City 2 Wolves 2.

The final whistle blows and the players celebrate with the fans. A hard-earned draw against top of the table opposition. Robin walks with his chest out and feels ten feet tall.

'Good game,' says Jimmy.

Imagine if I'd a been on the whole game, you silly old fucker.

'Yeah, got the result we deserved in the end,' says Robin, walking away.

*

Sunday 10 April 1977 —
A hotel room, Winchester —

'So what do you reckon about tomorrow?' asks Robin.

'I reckon we need some kip first,' says Wenty.

'I can never sleep away; it's like being on holiday.'

'You don't say.'

'I think we'll be all right tomorrow.'

'I hope so.'

'What are you doin'?'

'Lying here listening to you keeping me awake.'

'I wonder how many people have had nookie in 'ere over the years?'

'I don't know, and you're not my type.'

'Fuck off, you should be so lucky. I mean, it must be a lot of people, and we're lyin' here in the beds.'

'Where's this going?'

There's rapid movement under the sheet, slap, slap, slap.

'What the fuck are you doing?'

'Having a wank! If you can't beat 'em, beat it.'

'Haha, stop pissing about you daft sod.'

'I'm bored.'

'Then go to sleep.'

'I would if I could.'

'Stop yapping and maybe you will.'

'I'd love a bird tonight.'

'Have one tomorrow night.'

'Maybe.'

'Now, let's get some shut-eye, night, mate.'

'Night, Wenty.'

The room falls silent.

*

Monday 11 April 1977
Southampton v Cardiff City —
Clothes off. Cardiff shirt on. Shorts on…touches them…wishes them good luck.

The floodlights beam down onto the biggest crowd that Robin has ever entertained – twenty-two thousand six hundred and seventy-four punters.

At half-time, it's 1–0 to Southampton. The Dell sing their praises to the Saints. The Saints come out for the second half with their chests puffed out and walk onto their hallowed turf. An onslaught almost washes the Cardiff players away into the Solent as the Saints go marching on. Saints score and the crowd begin to roar. In the sixty-second minute, they score again and it's 3–0.

Am I the only fucker tryin' here? The only one who gives a fuck.

He runs and he chases. He harries, batters, pushes and pulls.

In the seventieth minute, Steve Grapes chips a free kick to Tony Evans. Evans flicks the ball into the six-yard box and Robin throws himself head first at the ball and powers it past the keeper to score. Southampton 3 Cardiff City 1.

Cardiff throw the kitchen sink at it. Jimmy shouts from the bench. In the eighty-eighth minute, Evans runs onto a long ball and powers a header into the back of the net. Southampton 3 Cardiff City 2.

Grapes runs out wide and crosses the ball, and Robin crashes into the box, heads the ball, which fizzes just inches wide of the post – Robin shakes his head and looks up to the sky, arms aloft.

The final whistle blows, the piercing shrill ending the comeback. Too little, too late, and what could've been, should've been, falls away, along with the crowd.

The dressing room is full of heads looking down at the quarry-tiled floor, looking for a hole to appear and swallow them up, and it stares them all back in the face: R-E-L-E-G-A-T-I-O-N.

Robin Friday thinks of the Third Division. *No, not for me, been there, done that.*

*

There is an itch that can only be scratched with a needle.

*

Friday 15 April 1977
Welsh FA Disciplinary Commission, The Royal Hotel, Cardiff —

Here we go, yes, sir, no, sir, three bags full of grovel, sir.

Robin sits arms folded on the bench, jeans and a long-sleeved terry-towel T-shirt with collars – eyes dark and hair wild. Jimmy Andrews sits dressed in suit and tie. Jimmy thinks and plans.

There is a disquiet which hangs in the air like old smoke.

'The photographers are here for you. I saw them on the way in,' says Jimmy.

Robin sighs. 'Well let's hope this hearing works out all right, otherwise I'll be sticking their cameras up their arseholes.'

'Best not to. Look, just tell the commission how it is and I'll back you up.'

The door opens. 'Come on in, gentlemen.'

He faces a large wooden table, papers in files, wooden walls, and wooden people making sure the rules are followed.

'Okay, the next item,' the man says looking down at his notepad. 'We're here to discuss Mr Robin Friday's disciplinary record. Suspension comes about at twenty points, and Mr Friday is currently on twenty-eight due to recent disciplinary infringements.'

'That's right, sir,' says Robin, staring across the table.

The heads in the room turn and look at Robin. Jimmy grips his chair.

'But, but…' they stutter.

'Let's discuss it. I'm more than happy to.'

'Okay, go ahead.'

'First of all, I'm really sorry. I just want to play football for Cardiff, but it's 'ard when it seems that I'm already a marked man before a game begins. That last sendin' off I got was for telling the referee to "sort 'em out" as Hereford had picked up the ball and kicked it away at a free kick – they wasn't even given a warnin'.'

'He's right, and my team captain backs that up. That's all he said to the referee. I've never seen a player take as much abuse as Robin does on a Saturday afternoon. He's often kicked black and blue, and unfortunately they know he'll retaliate,' says Jimmy.

'I know I've got to get a hold of my temper, but it's 'ard when all I want to do is play football and I'm getting kicked about.' He looks them in the eyes, their fat heads on sticks. 'I'll do my best not to retaliate, and once again I apologise for my past conduct.'

They've already decided, they already know, it's on their faces.

There's whispering, pointing at paperwork.

'After taking into consideration your previous conduct at Reading and now at Cardiff, and your apologies to this commission, and your assurances about your future conduct, we have decided that you will be suspended for two matches. To begin after tomorrow's fixture against Luton Town.'

'Okay, fair enough,' says Robin, nodding as he gets up and leaves the room. He walks out into the corridor. Jimmy thanks the commission and jumps up to follow Robin.

'You'll miss the Forest and Wolves games, big games,' says Jimmy.

'Well, it could've been worse, it could've been a three-match ban. At least I'm playin' tomorrow.'

'If I pick you.'

'It's your call,' says Robin, shrugging his shoulders.

'I want the Robin Friday that played against Fulham on New Year's Day, that's what I want.'

‘I’ll be that man, Jimmy. Tonight I’ll be tucked up in bed nice and early – have no fear.’

‘I’ll see you tomorrow then. I’m just going to pop to the lavvy,’ says Jimmy, wandering off up the corridor.

‘Yeah, see you tomorrow.’

Robin walks out of reception and out of the doors onto St Mary Street.

‘Hello, Robin, how’d it go? Can we have a couple of photographs, please.’

‘As expected, I suppose. They gave us a two-match ban, which starts after tomorrow’s game.’

A bulb flashes. He stands staring into the distance, folding his arms, and watches yesterday’s newspapers blow past him down the street.

‘That’s it, I’m off.’

‘Sure, just a couple more,’ says the photographer, backing away down the street, still click-clicking with his camera.

‘That’s enough, you got your pictures.’

‘Okay,’ *click, click,* ‘okay, thanks,’ says the newsmen, as they walk away, back towards the hotel, to wait for Jimmy.

Robin strides back to his hotel, to brood, to call on all he’s got, to show them what he can really do. *I’ll give ’em a fuckin’ picture!*

*

He stands up on the scaffolding, up high, reaching out for the rope, starts to fall backwards —

He screams himself awake, sits in a cold sweat, fights the chatter in his head. *You’re just not good enough for her, you’ve gone too far this time, left it too late. You’re here stranded while she’s there in Reading. Can you handle it, can you? How did the last marriage work out? History repeats, history repeats, you know. Charlie said you shouldn't have got married. Charlie says you're not the player you were, not the player you were, the player you were, player you were, you were* — it becomes too much, and he passes out back into the darkness.

*

Saturday 16 April 1977
Ninian Park, Cardiff City v Luton Town —

He goes to his usual spot in the dressing room. Clothes off. Cardiff shirt on. Shorts on…touches them…wishes them good luck.

His teeth clenching, eyes staring, feet pumping, studs click-clacking against the tiled floor. The taste of copper on his tongue, and adrenaline surging through him, stomach tingling. The dressing room chatters in anticipation.

Jimmy Andrews quells the noise, talks of tactics, scratches white chalk across the blackboard: arrows here, arrows there; do this, don't do that.

This is my game, and I'll play it my way.

He goes out with Cardiff onto the pitch, swells and grows ten feet tall in the atmosphere, not a care in the world, the freedom of just playing. Ten thousand four hundred and sixty fans have come to watch Cardiff City take on Luton Town.

He follows his own script, makes runs which confuse, pinches player's arms, laughs and blows kisses, throws his body into each and every challenge.

In the ninth minute, 'Leo' Sayer pops one away and it's 1–0 to Cardiff. The crowd cheer. In the eleventh minute, Luton stick the ball in at the other end. Cardiff City 1

Luton Town 1. *Not again.*

Robin hurtles into the keeper, Aleksic, over and over, makes the keeper sick of him. He goes in hard again and knocks the keeper back.

'Sorry, mate,' he says, holding the keeper's wrist, hard, controlling, like a vice.

'Fuck off!' says the keeper, pushing Robin's hand away.

'What?' says Robin, laughing and staring at the keeper. He opens his palms in forgiveness, as he sees the fire in the keeper's eyes.

'Right, that's enough from both of you,' says the ref.

'I was just apologising, Ref, I don't know what his problem is,' he says, pointing at the red-faced keeper.

'Look, just calm it down, okay?'

'No problem.'

Robin walks away, looks over his shoulder at the keeper and knows he's got to him.

He sees Wenty out wide. Robin steams into the area alongside Phil Dwyer. Wenty lobs a high ball which loops into the box. The keeper looks up, eyes wide, and Robin slots the ball straight past his despairing dive. He shakes his head as Robin turns away and heads out towards a sea of blue voices who salute him with arms to the sky. Cardiff City 2 Luton Town 1. His teammates surround him and rub his head.

Cardiff come at Luton in waves, the crowd pushing them on.

Robin sees a dawdling defender on the ball and swoops on him, stretching down low, scooping the ball out from under the defender's legs. He runs off like a jackrabbit towards goal. Robin eyes the angle and hits the ball low across the deck as he loses balance and crashes into the ground, and watches the ball nestle into the bottom left-hand corner. He roars, and watches the goalkeeper sitting bereft. Robin wheels away towards the ecstatic crowd and kisses his hands and gestures towards the crowd. He stands arms aloft as his teammates crowd in on him and celebrate in his shadow. As he runs back for the restart, he flicks the V-sign at the goalkeeper, who looks back in disgust. The crowd laugh and cheer.

In the second half, Cardiff let their foot off the gas, and Luton push them back and find gaps in their defence.

In the sixty-seventh minute, a low shot from Luton clips in off the post, and it's Cardiff City 3 Luton Town 2.

Robin breaks through onto a ball and goes one on one with the keeper. Robin has one eye on the keeper and one eye on the ball. The keeper goes in studs high and crashes into Robin's knee. Sends Robin sprawling to the ground.

'Cunt,' he says, holding his bloodied knee.

The keeper stares down and Robin struggles up from the ground, and it's clear he can't carry on. He signals to the bench and is replaced. He looks back at the pitch one last time, hopes that Cardiff can hold out.

There are handshakes and pats on backs, and Harry Parsons cleans up Robin's knee and rubs it down with liniment.

Robin watches the rest of the game from the dugout. Hopes that they can hold them off. In the eighty-second minute, he watches Phil Dwyer put the ball in the back of the net. Cardiff City 4 Luton Town 2, and that's how it ends.

Robin hobbles towards the tunnel with the rest of the team as they make their way towards the dressing room.

Jimmy appears at his side. ‘Great game, today, Robin, just what we needed, and just what you promised.’

‘Feels good, apart from this,’ he says, pointing to his knee.

‘You and Aleksic, eh? That was a battle, and you beat him by putting the ball past him twice, and that’s why I thought giving him the two fingers was wrong. It’s not sportsmanlike, is it.’

‘Did I?’

‘You know you bloody did!’

‘I don’t remember, honest. I just remember we was celebrating with the crowd.’

‘Well, you did. We don’t need it. You’re good enough not to need to do that, okay?’

‘Fine.’

Robin watches Jimmy walk away, and thinks: *I score two goals, flick the Vs, and all you do is focus on the fuckin’ negative. What’s the fuckin’ point, eh? It’s about entertainin’ the crowd. The silly sod don’t know that though. He’s all about formations, systems – well a fat lot it’s done us this season.*

The mood in the dressing room is buoyant. Jimmy raps his knuckles on the door. When he’s got everyone’s attention, he says, ‘We’ve six games to go, six games to secure our safety. If we can play like we did for spells today, then we’ll be fine. We’ve just got to tighten up, and that’s why Luton got two today. Two tough games coming up, so let’s see you all on Tuesday morning.’

Robin can’t be part of those two games, knows it’s in the hands of the other lads – hopes they can do it.

He limps out of the ground and towards the train station, heads back to London.

*

He meets his connection under a railway bridge, under orange streetlights, swaps some notes for heroin and ambles away.

*

Faces push up against a television screen, their voices as one crackling murmur. He tries to make it out, but he can't. Listens, gets closer, presses his face up against the screen. Swears he can see them. 'They're in there, and they're watchin' me,' he says, turning and scowling around the room, but no one is there.

*

Friday 22 April 1977
Jimmy Andrews signs a four-year contract with a one-year extension option. Some eyebrows are raised in the dressing room.

*

Saturday 23 April 1977
Saturday afternoon, he watches the results come in – Nottingham Forest 0 Cardiff City 1. Goes out in London. Disappears into cubicles to snort coke through a dirty rolled-up five-pound note. Comes back to drink more, misreads a situation and fights his way out of it. Gets out of the bar, gets back home, gets away. Wakes with blurred memories and anxiety pinning him to his bed. He scrambles through his jacket and finds a packet of gear. He opens the tin with a click and pulls out the syringe, hands shaking…

*

Tuesday 26 April 1977
Cardiff surrender to Wolverhampton Wanderers at Molineux, letting in four second-half goals to lose 4–1.

They are booed and jeered as they walk from the pitch. They sit in seventeenth place, three places above the relegation spots.

*

Wednesday 27 April 1977

Robin walks into the dressing room.

'What happened last night, lads?' asks Robin.

'We got well and truly mauled in the second half,' says Phil Dwyer. 'Could've done with you, mate.'

'Yes, we certainly could, but I'm sure Robin will pay us back on Saturday,' says Jimmy. 'Now get yourselves together and get out on that pitch; this will be no routine training session.'

Robin goes through the training, listens to the moaning, feels like he's not part of this – feels as if he's being held responsible in some way. In the five-a-side he's not himself and doesn't get out of first gear.

*

The night before the Burnley game he starts to feel unwell, sweaty, shaky and his stomach cramping. He knows how to heal it but can't get hold of what he needs.

*

Saturday 30 April 1977

Ninian Park, Cardiff City v Burnley —

He goes to his usual spot in the dressing room. Clothes off. Cardiff shirt on. Shorts on…touches them…wishes them good luck. Eleven thousand and sixty-four fans watch from the Ninian stands.

The game kicks off.

In the sixth minute, Robin watches a Burnley cross fly into Cardiff's area; an unmarked player sticks his foot out and puts the ball into the back of the net. There's a wall of blue silence punctuated by cheers and claps in a small claret and blue pocket in one corner of the ground. Cardiff City 0 Burnley 1.

Burnley launch attack after attack, but somehow Cardiff keep them out.

Robin chases and harries and makes a nuisance of himself amongst Burnley's backline. He makes up for lost time. Just before half-time, Robin gets a ball in the area and shoots, but it ricochets off the post and out of play.

The sun shines down on Ninian Park, but only on Burnley it seems. The Burnley goalkeeper wears a cap to keep the bright sun out of his eyes. He holds the ball tight to his chest.

'You drivin' the train home?' asks Robin, with a cheeky grin.

'Yeah, if we win,' says the goalkeeper.

'Blindin',' says Robin, pulling the hat's peak down over the goalkeeper's eyes as he moves back, laughing.

The goalkeeper pushes his peak back with his arms, making sure that both his hands are still on the ball, safe and sound.

The game peters out, and the final whistle blows. Cardiff City 0 Burnley 1. There are boos from the Cardiff City fans. The Cardiff players move away down the tunnel as the Burnley players go and greet their fans.

Robin walks towards the crowd, smells the Bovril and the pies. Signs autographs, tells the fans that it'll all be all right. He walks down the tunnel, along the corridor and into the dressing room, and the team are quiet, huddled around a transistor radio as the football results come in.

Jimmy sits clutching today's programme with the league table. The results crackle out across the airwaves.

'Jesus, we're twenty-first,' says Jimmy. Harry Parsons looks at him with wide eyes.

'Second from bottom,' says John Buchanan.

'If this doesn't shock some of you into action then nothin' will,' says Robin. Wide eyes stare back. 'I'm not going back to the Third Division.'

Jimmy asks everyone to sit down.

'There can be no sugar-coating this, boys, we're in trouble, but I know we've got the quality to get out of this. The games against Luton and Forest proved that. We've got two away games coming up against Hull and Bolton; we've got to believe in ourselves. Today we were poor, and I feel sorry for the fans that paid to watch us. Where were *you*?' says Jimmy, pointing at Pontin.

'Now hang on,' says Robin, 'let's not turn this into a blame game. He's young, only just out of the reserves. We can do this, together, we can get out of this.'

'You just concentrate on your game, Robin, and I'll sort the team out, so no retaliation, right?'

'Right,' says Robin, 'and I'm just saying this is no time to look for scapegoats. It's not going to help is what I'm sayin'.'

'I see, I see...get yourselves changed, and we'll sort this on Tuesday.'

The dressing room starts to steam as players march in and out, towels around their waists. Shit, shower and dress, and Robin makes his way to the players' lounge. They sip their pints with guilt but feel better after the second.

'What you up to tonight?' asks Phil Dwyer

'Back to London – got some stuff to sort out, you know,' says Robin.

'Yes, it'll be a quiet one for me and all, I reckon.'

'I'm not promisin' mine'll be quiet, but you never know, stranger things have happened.'

'Do you need a lift to the station?'

'Yeah, that'd be cool, cheers.'

'Right, we're off, lads,' says Dwyer.

'See you Tuesday,' says Robin.

*

Robin feels like he's coming down with the flu; there's an ache deep in his bones and he feels clammy. He reaches into his jacket and takes out his works – *eases the worry, the pain, the anxiety. Robin searches for Janis, but he can't find her. There's only darkness.*

*

Robin and Liza argue over the bills, over his dope, over his late-night comings and goings, over his disappearances. Robin sleeps on the settee, a thin blanket for company; he hears the voices again. Faceless voices in the dark that know him so well, that turn his thoughts inside out, backwards and drive them into him like shards of coal, blackening his heart. He listens and finds his tin; he breathes in shallow gasps, eager not to make a sound. *Just a small hit, to take the edge off, like,* he thinks. The voices encourage him to make them silent. *Go on, just a bit won't hurt; we sleep, you sleep.*

*

Robin thinks about calling Jimmy Andrews, but he doesn't.

*

Thursday 5 May 1977
Ninian Park, Cardiff—

Robin walks into the car park and spots Paul Went getting out of his car.

'All right, Robin, where've you been?' asks Wenty.

'All right, mate, yeah, been full of flu. Much better now though.'

'Glad to hear it. You missed a right to-do here yesterday.'

'Yeah, what's that then?' asks Robin, folding his arms.

Wenty looks around, checking the other cars in the car park.

'We had a meeting with the directors yesterday, right, telling us what Third Division football would mean.'

'We fuckin' know what that means, right?'

'Yeah, they were just talking about the finances though. But that's not the half of it. A couple of the board, Latner and Clemo, went blabbing to the papers, and so we all knew by Monday that there was going to be this talk yesterday.'

'Do they think we're stupid? We know what relegation means to us…and the fans.'

'They probably do think we're stupid. The chairman has come out and said that it was a private matter between the board and the players, so Latner and Clemo have egg on their faces.'

'Sounds like a ridiculous meetin', glad I missed it. Has Jimmy said anything about it?'

'No, he's tight-lipped about it really, but he says that we've just got to get on with our jobs and survive.'

'Yeah, right,' says Robin. 'Did they ask where I was?'

'Jimmy just said you were ill, that's all.'

'Cool.'

'Let's go and kick some leather,' says Wenty, walking towards the entrance.

‘Let’s do it,’ says Robin, looking down at his white plastic bag.

They walk down the corridor and into the dressing room.

‘Look who I’ve found,’ says Wenty.

The lads in the dressing room look up with wry smiles, and some with wary faces amongst them.

Jimmy Andrews turns around and looks Robin in the eye, testing.

‘Can we have a word?’

‘Sure, Jimmy,’ says Robin.

‘Where’ve you been?’

‘Had the flu. In fact, I didn’t feel right the night of the Burnley game,’ says Robin, looking straight at Jimmy.

‘So, how are you feeling now?’

‘Much better.’

‘Why didn’t you call me?’

‘The phone’s been cut off, and I didn’t feel well enough to make it down to the phone box.’

‘What about your wife?’

‘She’s staying at her folks. She don’t want the flu, does she, not in her condition.’

Jimmy reads between the lines, remembers who he’s talking to and treads with care.

‘Yes, you’re right. Just to let you know, we had a meeting yesterday between the players and the board.’

‘Yeah, Wenty told me about it.’

‘Did he tell you we’ll have to cut down playing numbers if we go down?’

‘No, he didn’t mention that.’

‘Right, well, it’s something for us all to think about. We’ve got to pull together for these last few games. We’ve got to get through this.'

'I'll give it everything I've got.'

'You better had.'

*

Saturday 7 May 1977
Hull City v Cardiff City —

Robin sits hands on knees on the bench in the away dressing room. His fellow players sit with him, all eyes on Jimmy Andrews.

'We've three games to go, and we need to win them all, starting today. I want you all straight out of the blocks as if your life depends on it. I don't need to spell it out for you – the board of directors have already done that. I want to get on that bus tonight with two points so that you or I don't dread going back to Ninian Park. You've all got your jobs; you know what to do. Now get out there and win!' says Jimmy, pointing at the dressing room door.

Robin bounces up and down, thinks of nothing but this moment – thinks of throwing himself about in the game. The Cardiff team head out into the corridor and onto the pitch.

'Fuck me, I've seen bigger crowds in the Fourth Division. They've no support, this lot, proper fuckin' khazi country. Let's do 'em,' says Robin to himself. The attendance is three thousand five hundred and eleven.

In the nineteenth minute, John Buchanan sends in a through ball; 'Leo' Sayer sprints into the box but is blocked and held by the Hull City keeper. The referee points to the penalty spot. Robin and Tony Evans talk about who will take it; neither is keen. Buchanan steps up and takes the ball and places it on the spot. He runs up, fires a shot which the keeper gets his hand to, but the ball spins into the back of the net. There's a small cheer from a corner of the ground where a couple of hundred hardened Cardiff fans cheer.

In the thirtieth minute, Wenty crashes into a Hull player in the box and the referee points straight to the spot. Dwyer and Wenty argue with the referee, who shows them both a yellow card for their troubles. Jimmy looks through piercing eyes, shouting at them to calm down. Hull make no mistake from the spot kick. Hull City 1 Cardiff City 1.

Robin, 'Leo' Sayer and Tony Evans keep running at Hull's defensive line, running on to golden threaded balls from Buchanan.

Robin takes a pass from Evans and moves along the byeline. He sweeps past two Hull players and knocks in a pass to Buchanan, who thunders in a shot from fifteen yards. Robin runs over to congratulate Buchanan and they make their way to the corner to wave at the travelling blue contingent. Boos ring out from the Hull crowd.

At half-time, it's Hull City 1 Cardiff City 2.

In the second half, Cardiff keep a tight backline; Hull can't break through. Robin keeps up his work rate, keeps chasing the ball in the hope that the demons will leave him. Doesn't want the final whistle to go, is happy to play away all day.

Finally, the ref blows up and it's all over, and Robin feels some relief. He heads over to the Cardiff fans and signs autographs. Signs his name again and again, gets into a groove, is happy to talk all day to the fans, comfortable with his own kind.

*

Robin goes back to London and drinks enough to set him free, and chips away at some golden-brown powder, just enough to keep sickness at bay. He forgets all of his troubles.

*

Monday 9 May 1977
The Cardiff City treatment room is full, and Robin has his knee worked over. John Buchanan and Doug Livermore wait in the queue.

*

Tuesday 10 May 1977
The Cardiff City bus retreats back down the motorway, full of sorrowful players and disgruntled directors. The bus whirrs along. Robin listens to the sound, rocks and rolls with the movement of the bus. He swigs at his bottle of Cinzano Bianco, looks out of the window. *Half-chances flicker through his mind, his legs twitch at the thoughts, sees the score on the board: Bolton Wanderers 2 Cardiff City 1. Hears the cries of joy from the Wanderers' fans, and the boos from the Cardiff fans.*

Cardiff's fate now hangs on the last game of the season.

*

Robin wakes up in a hotel room, the light breaking through a chink in the curtains. The room smells of cigarettes, stale booze, and sweat. He smells sweet perfume and sees a woman lying fast asleep next to him. Looks at his watch and it's after three o'clock on Wednesday afternoon. The speed that drove him through the night has left a hollow feeling inside him. He tries to block the thoughts of yesterday, of all of this mess. There are two cures – sex, of course, but once the seed is spent, the thoughts will flood back in like a riptide. There is another, and he starts to rummage around in his jacket for it. It will even everything out, coat his thoughts honey brown.

*

Thursday 12 May 1977

Jimmy Andrews sits on a chair in the dressing room, his back to the wall. 'Have a look at this.' He hands round a bunch of newspapers to the lads sat on the benches.

'That's yesterday's paper. Now look at the league table.'

		P	W	D	L	F	A	Pts.
14	Hull	40	10	16	14	44	48	36
15	Burnley	41	11	14	16	46	62	36
16	Fulham	41	11	13	17	54	60	35
17	Bristol Rovers	40	11	12	17	48	65	34
18	**Cardiff City**	**41**	**12**	**9**	**20**	**55**	**66**	**33**
19	Carlisle	41	11	11	19	48	74	33
20	Orient	40	9	14	17	35	53	32
21	Plymouth Argyle	42	8	16	18	35	53	32
22	Hereford Utd	40	7	14	19	54	77	28

Jimmy continues, 'It tells us everything we need to know, pure and simple. We must beat Carlisle here on Saturday to be sure of safety. We forget Bolton, just forget it, all of it.' Jimmy looks around the room, his eyes settling on Robin.

'Saturday is a cup final. Nobody here wants to play Third Division football. We've done that, and we're not going back. We need to believe, each and every one of us.'

Robin looks around the room and feels he doesn't need motivating, but some of this lot do – there's a weakness here. He'll make sure that he's on that team sheet come Saturday afternoon.

*

Saturday 14 May 1977

Ninian Park, Cardiff City v Carlisle United —

A game of survival.

Saturday comes, and there's tension in the streets surrounding Ninian Park. The fans file through the turnstiles, the last league game of the season, perhaps their last game in the Second Division. There's nervous chatter in the stands and down in the dressing room.

Robin goes to his usual spot in the dressing room. Clothes off. Cardiff shirt on. Shorts on…touches them…wishes them good luck.

Robin bounces on his toes, turns to Phil Dwyer. 'We're gonna rip 'em up.'

'Yeah, we're going to do them,' says Dwyer.

Robin's eyes are fixed, staring. He starts to jump up and down, throws punches into the air: left jab, right cross, left uppercut. Dwyer takes a step back.

Jimmy Andrews looks at Robin, swinging with power into the air.

'Come on, come on, you cunts,' he says, thumping his fists into his biceps.

Jimmy walks over to Robin and puts a hand on his shoulder and whispers, 'No cards today, okay?'

'No problem. I'm just getting it all out now.'

'Good man,' says Jimmy, patting him on the back.

The players sit down in their kits. Robin sits, legs still bouncing, his knees dancing up and down.

Jimmy addresses the team. 'Lads, this is it, don't let me down. Hit Carlisle early and hold on. They'll be throwing everything they've got at us. Make sure it's them that are relegated and not us!'

'Come on, you fuckers, let's be 'avin' you. We've a game to win,' says Robin, jumping up off the bench.

The lads look up, and Jimmy looks at them and says, 'You heard him, what are you waiting for?'

The players line up in the tunnel. There's a tension so tightly wound it's as if two ropes are woven through the players' intestines, and they're dragging their supporters behind them, their guts squirming with the expectation. Some feel their legs turn to jelly, others stand tight-jawed, legs flexing.

Robin stands uneasy in the quiet of tunnel, where time seems to be standing still.

He heads out into a sun-filled Ninian Park. The fans are singing 'Men of Harlech' at the top of their voices.

'We've nothing to worry about with this lot. Look at 'em, they're shittin' it! I can smell 'em.'

There are laughs from both teams, calls of 'Fuck off' from the Carlisle players – the tension eases for a moment.

'Let's put on a show!' says Robin. He walks over to some of the fans, gives them a clap and a wave before heading back to his teammates.

Fifteen thousand eight hundred and one fans have come to watch this relegation dogfight.

The whistle blows and the game kicks off.

In the first minute, Wenty falls over onto his shoulder. He feels a shooting pain and leaves the field. Cardiff play on with ten men. Harry Parsons works on him with Doc Hamilton, and they pop his shoulder back into the socket and give him an injection. Wenty runs back onto the pitch to cheers and applause from the Cardiff fans.

In the seventeenth minute, Alan Campbell breaks on the right, cuts to the edge of the six-yard box, and pokes in a shot from a tight angle. There's a massive roar from the crowd. Robin runs up with the rest of the players, patting Alan Campbell on the back, ruffling his hair. Cardiff City 1 Carlisle United 0.

Carlisle kick off and attack from the off. In the nineteenth minute, a booming twenty-yard shot sails into the back of the net. Cardiff City 1 Carlisle United 1. Cardiff stand as one, silent in their majority – stunned. Robin shakes his head, and through gritted teeth he says, 'Come on, you cunts, don't do this to me.'

Half-time, and talk of holding on, putting the game to bed.

In the sixtieth minute, Robin receives a ball from midfield, goes around one player, moves into the area, moves the ball from his right to left foot and goes around the goalkeeper, eyes on the goal, and the goalkeeper throws his arms around Robin's legs and brings him down.

'You fuckin' cunt,' says Robin, 'I was gonna score.' He looks at the referee, who points to the spot, awarding a penalty.

'Now you're fucked,' says Robin to the goalkeeper, who ignores him.

John Buchanan puts the ball on the spot, runs up, and hits the ball too close to the keeper, who parries the ball away. Steve Grapes runs onto the rebound and hits the ball wide. Ninian Park erupts with a moan – hands over mouths, stomachs churning. Robin holds his head and clenches his fists. Jimmy looks to the sky for answers.

In the final minute, Carlisle break through, and Ron Healey is taken out by a Carlisle forward, the ball is knocked back across the goal, and Robin, fearing the worst, steams back towards the melee. Jimmy looks on in horror as he sees Robin's eyes locked onto his target. Jimmy holds his head and expels, 'Jesus Christ, no!' Robin swipes at the ball, misses, and almost catches a Carlisle player. The ball is cleared off the line by Dwyer and to safety.

Robin looks up, and there are pushes and shoves as Cardiff players bunch around the offending Carlisle forward, who is sent to the ground. The referee runs over, and Robin sits breathing heavily, looking up from the floor at the melee unfolding.

The final whistle goes, and there's pandemonium. Jimmy runs onto the pitch, clapping his players and the fans, who have stood all season through thick and thin. The Carlisle players drop to the floor, knowing their fate is now out of their hands.

Jimmy shakes the hand of every Cardiff player; he shakes Robin's hand. 'Thanks, Robin.'

'No problem,' says Robin.

There are shouts of joy from the Cardiff fans, and Robin heads towards them. Blows kisses and waves at the fans. He signs autographs, takes a scarf from a fan and hands them his shirt.

He heads off the pitch, down the tunnel, and along the corridor into the dressing room. He walks into Jimmy handing out bottles of champagne. Corks pop and players slurp and swig at bottles. *Survival is a victory*, thinks Robin.

Jimmy sends a bottle of champagne into the match officials' room.

Robin strips off and sinks into the hot bath, the salts sinking into his cuts, stinging away. 'Thank fuck for that, eh lads,' says Robin.

'Thank fuck indeed,' says Phil Dwyer. 'How close was that at the end?'

'Too fuckin' close. Can't believe I missed that bloody penalty,' says Buchanan.

'No, nor can I, but Grapes' follow-up couldn't have been bettered by Stevie Wonder,' says Robin, laughing.

'How'd he miss?' asks Dwyer.

'Fuck knows, but at least we're not that lot next door. Imagine sitting there waiting for Orient to finish their season.'

'Orient'll do it, I think,' says Buchanan.

Wenty comes into the room holding a full bottle of champagne.

'Here he is, the one-armed bandit. Where'd you get that one?' asks Robin, taking a swig from his plastic cup.

'Jimmy gave it me, for bravery,' he says, laughing. 'Ref sent it back.'

'Course he did, the cunt. We was just runnin' out in 'ere an' all,' says Robin.

Wenty steps into the bath, takes a swig from the magnum and passes it to Robin.

'Cheers, how's the shoulder?'

'The injection worked a treat, but I'm sure it's going to be hell later,' says Wenty, sliding down into the bath water.

*

Thoughts turn to the Welsh Cup final, a two-legged affair, with the winners (so long as they're Welsh, of course) being able to play in the following season's European Cup Winners' Cup. The board of directors have laid down big player bonuses if Cardiff City can retain the cup. Robin rubs his hands.

*

Monday 16 May 1977
Ninian Park, Cardiff City v Shrewsbury Town, Welsh Cup final, first leg —

This isn't Wembley but it's a cup final, the chance of glory, a piece of silverware to hold if only for a moment – the chance to play in the European Cup Winners' Cup.

Robin thinks back to a decade ago: *Wembley, Saturday 20 May 1967. A sea of fans in the stands; the Chelsea and Spurs' scarves and flags in the FA Cup Final. The standing ovation as the teams filed out onto the pitch.* He sees it like it was yesterday. He can taste that day, smell it – but he wasn't playing then.

Today, Shrewsbury Town of England and the Third Division are the opposition, on a Monday night in May, but somehow this seems like a pre-season friendly – the atmosphere hollow, like a reserve match. Ninian Park with half-empty stands. An English team in a Welsh Cup final.

The game kicks off and Shrewsbury start on the front foot. Shrewsbury's front three of Bates, Lawrence and Maguire cause havoc with Cardiff's defence, which sees the young Keith Pontin deputising for the injured Wenty.

In the eighth minute, Hornsby chips the ball over Ron Healey's outstretched arms and the ball bounces over the line. Cardiff City 0 Shrewsbury Town 1.

At half-time, the Cardiff players trudge off the pitch and into the dressing room, the players' heads down. Jimmy stands brooding. 'Get yourselves a bloody drink, then sit down and listen.' The players grab their sugary tea and sit on the benches. Robin sits, sweat dripping down his face, his hair damp.

'We might as well knock on next door and hand them the cup because that's about as poor a performance as I've seen in a long while. Is a win bonus not enough for some of you? It's like an open barn door at the back there. Pontin, sort yourself out and get tighter on your man.'

'Come on, leave it out,' says Robin.

'Well, what do you suppose I do, tell everyone it's okay?'

'No, you bollock the rest of 'em for not helpin' him out, that's what.'

Jimmy looks at the rest of the defenders; they look away.

'You've all got your responsibilities out there. I don't need to tell you, do I?' There's no reply.

'Let's at least finish this season with something positive, something we can tell the grandchildren. Now get yourselves back out there and win this tie.'

There are nods, and 'Yes, Boss' and 'Yes, Jimmy' as the players finish their tea and head out back down the corridor and down the tunnel, where Shrewsbury wait.

Cardiff City try to dig their way back into the game, push, pull and fight their way back. In the eighty-sixth minute, there's a scramble in the box and Freddie Pethard hooks the ball into the back of the net. Cardiff City 1 Shrewsbury Town 1. Freddie Pethard picks the ball out of the back of the net and runs back to the halfway line.

In the final minute, 'Leo' Sayer swings a corner into the Shrewsbury area, Robin watches the ball, there's a scramble in the box, and a Shrewsbury player tries to get a foot to it, but the ball is collected and sent back into the mix. The ball swirls into the air, and as it comes down, Robin throws himself at it, head first, and the ball flics into the back of the net. Cardiff City 2 Shrewsbury Town 1. Cheers and applause ring out. Robin reels away, punching the air, grinning, and jogs back to the halfway line. His voice is announced over the tannoy and there's another cheer.

Shrewsbury kick off, but the referee blows up for full-time.

'That should do us for today, lads!' says Robin to his teammates.

'You're a bloody life saver,' says Phil Dwyer.

'We were lucky out there,' says Jimmy.

'You make your own luck,' says Robin.

'Aye, you're right,' says Jimmy.

'Don't seem right though, playin' a final over two legs. What's the point?'

'The point is consistency and tradition. To win over two legs, you can't fluke it. We got away with it today. Things'll be tough at Gay Meadow on Wednesday, mark my words.'

'We'll be all right. We just need to shore it up at the back.'

'Tell me something I don't know.'

*

Wednesday 18 May 1977

Gay Meadow, Shrewsbury Town v Cardiff City, Welsh Cup final, second leg —

The silver cup sits on a table in the stands, contested for almost one hundred years. The winner's names engraved, never to be forgotten.

Robin Friday wants to hold the cup, wants photographs of himself with the cup, wants the win bonus. Wants it all.

Jimmy Andrews goes through the tactics, tries to address Monday's inadequacies. A bright orange sun stains the sky as the players head out onto the pitch. The last game of the season.

In the second minute, the ball is in the back of the Cardiff net. There's a cheer. Shrewsbury are alive and kicking, and some of the Cardiff players already seem to have their deckchairs out. Shrewsbury Town 1 Cardiff City 0. Shrewsbury attack and attack, and Cardiff fight to hold them off.

In the sixty-first minute, Pontin puts the ball into his own net: Shrewsbury Town 2 Cardiff City 0. Shrewsbury's confidence grows, and they can see one hand on that silver cup. Robin tries to fight back but feels the tie slipping away.

In the sixty-seventh minute, Shrewsbury put away their third goal. The Shrewsbury fans wave their blue-and-amber scarves in the air.

Robin shouts and screams, but Cardiff will not wake up.

The final whistle goes. There are laughs and smiles from the Shrewsbury players and fans. Robin walks up to collect his runners-up medal, looks at the cup, large and silver. The Shrewsbury players collect the cup, hold it aloft, and walk around the pitch with their winner's medals.

There is quiet amongst the Cardiff players; champagne corks and cheering sounds come from next door. Thoughts of what could've been hang in the away dressing room's stale air.

There's quiet on the bus. Jimmy sits with arms folded. The directors sit with Welsh FA reps. It wasn't meant to be this way.

Robin sits on his own, fidgets in his seat, rubbing his chin, sits stewing in the misery of defeat, the misery of his thoughts. *This lot didn't even try. The magic of the cup; the magic my arse!* The itch starts again.

*

The Prince Rupert Hotel, Shrewsbury —

The players, management, and directors head to the hotel bar. They drink to forget, but not too much, apart from one.

Robin gulps pints down, chatters, heads to the toilets and goes into a cubicle. He takes out a wrap of paper and dabs its white powder onto the back of his left hand, covering his right nostril with his right hand. Snorting hard, he pulls the white line of cocaine up his nose. A bitter taste hits the back of his throat. He licks the residue off the back of his hand and folds the wrap up and places it in his pocket.

Some of the lads play snooker. Robin orders a pint, downs it, takes another, and another. The players stand around laughing, joking, the directors talking, smoking cigars bigger than their cocks.

The buzz of the cocaine starts to wear off, and Robin throws down another drink —

These lot, they're all cunts. Look at 'em. Talkin' about me, I fuckin' bet.

'What's your fuckin' problem?' he says, looking at the barman. 'Get me a fuckin' drink, them cunts are payin' for it,' says Robin, pointing at the directors.

He takes the pint, his blood swimming in alcohol, and staggers towards the snooker table.

'Any of you cunts fancy a game?'

Shocked faces stare back at him.

'No? I'll show you how to play better than you did today!' he says, jumping up onto the snooker table. Robin puts his beer down and kicks a snooker ball off the table, it crashes off the wall. There's movement, people group together, strength in numbers. Robin picks a snooker cue up and swings it, and players move away.

'You're all useless fuckin' wankers!'

The board of directors and the management move towards a far wall, backs pressed against it.

Robin has the attention of the whole bar.

Phil Dwyer steps forward. 'Come on, mate, get down,'

'Fuck off, you cunt, or you'll get some off this!' he shouts, swinging the snooker cue.

Robin picks up a ball and throws it across the room. It smashes into a wall light, and glass shatters and the ball crashes to the floor.

'You fuckin' lot, board of cunts, well I'm fuckin' bored of you. 'Ave some of this,' says Robin, scooping snooker balls off the table.

He throws them straight at the directors. They jump about, their heads bobbing and weaving like a live coconut shy. They run and take cover behind the bar. He throws a ball and breaking glass crashes behind the bar. Throws again, *smash*.

'Doug, you're the captain,' says Phil Dwyer.

'This is madness,' Doug Livermore whispers. 'Let him throw the last one, and let's rush him and get him to bloody bed.'

Robin hurls another snooker ball and it ricochets off the bar and into the bottles behind. He jumps down off the snooker table and lands on both feet, admiring his work.

'You comin' out, or what, you cunts?' he says, seeing eyes peeping over the bar.

'Now,' says Livermore, as Dwyer and a vanguard of players surround Robin. Dwyer swings his arm around Robin. Robin's feet start to go from under him, his balance gone, and the players carry him away up the stairs to his room. They put a bowl by his bed and lie him on his side.

'Come on, mate, that's enough,' says Dwyer. Robin doesn't answer.

*

In the morning —

He wakes, opens one eye, sees the breeze blowing through the curtains, tries to get up and feels a sickening pain sear through his head. He looks down at the bowl, spits into it, saliva dripping from his mouth as he spits it away. Then it comes, the first violent hurl from the pit of his stomach, almost falling off the bed, the puke splashing into the bowl. He heaves a second time, third, and a fourth and final dry, agonising retch. He spits and wipes his mouth.

'Fuck, me,' he says, heading for the toilet. He turns on the tap, swills his mouth out, tries to spit away the taste of sick. He looks into the bathroom mirror, sees his hair wild, his eyes puffy, bloodshot.

Something isn't quite right, and through the darkness of his mind he sees shocked faces, balls hitting walls. Oh, fuck.

The anxiety hits him like a cold hammer. He sits down on the edge of the bath.

Well, son, you've outdone yourself this time. How the hell are you going to explain yourself? Madness for all to see —

No silver cup, a loser's medal, apologies to make, and repair bills to swallow.

He feels another surge of nausea and grips onto the toilet, throwing the poison and the bile out of him. The puke spatters into the toilet until he retches himself empty, his eyes watering and saliva dangling from his lips. He wipes his mouth and swills it out with water and toothpaste.

There's a knock at the door.

JESUS, they're coming for me. He looks at the open window. *Don't be stupid, you'll break your bleedin' neck.*

Robin opens the door. Jimmy Andrews and Phil Dwyer stand there looking at him, and into his hotel room, the caustic smell of vomit hitting them.

'How are you feeling?' asks Jimmy.

'I've felt better, come in,' says Robin.

'That was some blowout you had last night. You remember any of it?' asks Dwyer.

'Bits,' says Robin, sitting down on the bed as Jimmy stands next to the open window, looking down onto the street below.

Dwyer sits on the other empty bed.

'I was arseholed. I just wanted to win that cup. I'm so sorry, so fuckin' sorry.'

'Well, you livened the place up, that was for sure. The bar looks like a scene from a Western.'

'I'll pay the repair bill,' says Robin.

'You'll have to do that, and apologise to the board. To say they are not impressed would be an understatement,' says Jimmy, still looking out of the window.

'I'll apologise to all concerned, Jimmy, I will.'

Jimmy looks at Robin sitting on the bed, and says, 'I've never seen anything like it, Robin, never in all my years. We're lucky they didn't call the police. We had to talk them out of it; they'd have carted you off to the cells.'

Robin sits with his head in his hands. 'Well, at least it's helped us all forget about the cup final,' says Robin with a sarcastic smile.

‘It’s definitely done that,’ says Dwyer, trying to hide his smirk. ‘It was like having a night out with Keith Moon.’

Jimmy looks at Robin, sitting there dressed as he was last night, hair a wild mess. ‘There’s one positive, and that’s that you’ve got the summer break to get yourself sorted out. We’ve got to get you up to Cardiff.’

‘I’m not having that conversation now, Jimmy, not when I’m like this, that’s a f— liberty.’

‘The liberties were all taken last night, Robin.’

There’s a glare from Robin. ‘Just leave it out, Jimmy, we’ve got the baby due soon.’

‘I’d leave it today,’ says Dwyer, looking at Jimmy.

‘Aye,’ says Jimmy, ‘we’ll be leaving soon, so get yourself together.’

‘I’ll be two minutes,’ says Robin, as Jimmy Andrews and Phil Dwyer walk out of the room.

He splashes his face with cold water. Looks in the mirror. Looks at his dark eyes. Fights the anxiety inside his chest, thinks of the apologies he’s got to make at the foot of those hotel stairs and beyond.

Liza, what the fuck am I going to tell her? ‘Sorry, love, we’ve a bit less money cos I smashed up a hotel.’ No, no fucking way, not in her condition.

He hears the voices again. They come through the wall into his ears, and into his mind.

You useless cunt. Look at you, acting like a fuckin’ arsehole when you should be acting your age. When will you learn, eh? This is your second go, remember? The first, Maxine, do we need to go there again, no, no, I didn’t think so, you silly cunt. You fucked it up at Reading, now you’re fucking it up at Cardiff – well done, son!

'Fuck off!' says Robin.

No, I won't, I'm here to help, here to straighten you out, to make sure you get back on the straight and narrow path that you've always strayed from, here to see you right, pal. Can you hear them talking about you downstairs? Listen, just listen. 'Why the fuck did we sign him? He's mental!' That was Phil Dwyer. 'It's the worst signing we've ever made. We've got to get rid of him before he takes the club down with him.' That was the board, crowing in cigar smoke. 'Let's make an example of him. If we do that, then it'll keep the rest of them on their toes,' says Jimmy Andrews. You can hear them, can't you. See, I'm here to help. You'll hear Liza, too, if you want?

Robin pulls himself out of his thoughts, his chest tight. He breathes in…and out, fumbles in his pocket for his inhaler. Takes a blast. Watches his face morph in the mirror. Sees horror in his eyes, sees beyond himself, and it petrifies him.

Robin rubs his face. 'Let's get this over and done with,' he says, opening the door and closing it behind him.

Fuckin' Shrewsbury; fuckin' hotel; fuckin' anywhere but here.

He heads down the corridor, and to the stairs, pauses for a moment and takes a deep breath. Heads down the stairs and hears the Cardiff City group in reception, chattering, chattering, then it stops…

*

In the off-season —

Robin hires a mate with a lorry and moves himself and his heavily pregnant wife to Bristol: a halfway house between Cardiff, Reading, and London.

PART THREE
CARDIFF CITY
SEASON 1977/78

A baby cries and a cool breeze blows in through the curtains. The sunlight makes shadow puppets with the curtains. Shapes dance across the walls.

*

To make it safe for the fans, the board have to pay a significant six-figure sum to improve Ninian Park. They are eager to get it ready to host the World Cup Qualifier between Wales and Scotland, and they have until Wednesday 24 August 1977 to prove they are ready. In the meantime, the capacity is reduced to a maximum of ten thousand spectators.

*

Thursday 14 July 1977
The first day of training. There are catch-ups, stories, and smiles. Congratulations given for babies being born.

Robin runs up the Wenallt, among the ferns and the bracken, up and down, up and down. He runs on paths that criss-cross. Scars on the landscape. Some players bolt up and down the hill. Robin is in no rush; he feels the wind in his face and the sun on his back. At the end of the morning's session, Robin approaches Jimmy.

'Jimmy, can I have a word?' asks Robin.

'Yes, sure, is everything okay?'

'Well, yeah, sorta, you know I've moved to Bristol?'

'No, no, I didn't actually,' says Jimmy with a frown.

'Right, well, it's gonna cost about fifteen quid to travel up 'ere every week, so how do I claim it back?'

'Claim it back?'

'Yeah, for the travel, like.'

'I asked you to move to Cardiff and you refused, and now you're asking for expenses. I want all my players to live as near to the club as possible.'

'So, you're not going to pay 'em?'

'Absolutely not, no.'

'You sure about that?'

'Yes, it's your choice to live in Bristol, so any costs relating to that should be paid by you and not the club.'

'Right, well, I ain't payin' fifteen quid a week out me own pocket.'

'I'm afraid you're going to have to.'

'I ain't.'

'Then move to Cardiff and you won't have to pay anything.'

'I don't want to move to Cardiff. I've been in Bristol almost two months now. We're settled.'

'That's up to you, but you'll pay your own travel.'

'So you're not going to pay it?'

'No.'

'Okay, see you, Jimmy,' says Robin, turning and walking away.

'See you tomorrow,' says Jimmy.

Robin doesn't turn around.

*

Friday 15 July 1977
Jimmy Andrews sits and waits for news. He huffs and he puffs, moans to coach, Alan Sealey, moans to anyone with an ear. The phone doesn't ring. Robin Friday is on the missing list.

*

Monday 18 July 1977
Robin phones Jimmy Andrews.

'Jimmy, it's Robin.'

'Robin, what's bloody going on?'

'Are you going to pay my travelling expenses?'

'No, and don't push your luck. Where were you on Friday?'

'I wasn't at training because I'm not payin' for travellin'.'

'And I've told you we won't be paying for it.'

'I'm not payin' out of my own pocket. The club should pay it.'

'Right, Robin, if you want to play it that way then I'm going to fine you because you're in breach of your contract. Do you understand me?'

The phone goes dead.

*

'What's going on?' says Liza. 'How're we going to pay the bills? They'll cut off the phone and electricity.'

'Just leave me alone, I'm off out,' says Robin.

'Where?'

'Anywhere,' says Robin, picking up his denim jacket and slamming the door behind him.

*

Robin gets on a train to London and stays away for a few days. Smokes blow and drinks lager. Crushes up pink Diconal tablets and sets out his works.

*

He walks up the garden path wishing each step took longer. Robin puts his key in the door, turns it, feels the atmosphere change, feels unwell, queasy in his stomach – knows inside that he's been chipping too much these last few months. If he doesn't take his medicine he'll get ill, and this medicine isn't always easy to get hold of – *dark corners, seedy pubs, and moody contacts.*

He walks into the hallway, listening, but the house is still. He feels a temporary stay of execution, then he sees the note: *tired of waiting…sick of this…of you…no money…gone home.*

'Fuckin' hell,' he says, reaching for the telephone. He picks it up and starts to dial, but there's no dialling tone.

'Jesus, this is all I fuckin' need,' he says, and sighs.

A well of panic opens up inside him, like a black hole sucking everything out of him. He kicks the door through into the kitchen. Stands with his hands on his head. 'For fuck's sake, silly cow.'

He pulls out a chair and sits down, head in his hands, feels the pain swell inside his heart, feels the tears start to trickle down his face. 'Why am I so fuckin' stupid? I should've come home,' he says.

Right, pull yourself together.

He checks his pockets for shrapnel. Jangling the coins in his pocket he heads back out of the house and down the road to the red phone box.

He dials the number and waits for the connection.

‘Hello,’ says Mrs Deimel.

‘Hello, Heather, it’s Robin, can I speak to Liza? Is she all right?’

‘She doesn’t want to speak to you.’

‘Look, come on, I just want a word, to know that she’s all right.’

‘She’s fine, Robin, now she’s here.’

‘Please, can you ask her to come to the phone.’

‘No, sorry, enough is enough.’

‘Then I’ve got no choice: I’m coming down to Reading.’

‘You can, but I won’t let you in.’

‘I don’t care, I’ll knock the bleedin’ door down.’

There’s a pause at the other end, then a click, and the line is dead.

‘Bollocks,’ he says, smashing the receiver down.

*

Boards a train from Bristol to Reading —

Walks from the station, head down, collar up.

Walks down Connaught Close. He knocks on the door, hears movement. The door opens and it’s Mrs Deimel.

‘Robin, I’ve told you, she doesn’t want to see you, she’s resting.’

‘Look, can’t I just have a word? I want to say sorry.’

‘You disappearing at all hours and not coming home? She just doesn’t need that. She needs looking after.’

‘Can I just see her for five minutes, please?’

‘No, and that’s final.’

He sees himself barging through and confronting Liza – and knows it would be a horror show that wouldn’t do anyone any favours.

‘Can you give her these?’ He takes out a box of Milk

Tray chocolates from out of a white plastic bag.

'I'm sorry I've bothered you or caused you concern; the last thing I want to do is upset Liza.'

'You've got to change.'

'I'll try.'

'It'll have to be more than *try,* Robin.'

'Yeah, I know,' he says with sad eyes.

Mrs Deimel looks at the hurt in his eyes. 'Just give it a few days, Robin. You need some thinking time too.' She closes the door.

Robin turns on his heels and walks back up the path and down Connaught Close. He looks back over his shoulder at Liza's folks' house and sees an upstairs curtain twitch; he waves, hoping she's seen him. His legs feel heavy as he makes his way back to Reading train station.

*

Wakes on Monday, rubs his eyes, and for a moment he feels just right, until he remembers Liza, and the training he's got in Cardiff. His stomach gurgles with emptiness. He looks at the clock and realises he should've left at least half an hour ago. He fights the part of him that wants to get up and get on with it. He shifts in his bed but still lies as if pinned to it.

The flu, that's what I'll tell Jimmy. He won't want me there with that – works every time. A couple of days' grace, to try and sort me head out. Got to pay the fuckin' bills, pay for the train fares, pay for the property, pay for the dope, pay for the new baby. Pay the fuckin' man. Money...

Robin pulls himself out of bed and walks in his blue Y-fronts towards the phone, and just as he's about to pick up the receiver, he remembers the phone's been cut off.

'Bollocks.' He shakes his head and slopes back to the bedroom and falls back into bed.

*

Monday 25 July 1977
Robin phones Jimmy from a red phone box and tells him that he's got a chest infection. Tells Jimmy that his doctor is looking after him and that he just needs some rest.

*

Wednesday 27 July 1977
Cardiff play Swindon Town in a friendly, without Robin. Cardiff win 4–1 and Tony Evans scores four.

*

Robin knows that he's got to return to Elm Park on Saturday, to see his old teammates. To play in a friendly against his former club. They'll ask him how he's doing. They'll see it in his eyes. And when he plays they'll tell him he's not the player he was. Robin doesn't want to go back to Elm Park. He retreats to London.

*

Thursday 28 July 1977
Robin phones Jimmy and tells him he can't make the game on Saturday. Doesn't want to make the game on Saturday. Too many questions to answer; too many lies to tell. He eats the pink Diconal tablets like sweets. Hides away in fields of pink cotton wool.

*

Monday 1 August 1977
Robin arrives for training and is under doctor's orders to only do light training. He runs in the sun with David Giles and Phil Dwyer.

'You better?' asks Giles.

'Startin' to get some energy back, Gilo, but this illness

has wasted me…Look,' says Robin, pointing at his ribs, which poke out from under his skin, 'it's not like I had much fuckin' weight to lose, is it?'

'No, but I'm glad you're on the mend,' says Giles.

'How've things been while I've been away?' asks Robin.

'It's been okay to be honest, Robin, but there's a lot going on,' says Giles.

*

A monkey whispers into Robin's ear, but he tries to ignore it.

*

He trains, but the *sickness* starts to come back in waves. His body doesn't know if it's coming or going.

*

Thursday 4 August 1977
He runs around the training pitch but stops and puts his hands on his hips. Robin bends over double and pukes. His face is pallid, cold sweat dripping down his face. He hurls again, and his stomach feels like its clenching up inside him. He goes to ground and steadies himself. Concerned faces look on. Jimmy sends him home.

*

Robin makes the sickness go away with an injection.

*

Monday 8 August 1977
Robin phones Jimmy —

'Jimmy, it's Robin. I'm still not well…no…yeah…I can't shake this bug…they think it's gastroenteritis…yeah, I'll let you know.'

*

Robin prepares to detox. Needs to rid his blood of the poison; he locks himself away.

He sleeps in fits and starts, tries to read but can't. Smokes fag after fag. Ignores the outside world. Everything is happening inside, and it hurts. Dreams and reality meld their boundaries.

He sweats and shivers, pulls the blanket close around him. *He sees the light of the full moon breaking through a gap in the curtain. Sees a face on the moon, stares at it – sees it change into a large round skull inside a space helmet. He sees Death at the foot of his bed. He grips the sheets. He wishes it was Steve, but it's not. An arm with a bony finger points at him, and he jolts up in bed, mouth open, screaming, breathing hard, heart beating fast.*

He sees dark horses running through fields into the night. The voices come: you're not good enough, you cunt! Who the fuck are you trying to kid? Robbie big bollocks, we're coming for you, and we want our money, you owe us the fucking money, you mug. I'd pay if I were you. I'd pay if you wanna play football again. We'll tell Cardiff about your little habit. We'll tell Jimmy Andrews that his centre forward is a good-for-nothing junkie. All the smiles in the world won't gloss over that, will they, Robbie? No, they fuckin' won't. Breach of contract, I think they call it, no more money from Cardiff then, eh? Of course, we can shut up if you want? I mean, you don't want us to talk about your failed marriages? No, that would be going below the belt, wouldn't it? I wonder where Liza is now, what's she doing? You'll never know because you're lying here and rotting. Shall we talk about the kids?

Robin sits up holding his chest. He can't breathe, reaches for his inhaler and presses and breathes in, once, twice, and another for good luck. His bed is soaked. He turns and switches a small transistor radio on, listens and is glad of the company. He lies awake, shivering, craving one more hit. Holds himself tight.

*

Monday 15 August 1977
Ninian Park, Cardiff —

Robin hears the banging, sees the building workers busy in the stands. He holds his stomach, tries to ignore the cramps which push and pull. His body craves another hit, but he has to ride this out. Has to lose the monkey that sits on his back.

Robin walks into reception and down the corridor and into the dressing room. David Giles is just finishing up tying up his laces; he looks up.

'All right, Robin.'

'All right Gilo, late as well then?'

'No, I've just been to the toilet. You hurry up and we'll go out together.'

Robin gets undressed, gets changed into his football gear. There's small talk. Robin visits the toilet. He reaches into his sock and pulls out a small bag containing powder and rubs it around his gums. He tries to empty his bowels and washes his hands.

'Right then, let's get out there.'

They walk down the corridor and turn into the tunnel. The players are grouped together around Jimmy Andrews, who is flanked by coach Alan Sealey and an unknown well-built middle-aged man.

'Lateness will not be tolerated any more,' says Jimmy, pointing at Robin, 'unless you've got a valid excuse. I was just telling the lads that Mr Tudor Jones here is a former

Welsh Guardsman. He's your new trainer and physio – he is also here to improve discipline, something we sadly lacked last season. All of you have to step up, all of you. We've little money now for players.' Jimmy points at the stands, which bang and clang with workers. 'Six hundred thousand pounds that lot has cost the board, which is why we have to focus on our discipline, on our game. We've an uphill climb this year, and it'll be even harder than last year…'

Jimmy keeps talking, but Robin doesn't listen. His insides squirm, and he just wants to kick a ball, not be forced to listen to this. Alone in his thoughts, he feels a tap on his shoulder.

'Robin, why were you late?' asks Tudor Jones.

'I've got stomach problems, mate.'

'That's no excuse,' says Tudor Jones, looking Robin up and down.

'It is when you've got the thre'penny bits.'

'I don't care. You need to be here on time. I'm fining you two quid.'

'All right, take it easy, mate.' Robin takes the bollocking on the chin; he's not got the energy to fight – feels weak to his core.

Jimmy gets training underway, and Alan Sealey takes over – drills, drills, drills. They play a game of two-touch football. Robin falls foul of too many touches, doesn't like the restrictions. Doesn't feel the need for it. Wants the five-a-side to be simple so he can play as he should, with freedom.

*

Tuesday 16 August 1977

The sun scorches down onto Ninian Park. The training is

hard today, and Robin can feel it in his legs, his lungs; his body aches and his stomach cramps. He still tries to run, to chase the ball, but he's way off the pace – it's not there, the power is gone. Players call for the ball, and their voices echo off the stands – sometimes clipped short by the bangs from the workers in them. Robin feels saliva in his mouth. He starts to feel sick inside. A wave of nausea sweeps over him and his stomach pushes up the little breakfast he's eaten. He falls to his knees and vomits yellow bile; there's a second wave and a final dry retch. He coughs and tries to spit the vile taste out of his mouth.

'Fucking hell, Robin, you okay, mate?' asks Phil Dwyer.

Robin looks up, his face grey, and laughs. 'I've felt better, that's for fuckin' sure.'

Phil Dwyer takes Robin by the arm and helps him up. The yellow bile forms a web in the grass and glistens like a broken egg in the sun.

Alan Sealey and Jimmy approach, their faces full of concern. 'Here, have this,' says Alan, and he passes a white plastic cup of water to Robin.

Robin takes the cup, takes a mouthful and spits it out, and wipes his mouth with his sleeve. 'Thanks,' says Robin, taking another sip of water.

'Get yourself home, Robin,' says Jimmy with concern.

'I'll be okay, just give us a minute.'

'We don't know if you've got a bug, and the last thing I need is more players calling in sick.'

'All right, Jimmy, I'll keep you posted.' Robin trudges off the field, down the tunnel, into the corridor, and back into the dressing room. He feels faint and gets changed as quickly as he can, but everything is an effort.

He rolls his kit into a ball and stuffs it into his white plastic bag. He leaves the dressing room, heads down the corridor and out through reception, into the car park. The sun beats down, and Robin squints at the daylight, its rays causing him more distress.

Robin spends the night alone in Bristol, wakes the next morning and heads to the train station and waits for the train back to London.

*

St. Stephen's Hospital, London —

Robin lies in bed, an intravenous drip-feeding water into his dehydrated body. The doctors come and go, prodding and poking him. He's well fed. They test his blood, test for everything, but nothing is conclusive. It's inconclusive. *He looks out the window and hopes the habit is no more, but he still hears the call of the monkey and the flap of the dragon's wings. He knows that if he wants to get back on the pitch he's got to kick his habit into touch. His body still craves the euphoria, the calm, and the quiet. He owes Jimmy Andrews, and he owes Cardiff City.*

*

Thursday 18 August 1977

Jimmy tells the press that Robin is still unwell and that he could be out for a month at least. He tells them that Robin's weight has dropped from 13st 2lbs to 12st 6lb.

*

Jimmy hasn't heard from Robin for days and has no phone number for him. He needs Robin Friday back fit and in his team. Jimmy gets into his car and drives out of Cardiff and over the Severn Bridge into Bristol. He clutches the steering wheel, eyes on the road. He looks out across the estuary, out to sea. He moves against the tide. He pulls his car up near Bristol and pulls out his Bristol A–Z looking for Robin's street on the map. He studies the map and then drives off.

He finds the street and parks up outside the small semi-detached house. He strolls down the path and is greeted by milk bottles on the step; he counts them one by one. They are full; some of the older ones have been got at by the birds, and others have cottage cheese poking out of the top. Jimmy knocks at the door. He knocks again, louder this time – but the house is still and quiet. He knocks on the window and tries to find a gap in the closed front curtains, though no gap exists. Jimmy scratches his head and walks to the next house and knocks on the door. He waits and hears movement. Footsteps approach the front door. The door opens, and an elderly lady answers the door.

'Yes, may I help you?'

'Erm, I'm after Robin, next door,' he says, pointing over the fence, 'but he doesn't seem to be in. Have you seen him lately?'

'No, not for a while. I don't get out much you see; it's my knee. I haven't heard any music or shouting for a bit.'

'Shouting?'

'Yes, bawling at each other, slamming of doors, and the baby crying.'

'Right, thank you…erm, I'll be going then,' says Jimmy, backing away. 'Cheerio, take care.' He waves and turns his back, and heads to his car, gets in, sighs, and starts the engine. He heads back to Cardiff, knowing nothing more than when he started out on his journey over the Severn. Jimmy grips his steering wheel and crunches through the gears – teeth clenched.

*

Robin convinces Liza to return. He says he's sorry and that'll he'll change.

*

Robin stands over a toilet and pisses. He reads 'Armitage Shanks' written in blue on the porcelain, even though he's read it thousands of times, thinks of Bill Shankly at Liverpool – thinks of winning cups. He looks down and sees his stream of brown piss pollute the bowl below, like an oil slick at sea. Inside he feels anxious, knows that he could solve this problem very quickly with a little trip out, but he wants to sort himself out, needs to. *He must phone Jimmy. Must phone him* – guilt wells up inside – *maybe tomorrow,* he thinks.

*

'I've told you, you're not going out dressed like that.'

'I'm only going out to see my sister,' says Liza.

'Look, I don't like it, the way other blokes look at you.'

'I'm going to see my sister, what's the problem? You're just being paranoid.'

'No, I'm not.'

'So it's all right for you to disappear off out until the early hours and sometimes not even come back. That's okay, is it?'

'That's different, isn't it. I've told you, now just leave it.'

'Or else what?'

Robin stares at Liza and says, 'Don't fuckin' push it.'

*

Thursday 25 August 1977

Jimmy Andrews knows without Robin Friday he needs another striker. Keith Robson is signed from West Ham

United for £30,000. Jimmy hopes that Keith Robson will deliver what he needs: goals.

*

There's a loud rap on the door, and Liza peeps through the curtains. She opens the door, and there stands Jimmy Andrews.

'Hello, is Robin here?'

'No, he left about half an hour ago.'

'Right, where's he gone?'

'He didn't say.'

'Okay, sorry to bother you.' Jimmy looks at his watch. 'Tell him I called, and please ask him to call me, it's urgent.'

A car door slams outside and a car screeches off up the road.

Liza walks up the stairs to the bedroom and looks at Robin. His eyes are heavy, barely open, and his works are laid out next to him, his arm still with the rubber tourniquet in place, slack, but like a small serpent around his bicep. Tears roll down her eyes, and she knows that this can't go on, that this is finished, and that he's finished. The pain rolls up inside her and presses deep within her chest. She feels everything right now that he can't. She has to think about herself and her young family.

*

Infighting in the boardroom continues. Ninian Park won't host the Wales World Cup qualifier, it will go to Anfield, England. The vile plague that started in the boardroom infests the whole club, seeps into the team, robs them of spirit. It's every man for himself.

*

Wednesday 14 September 1977
Cardiff City, without Robin Friday, play FK Austria Memphis in the first round, first leg, of the European Cup Winners' Cup. The game finishes 0–0.

*

Monday 19 September 1977
He heads to the red phone box —

Picks up the receiver and dials, places his five pence into the slot. He hears it fall amongst the other coins.

'Jimmy, it's Robin, how are you?'

'I'm good, Robin, very good, but more to the point, how are you, feeling better, I hope?'

'Yeah, starting to feel a bit stronger, and getting my appetite back, like, so yeah, getting there, thanks,' says Robin, watching the traffic pass up the road.

'We've got Fulham at home on Saturday, Best's playing.'

'I know, that's why I'm calling. I'm gonna come up and watch.'

'That'd be good, the lads'll be pleased to see you. They've all been asking after you.'

'Tell them I'm on the mend and I'll see them on Saturday.'

'Okay, take care, Robin, bye for now.'

'See you, Jimmy.'

Robin drops the receiver, pushes at the door, which swings open. He walks up the street with a spring in his step.

*

Wednesday 21 September 1977
Piccadilly Circus —

The evening rush hour traffic hums by, stops, horns

beep and peep, and it continues through the arteries of London. There is the smell of tobacco, liquor, perfume, and car fumes. Words pass by on the lips of strangers, snippets of conversations caught. The bright lights of the adverts give Piccadilly a luminescence: Cinzano, VW, Carlsberg, Coca Cola, Wrigley's Spearmint. The lights flash. The   flash. The lights flash. The   flash. The lights flash.

Anteros watches over the Circus, his bow always ready to strike, reaching up on high above his statue. People sit on the steps below and the evening light begins to fade.

Robin walks amongst the crowds, looking for a mark, someone who looks like they might be a carrier of a few pills, powder, or dope – anything will do for personal use, or for resale.

He waits on a corner, starts to suss out the scene, sees one standing on her own. She smokes a fag, blowing the smoke up into the air, looking at passers-by. He looks at her and smiles. She gives a faint glimmer of a smile back before looking down at her feet. She takes out her lipstick and presses its rouge onto her lips, pulls out a mirror and smooths the lipstick with a finger.

Robin moves across the pavement and heads to his mark. 'Excuse me, miss, can I ask what you're doing here?'

'I'm just hanging around, you know,' she says, looking Robin up and down.

'Well, I'm with the Met, undercover, drug squad' – Robin flashes a card with his photograph on – 'and I'm going to ask you if you're carryin' any illicit drugs. Now, we can do this two ways: you can surrender whatever you're carryin', or I can frisk you and confiscate any drugs which may be in your possession and then arrest you under the Misuse of Drugs Act nineteen seventy-one. So, what'll it be?' asks Robin.

She looks up at him, lips pursed. 'Now that's something to consider, isn't it?' She pauses, then reaches into her purse and starts to root around. 'I was wondering how you're fixed for tonight, sir?'

'You what?' says Robin, raising his eyebrows, and tucking his fake card away in his pocket.

'Well, you've played your card, now it's my turn.' She flips out her police identity card. 'Now I think that trumps your card, don't you?'

Robin is frozen to the spot, mouth open, no words, he's not breathing. And then, just as he's starting to come to, to grasp this little situation, to look for escape routes—

'Now, before you think about doing a runner, there's one of ours there,' she says, pointing to a big man in a dirty suit, 'and one there,' she says, pointing to a short, stocky guy in a Crombie. 'Now, I'm arresting you for falsely suggesting that you were a police officer. You are not obliged to say anything, but anything you do say may be given in evidence,' she says, clicking the handcuffs onto one wrist, then another.

'Fuck. I've really gone and done it this time,' says Robin, shaking his head.

'Well, I'll give it to you, you made a good job of the card,' she says, pulling it out of his pocket and inspecting it. 'Not bad, sir. Now let's get you down to the station.'

The big man in the dirty suit walks up behind Robin and looks at him. 'Don't I recognise you?'

'Dunno, do you?'

'You seem…familiar somehow.'

'Nah, I've just got one of those faces.'

'What's your name?'

Robin goes quiet.

'What's your name?'

Robin shakes his head.

'Cat got his tongue, I think, love.'

A dark blue police van pulls up, and Robin is pushed into the back of it. He sits down, drops his head, looks at the handcuffs. *Even Houdini couldn't get out of this one. What the fuck am I going to do?* Thoughts flood his mind: *Liza, the baby, folks. Jimmy Andrews and Cardiff City, two hundred and fifty nicker a week up in smoke.* He shakes his head. *This could only happen to me. Right. Now. At. This. Moment. Jesus. Fuckin' Christ.*

The van weaves through the traffic and reaches Bow Street station. The large wooden doors swing back and the van passes through. Robin looks around and sees stern faces.

They book him at the desk. No one raises an eyebrow when he gives his name. They take him into a side room and take his fingerprints. He gives Liza's parents' address in Reading as his address. He's told he gets one telephone call.

Robin is led into a cell with dirty tiled walls and a concrete bed with a flimsy mattress. There's a smell of bleach and stale piss. He's patted down, gives up his belt, wallet, but gets to keep his fags and his inhaler. The metal door closes behind him. He pulls out a fag, asks for a match, strikes it and lights it. Takes a long drag and rubs his neck.

You stupid cunt. There's no bigger cunt in London right now. You are the capital of cunts, aren't you?

Problems with the missus? You just multiplied them by a thousand.

'Fuck off! I'm trying to think!' says Robin to the four walls of his cell.

Now, just got to plead guilty and hope that helps. Who the fuck can I call? Who? I've gotta hope that I go under the radar and don't get in the fuckin' news, or that's me done. Finito.

Robin sits on the concrete cell bed, thoughts cascading through his head. He breathes, takes another drag of his fag. B-R-E-A-T-H-E-S.

Let's be logical, let's simplify this. I've got nicked. Court tomorrow. I've just got to tell Liza and float that particular lead balloon. She's gotta know, and she'll have to help me out, get a solicitor, maybe. Must contact Cardiff with a plan as soon as I know the score.

He lies back on the concrete bed. Takes the last drag and stubs the fag out on the wall and throws the butt across the room into the slop bucket. Doors slam outside in the corridor, heavy footsteps. Cries and shouts echo out.

Robin bangs on the cell door. 'Can I have my phone call? I want my phone call.' He waits and then a small square opens in the door. 'Yes, what is it?' says a face through the square opening.

'Can I have my phone call now, please?'

'Okay, give me five minutes and I'll come and get you,' says the copper.

Robin paces up and down the cell, clenches his fists, each waiting second building up the anxiety of the phone call he doesn't want to make. The hardest call he's ever had to make.

The square panel opens and the same eyes peer through. 'Ready?'

'Yeah,' says Robin.

'Turn and face the wall, take a step forward, and show me your hands.'

He turns and faces the wall, puts his hands behind him and steps forward. The cell door opens. He feels a pull and cold bands of steel are placed around his wrists.

'Right, follow me.'

Robin is led to a room where a phone sits on a table with a notepad. The officer uncuffs Robin and offers him a seat.

'Okay, one phone call and that's it.'

Robin picks up the phone and dials. Waits. The phone rings out then pings.

'Hello,' says Liza.

'Liza, it's Robin. I'm at Bow Street. I've been done at Piccadilly…I can't go into it…Liza, are you there?'

There's silence on the other end of the phone.

'Liza?'

He hears a sniffle, and then, 'You stupid, stupid bastard. Don't think I'm coming to rescue you. We've got a three-month-old baby and you fucking drop this on me. You're so fucking selfish.'

He hears the sobs on the other end of the line.

'I'm sorry, love, really sorry.'

The phone clicks dead.

'Liza, Liza,' he says, looking down at the phone. 'Fuck it,' he says, holding his head.

'Don't worry, that's a pretty standard response. She's in shock,' says the copper.

'I'm fucked,' says Robin, feeling a lump in his throat.

The officer leads him back to the cell.

He lies down, closes his eyes and tries to sleep, but his thoughts turn over and loop. The night is full of howls, moans, banging and footsteps, which echo in from the corridor. There's no rest.

*

Thursday 22 September 1977

Bow Street Magistrates Court —

He is put into line with the other remands: tramps, alkies, junkies, burglars, pickpockets. He is amongst them; he is one of them. A court attendant ushers him into the dock. He stands, and a magistrate reads the charge: 'That on the twenty-first of September nineteen seventy-seven at Piccadilly Circus, West One, that you Robin Friday made a statement calculated to falsely suggest that you were a member of a police force, contrary to section fifty-two, sub section one of The Police Act, nineteen sixty-four.'

'How do you plead?'

Robin looks down and says, 'Guilty, Your Honour.'

'What do you do for a living?'

'Asphalter.'

'Address?'

'Six Connaught Close, Reading.'

'Please sit,' he says.

Robin sits on the wooden bench. There's whispering amongst the magistrates and the court associates.

'Right, given that you've pleaded guilty, I'm going to remand you in custody until October the twentieth of this year, nineteen seventy-seven. Bail is set at one hundred pounds for the charge, and a surety of two hundred and fifty pounds is set for remand without custody.'

Fuck —

The warehouse.

*

Saturday 24 September 1977
HMP Pentonville —

Robin stays at Her Majesty's pleasure. His name is now a number, but not a nine or a ten. This one is longer – it doesn't matter. He gets a haircut, short back and sides. Keeps his head down and nose clean. Robin can't get what he needs and starts to 'rattle'. He is given paracetamol and biscuits to help him ride the cold turkey.

He lies, eats, and shits in the same cramped, pokey room. He sits listening to the radio, listens to the scores coming in. There are reports from the Cardiff City v Fulham game. His name isn't mentioned, but George Best's is. He could be there. The room closes in on him. *Gotta get clean and sort my fuckin' head out.*

*

Monday 26 September 1977
Jimmy Andrews doesn't like lying but there's no other choice. He tells the press that Robin had phoned to say he was going to be at the Fulham game, but that Robin's medical adviser had phoned later to say that Robin was very unwell and had been admitted to a London hospital with hepatitis and could be out for several months. 'It's a big blow for us,' says Jimmy.

*

Robin thinks of his children and feels pangs of pain in his chest. Thinks of his mum and feels a lump in his throat. He wishes he could let it all out into his pillow, wishes he could cry.

There are voices, always voices. *If I know you're using drugs, it won't take them long to find out you're using them. If you could just settle down, work on your game. You shouldn't get married again* — He moves in his bed all alone; there's no comfort here —

Just boredom and time to reflect and time to regret.

*

He walks past cells, watches the screws, watches the other inmates out of the corners of his eyes: blurs. He walks slowly, shoulders in a hunch. His hands in his pockets, unsmiling, uncaring. Head down, ready at any moment for anything.

*

In the night-time —

The chase is on, and he runs screaming, eager to get away, runs into a building, climbs the stairs and hears them shouting. Still they come; they lunge at him; no, he fights them off. Runs up another set of stairs, and another, and then he's on the roof. A woman is there, she's with someone else, a man with arms like an octopus, reaching around, pulling at her clothes. She giggles. What? He screams, and his pursuers burst out onto the roof like wild dogs with callous smiles. She's gone. He's nowhere to go, moves towards the edge and falls backwards—

He sits bolts upright in his bed, beads of sweat pouring down his face. He comes to and buries his face in his palms and falls back onto the bed.

*

Paces in his cell. Slops out. Walks the prison wing landing, clanging along the metal, whistles to himself. Walks the exercise yard, around and around. Heads down the stairs towards the dining room. Eats dinner. Cell doors slam and the night comes.

*

In the night-time —

Jimmy Andrews sits in the corner of the cell, next to the slop bucket.

'Archie?' says Robin, with half-shut eyes, trying to focus.

'Don't Archie me, you cheeky bastard. Look at you, locked in a bloody room with a bucket full of your own shit and two other cons for company. Reaching for the stars, eh, lad?'

'I fucked up, I'm sorry, I won't—'

Jimmy interrupts, and in a mocking voice says, 'Do drugs? You'll clean your act up, you'll sort your head out? That it, eh?'

'I will. I'll get clean, train, move to Cardiff, honest.'

Jimmy is now dressed as a clown. 'Do you think I'm a soft touch? Think I'm daft, lad?'

'No, Jimmy.'

'It was a rhetorical question, cunt. I must be daft because I fucking signed you, a bloody druggie who doesn't know when he's had his fill. It's got you by the balls, lad, it's right under your fucking skin.' Jimmy leaves his seat and comes right up to Robin. Robin can smell his breath: Polo Mints. 'It's right in there,' he says, jabbing Robin in the chest, 'like a dirty, festering plague.'

'I, I, I'll sort it. The docs gonna put me on meds that'll sort it out, help me get clean.'

'Get clean for what? What's the point, you've gone too far, the line is about a thousand yards behind you,' says Jimmy, pointing behind him with his thumb. 'You're way past it, and we want our twenty-eight thousand pounds back, not tomorrow, but now! You thieving bastard!' Jimmy starts to throttle Robin.

His eyes spring open, staring at the ceiling, staring at the four grey walls. 'Oh, Christ, not again,' he says, reaching around for a fag and his lighter. He sparks up, sits on the end of his bed, the first glints of sunlight piercing the cell and bringing him around. Looks down at his knees, the scars of battles on the pitch, his knee still not right.

This is going to take everything I've got left…everything.

*

Wednesday 28 September 1977
Cardiff City play away against FK Austria Memphis in the European Cup Winners' Cup, first round, second leg. Robin sits in his cell rolling cigarettes, watching his back. Cardiff City lose 1–0 and exit the competition.

*

Thursday 29 September 1977
The cell door opens and Robin is told he's out on bail. He's led down the wing, down the stairs and into the processing area. He sits and goes through the motions. Answers the questions and nods. They tell him he's free to go and that his bail has been paid until 13 October 1977.

Robin walks out of the gates of Pentonville, but there's no one there to meet him. He looks behind him as the gates close. He heads back to Bristol on the train.

He sees the full milk bottles on the step, ignores them. Opens the front door and heads in. The house is cold. There's a note on the kitchen table from Liza. He reads it.

> *Dear Robin, I've gone to my parents and I won't be coming back. My mum paid the bail and surety money for you and she needs it back, all £350. I just*

can't do this anymore. Liza.

He sits down in the chair. Holds his head in his hands, elbows on the table, and he sighs. Closes his eyes and shudders. He looks down at the note, sees her handwriting and watches as his tears splash down amongst the words. Her words.

*

Friday 30 September 1977
Jimmy Andrews sits in his office preparing for Cardiff's away trip to Blackpool.

There's a knock on the door.

'Come in,' says Jimmy.

'All right, Jimmy, it's me,' says Robin, looking sorry for himself.

'Bloody hell, Robin,' says Jimmy, looking at his player, who looks thinner in the face. 'Take a seat, please.' Robin sits down.

'Look, I'm sorry about all the aggro I've caused, but my head is all over the place. I've been having problems with the wife, and it all got on top of me. Before you start, I'll be moving to Cardiff as of today. I'll sort out a hotel, and I wanna play in the next reserves' game. I just wanna put all this behind me and move forward and start enjoying my football again and proving to you what I can do.'

'Thank you, Robin. I think the move to Cardiff will be good for you. We've a game against West Ham reserves on Wednesday, and we'll be glad to have you back for that. Now, we have to talk about the serious stuff. I have a duty to this club and my players, and that includes you. I've lied to the press about you, and I've lied to the players. What happened with the arrest is over, we'll never mention it again after this conversation, and I don't expect you to mention it either. Is that clear?'

'Yeah, crystal.'

'Why were you impersonating a police officer?'

'So I could search 'em and nick stuff, like.'

'What sort of stuff?'

'Oh, you know, just a bit of wacky baccy, nothing serious.'

'What were you going to do with it?'

'Smoke it. It's a bit like having a couple of pints.'

'Do you do this all the time?'

'Nah, I just have a puff of it every now and then.'

'Right, well you can cut that out for a start and just have a couple of pints instead. That's legal.'

'Okay, not a problem.'

'Now, what have the courts said?'

'I'm bailed until the thirteenth of October and got to appear in court then, and I've to go back on the twentieth of October too. It's all okay. It basically means I have to keep my nose clean for the next twelve months.'

'Look, it's good to have you back, but I'm telling you now, I don't want any more trouble. Get yourself fit, get into that team, and prove to me what you can do. God knows we need you.'

'Don't worry, I will, I promise, Jimmy. I won't let you down.'

'This is a fresh start, Robin. Don't let me down.'

'Okay, Boss,' says Robin, shaking hands with Jimmy over the desk.

'I'll see you Monday at training,' says Jimmy.

'Yeah, I'll be the first here,' says Robin, leaving the room with a faint smile.

*

Monday 3 October 1977

Robin jumps on an early train, fidgets in his seat.

He arrives at Ninian Park for training, hopes that he can still do it. Hopes that his body won't let him down. He greets the other players with nods and grins. He says he feels much better and is on the mend. He watches the ball move and chases it down, but he's slow, slower than he was. When he gets the ball, he guards it, and some players don't come near him.

*

He prepares himself for games in the reserves with the also-rans, the 'stiffs', and the hoping to be back soons. He runs, legs heavy, thinner in the face, lighter in frame. Sees players look at him with questioning eyes.

*

Wednesday 5 October 1977

Ninian Park, Cardiff City reserves v West Ham reserves.

At half-time, he tastes copper in his mouth as he breathes in. He sips some water. He comes out for the second half, runs around, but his legs feel like jelly and his guts are weak. He loses his temper and is shown a yellow card. It finishes Cardiff City 0 West Ham 2.

*

He goes back to his hotel room and wonders where Liza is but tries to block it out. He reaches into his pocket and takes out his pink pills again.

*

Saturday 8 October 1977

Kenilworth Road, Luton Town reserves v Cardiff City reserves —

Robin plays away with the reserves at Luton Town, loses his temper and gets another yellow card. Luton Town 1 Cardiff City 1. Two games, two cautions.

*

He feels like he's in a washing machine, spinning around and unable to catch his breath, unable to get his feet on the ground. A cycle. He's got to stop and tries to stop with the gear and the lines and the pills. His mind machine guns thoughts at him, always dark, hard and biting. *Rat-a-tat, rat-a-tat, rat-a-tat, rat-a-tat, rat-a-tat!*

*

Robin misses the reserve game at Bridgend. Jimmy tells the press that Robin has a stomach strain and is still a couple of weeks away from full fitness. Jimmy Andrews seethes in anger.

*

He keeps running in training, but they look at his dark eyes, and he's quiet and not his usual self. He stares into space. Robin travels back to London and obliterates himself. Turns up for training in and out, in and out. Anger wells up inside when he's alone in his hotel room.

*

Thursday 13 October 1977
Bow Street Magistrates Court —

Robin stands in the dock and his charges are read out again. He tells them that he's okay, that he's learnt his lesson, and pays the remainder of his bail money. He shows remorse and hypnotises them. He is asked to return on Thursday 20 October 1977.

*

Saturday 15 October 1977
Leyton Stadium, Brisbane Road, Leyton, London —

The Orient v Cardiff City game is in full swing. There are cheers, whistles and boos. Robin ambles down the concrete steps of the Main Stand with a carrier bag in his hand. He heads down towards the dugout and clocks Jimmy Andrews through the Perspex.

He hammers his fist on the Perspex. *BANG-BANG-BANG —*

'Oi, Archie, it's Robin. I wanna play,' says Robin.

BANG-BANG-BANG —

'Archie, Archie, it's Robin.'

Jimmy Andrews does not turn around. Robin sees David Giles.

'Oi, Gilo, can you get Archie for me?'

David Giles smiles and taps Jimmy Andrews on the shoulder. 'Mr Andrews, Robin is here and he'd like to talk to you.'

'Just ignore him and focus on the game,' says Jimmy.

Giles looks back at Robin and shrugs his shoulders.

Robin shakes his head and finds a seat and watches the rest of the game. It finishes Orient 2 Cardiff City 1. They sit in twentieth place in Division Two. They've only won one game so far this season.

He gets up from his seat and heads out through the stand and into the street. A gang of young Cardiff City supporters gather around him and pester him for autographs. Robin sees Jimmy and the Cardiff players heading towards the team bus, they ignore him. He shakes his head and laughs.

*

Robin trains and does as he's told. Inside he churns. Voices whisper inside his head. It goes quiet when he enters the dressing room, people fidget when he's there, they hold back. It's all very civil on the outside, but he wants to swing at them, and they want to swing back. There is needle in the dressing room, but not the sort he'd like.

*

Wednesday 19 October 1977
Robin gets on a train to London and stays with friends. Has a quiet night.

*

Thursday 20 October 1977
Bow Street Magistrates Court —

'I hope that now, having had a taste of what life in the prison system is like, that you won't offend again. I note your marital problems, your medical issues. Your remorse is evident for all to see. I hope, and I'm sure, that this has taught you a valuable lesson. I don't want to see you again. I'm conditionally discharging you for twelve months,' says the magistrate.

'Thank you,' says Robin, looking at the magistrates, gripping the rail of the dock in front of him. He smiles and nods.

He walks out of Bow Street, the £250 surety money in his back pocket, the wind under his wings, and heads to the nearest boozer to celebrate.

*

Friday 21 October 1977
Jimmy Andrews sits the players down, talks to them about the crisis. He tells them that Albert Larmour and David Giles have been put up for sale because the club needs the money. Jimmy says they've got to cut the senior playing staff to eighteen. Robin shakes his head, folds his arms.

*

Saturday 22 October 1977
Robin travels with the reserves to Swindon Town's County Ground, runs as hard as he can, puffs out his cheeks, wipes his brow. In the second half, he breathes hard, holds his chest. Struggles to keep going. The game finishes Swindon Town 2 Cardiff City 1.

*

Jubilee Park —
Tudor Jones takes the Cardiff players for a warm up. Jones stands upright in his tight tracksuit bottoms and proudly wears the three-feathers on his chest.

'Right, boys, squats to start us off. Follow me…'

'What the fuck is this silly bastard doing?' asks Robin.

There are laughs from fellow players. Jones does not reply.

'Oi, Bonk, what are we fuckin' doin?' asks Robin.

There are sniggers.

'Just follow my lead,' says Jones.

'Fuck this, he'll have us doin' the hokey-cokey next,' says Robin, standing with his arms folded. There are laughs.

*

Wednesday 26 October 1977
Ninian Park —

Robin holds the ball up, runs in short spurts. In the second half, he runs and grimaces, breathing heavily. Makes a nuisance of himself at set pieces and tries to do what he can. The game finishes Cardiff City reserves 1 Birmingham City reserves 1.

*

Thursday 27 October 1977
The players go through the motions in training, Robin gets

stuck in and puts himself about in a five-a-side game. Phil Dwyer pulls up, limps off the pitch holding the inside of his thigh. Jimmy looks on with concern and folds his arms.

After training, Jimmy walks up to Robin and says, 'Not a bad session, Robin. How're you feeling?'

'Getting there, you know.'

'Right, well Phil Dwyer is looking doubtful for tomorrow, so I'd like you to be on standby for Brighton this Saturday.'

'Yeah, sure,' says Robin.

'Look, I know you're still not fully fit, but I know you can dig deep, and that's what we need right now.'

'I won't let you down.'

'I hope so, because I'm depending on you.'

*

Friday 28 October 1977
The Grand Hotel, Brighton —

Robin, wearing jeans, T-shirt and a denim jacket, and his red leather cowboy boots walks into the reception area with his kitbag and a full plastic bag stuffed with clothes. There is chatter as Jimmy Andrews and Harry Parsons sort out rooms for the players.

'All right, Archie. Okay, lads,' says Robin with a smile.

'I'm glad you could make it, Robin,' says Jimmy.

'No problem, you got the keys?'

'Right, you're in with Gilo,' says Jimmy, handing over the keys. 'Dinner will be at five 'o' clock sharp.'

Robin nods and heads towards the lift with David Giles. Robin presses the lift button and the doors open. Robin presses the button. The lift shudders upwards. Then it stops and the doors slide open. Robin and Giles head towards their room. Robin puts his key in the door and unlocks it and pushes open the door.

'Fuckin' lovely this, Gilo,' says Robin, eyeing the room and clocking the TV. He walks to the window and looks out at the sea view.

'Very nice, indeed,' says Giles.

Robin switches on the TV and puts on BBC1. He claims his bed by dropping his kitbag onto it and lies down. Stretches himself out and crosses his legs. 'This is the life,' says Robin, reaching for his fags…the hours pass…

'Robin, I'm heading down for dinner now. Are you coming?' says Giles.

'I'll be down in a bit.'

'All right,' says Giles, heading out of the room and shutting the door behind him.

Robin goes to his kit bag and takes out his Diconal and pops a couple into his mouth and swallows them. He turns off the TV and heads out of the room. He walks down the corridor and presses the lift button. Waits. The lift door slides open. He steps in and presses the button for the ground floor. The lift shudders down to the ground floor and the doors slide open.

Robin follows his nose and heads towards the dining room. He sees the players and management sat around in their blazers and ties. 'Evenin' gents,' says Robin.

Jimmy looks up from his soup and looks Robin up and down. 'Robin, you can't eat in here dressed like that. Now please go and put that nice velvet suit on.'

'All right, I will,' says Robin.

Down the corridor…in the lift…up in the lift…out of the lift…down the corridor…keys…unlock the door…opens door…heads to his plastic bag…takes his suit jacket out and wraps it around his right arm…pulls out the velvet trousers and wraps them around his left arm…heads to door…opens door…closes door…locks door…down the corridor…in the lift…down in the lift…out of the lift…down the corridor…into the dining room.

'Archie, I've sorted it,' says Robin grinning. The players look up and there is a roar of laughter. Jimmy stares down at his tomato soup.

'You look like the bloody Michelin Man,' says Giles, laughing. They all laugh, apart from Jimmy.

Robin sits down at the table. He sees the players' drinks: orange juice, and coke. Scanning the room, he sees a waiter. 'Oi, garcon,' says Robin, banging the table with his fist. The waiter looks over. 'Four lagers, pronto!'

Jimmy shakes his head and looks away. There is small talk at the tables. Robin throws his pints down his neck and gets stuck into his food.

The players head back to their rooms.

Robin sits on his bed. 'Gilo, can you do us a favour and get us two bottles of Cinzano?'

'Err, yeah, are you sure?'

'Yeah, course, I can't go down there because Archie'll be on the prowl. He won't suspect you,' says Robin, handing over a tenner. 'Hide them in this jacket,' he says, handing over the velvet jacket.

*

Saturday 29 October 1977

The Grand Hotel, Brighton —

Robin skips breakfast, skips lunch, and gets himself up and out of bed. He takes a big bag of peanuts from the mini bar and shoves them into his plastic bag.

'Gilo, look away now,' says Robin.

‘Why?’

‘Don’t worry,’ says Robin, reaching around the back of the TV. He feels for the chain that secures the colour TV to the wall. He pulls and twists, and there is a clunk as the chain comes away from the back of the TV. Robin picks it up and wraps it in his velvet jacket and then shoves it into his kitbag.

‘Right, you’ve seen nothin’, now let’s go,’ says Robin. Giles nods and picks up his bag and they leave the hotel room, go down in the lift, out through reception and they board the Cardiff City team bus which waits outside.

The bus moves through Brighton, towards the Goldstone Ground. There is nervous chatter amongst the players. Robin sits alone in his seat and shovels handfuls of peanuts into his mouth and crunches away.

*

Brighton & Hove Albion v Cardiff City —

Twenty-two thousand seven hundred and four are at the Goldstone Ground. The blue and white of the home crowd, Brighton & Hove Albion, mixed with the blue and white of Cardiff City.

The teams line up in the tunnel, Brighton in blue-and-white-striped shirts, Cardiff in yellow shirts. He remembers what Jimmy told him: *Don’t let them wind you up and don’t under any circumstance retaliate. Just don’t.* The roar from the crowd goes up as the players file out together onto the pitch. Brighton fans are baying for the Seagulls to peck out the eyes of the Bluebirds. Robin feels like a jolt of electricity is belting through him. His nerves jangle.

The first half starts and Robin is being marked by Brighton defender, Mark Lawrenson, who is like a shadow. Lawrenson kicks him, and Robin kicks and punches back twice as hard. The rest of the Cardiff City team are knocked about, but the referee lets it go.

Half-time comes, and Cardiff are two-fucking-nil down with another forty-five to play. The Cardiff team tramp down the tunnel towards the dressing room. Jimmy is waiting. Some of the lads sit down on the benches.

'Get up! No one sits down until we've worked out what the hell is happening out there!'

The lads jump up, and Harry Parsons makes himself busy with the tea.

'We've got to contain them, got to. If we don't, this'll end up as a cricket score.'

'We've got no fuckin' guts today, no bite, and it shows, and that fuckin' ref is bent. He's blown fuck all for us, and I'm being sliced to ribbons out there,' says Robin, showing the marks on his knees and shins. 'Look at Wenty…he's fucked, they've battered him.'

'We've got to play it a bit clever, Robin. As I said to you before the game, don't bite, that's what they want, they want you out of the game.'

'But I've got no protection; I've got a right to defend myself.'

'Look, just keep your cool and show them by putting in a couple of goals.'

'I'll fuckin' try if I don't get carried off on a stretcher first.'

Robin drinks down his sweet tea; he's bouncing off the walls and keen to get back out there. As Robin walks out of the dressing room, Jimmy taps him on the shoulder and says, 'Remember, don't lose it, or they've won.'

Robin nods and heads down the tunnel with the other

players. He comes out of the tunnel and looks up at the Cardiff fans as they chant with hope in their eyes. They pray for a comeback, a miracle.

The ref chucks the ball to Robin, and he places it onto the centre spot. He kicks off and passes it back to midfield as he makes a run forward. The ball is knocked over the top, and as it moves over his head, he runs onto it. As it lands, Lawrenson flies in hard and crashes into Robin. Lawrenson's knee catches Robin in the side and he feels a sharp pain that passes through his body all the way to the top of his head. The referee blows his whistle and awards Cardiff a free kick, but the free kick amounts to nothing. The ball is intercepted and played quickly up the line towards goal by the Brighton midfield.

Robin looks up at the clock in the corner of the stand: just over a half-hour to play.

He collects a loose ball on the halfway line and scoots past one, two of their players, and as he looks up towards goal, there's Lawrenson. Robin tries to nutmeg him, but Lawrenson flies into the tackle with both feet and smashes Robin in the shins, sending him crashing to the floor. The pain flows. *There's a red flicker.* He jumps up and sees the player still on the deck. Robin explodes and kicks Lawrenson in the face. There's a moan, and Lawrenson holds his face – Robin has lost his shadow.

The referee runs up and a ruck forms. There's a bunching of players and pushing, shoving, and shouting. Robin pushes and shoves. The referee tries to calm things down and calls Robin over.

Robin roars, 'Did you see what he fuckin' done to me? Did you? He should've been booked already!'

Alan Campbell approaches to support Robin. 'Ref, are

you going to book him!' he says, pointing at the Brighton defender who is being held back by his own teammates. 'Well, are you, or bloody what? How many times have you let them off this game?'

The ref orders Alan Campbell away, but he won't go.

The ref reaches into his pocket and shows Robin the red card.

'You biased cunt. He's been kickin' the shit out of me all game and you've not booked him. I'll ask you again, are you going to fuckin' book him?' says Robin.

'You need to go…now,' the ref orders.

Wenty puts an arm around Robin and helps him on his way.

Robin walks away to boos and shouts from the Brighton fans. He looks at Jimmy in the dugout; Jimmy is waving his arms and shouting; Harry Parsons puts an arm around Jimmy to calm him down. Jimmy looks across at Robin, and Robin glares back through stormy eyes. He shakes his head and looks back at the melee on the field that he's left behind him; he sees Alan Campbell receiving a yellow card from the ref. Jimmy drops his head into his hands. Robin walks down the players' tunnel and the noise of the crowd falls away. He turns right into the corridor and looks up and sees the sign: Home Dressing Room. He tries, but the door is locked. He crashes through the other door and into Cardiff's dressing room. He picks up his teammates' clothes off the pegs and benches; he sweeps along with his arms full and heads for the bath. He throws the pile of clothes into the huge bath; some sink, some float, but they all go in, like a tailor's soup. *That feels better.*

Robin goes straight to his peg and undresses quickly,

leaving his kit where it falls on the floor. He pulls on his jeans, then puts on his T-shirt, throwing on his denim jacket and pulling on his red leather cowboy boots. He clacks his football boots together and sends muddy chunks across the room. He puts his boots in his white plastic bag and takes out his bottle of Cinzano Bianco from inside his towel, unscrews the top, and takes a swig and screws the lid back on and wraps it back inside the towel. Robin grabs his TV laden kitbag and plastic bag. He storms out of the dressing room and down the corridor and out of the lobby doors into the car park. Robin sees the Cardiff bus driver, who looks up. Robin walks quickly past.

'Robin!...Robin!...Robin!'

He turns around and waves at the bus driver. The bus driver looks down at his watch, looks up with puzzlement on his face, hesitates and then waves. Robin is off through the gates. He reaches into his pocket and pulls out a fag and lights it up. He asks an old lady dressed in a brown raincoat the way to the train station. She mumbles and points down the road. Robin marches on towards the station, thinking only of getting back to London.

As the train moves towards London, Robin looks out of the window and watches fields and buildings fly by as dusk starts to fall. Darkness approaches. The carriage is half-empty. Robin unscrews his bottle of Cinzano Bianco and takes a large gulp. He lights up a fag and pulls on it as if it was his last one. He brings a Led Zeppelin tune to mind and taps his foot and hums.

I never want to go back to Cardiff; not for football, not for fucking, not for anything. I'm sick of this bullshit. He sits and squirms in his seat, fights the voices, sees Jimmy Andrews, spits fire at him and then jolts himself out of his thoughts and heads towards the toilet.

He sits down on the toilet seat and pulls his works out of his inside jacket pocket. Then he leans back, takes out a pink Diconal tablet and his teaspoon. Turns over his works tin and crushes the tablet into a rough pink dust. Holds the tin carefully. Stands up and presses the tap and takes a small amount of water into the spoon. Steadies himself. Sits back down. Sprinkles in the pink dust. Takes a syringe, draws up the pink paste and injects between his fingers. The hit makes him slouch on the toilet seat – time passes as he hangs onto the tail of the dragon, getting higher and higher. Robin's eyes flicker and his head rolls to the side. A stupor envelops him and he drifts off:

'Hey, man, how're you hanging?'

'Been better, Janis, but I'm all right now I'm here again, with you,' says Robin, leaning back into the cushions and pillows which surround him.

Janis sits cross-legged smoking a long spliff and pushes back her big round spectacles. Her tie-dyed clothes kaleidoscope in and out of the background of purple and lilac wall carpets. She takes a drag on her spliff. 'So tell me, what troubles you?'

'I just can't stand being told what to do any more. Do this, don't do that. I'm tired of all this bullshit. Tired of the arseholes. I can't do it any more – I want out.'

'Sounds like you got decisions to make, honey, gotta do what makes you happy.'

'I miss my little girls too, Janis. It breaks me up.'

'Sssshhh, ride the trip, man, it's all gonna be all right. Have some of this,' says Janis, reaching across and passing him the spliff. Robin floats along in his bubble of freedom, unshackled from the problems that press on

him...

There's a knock at the door, and Robin comes to on the toilet seat. He stretches, pulls himself up off the toilet. He pulls the window down, feels the cold air rushing in against his face – looks out into the passing green pastures. There's another knock at the door.

'Hang on, just give us a sec. I'm laying cables in 'ere.'

Robin takes a deep breath, opens the door, walks straight past the queue, and heads back to his seat. Back to the Cinzano Bianco. London is calling.

Robin heads through London, back out west to Acton.

*

But something keeps knocking at his head; he can't sit still, and thoughts fly around. He keeps seeing Jimmy's face. How's he going to explain this one? He knows he's safe in London. He tries not to think about training at Cardiff on Tuesday.

*

Monday 31 October 1977

Robin has a free day but he sits alone, and his thoughts stamp him into the floor. He lights up a spliff and pulls on it. His head is fuzzy and he pulls out a packet of Diconal. He presses a spoon over the pink tablets and crunches them to dust. Mixes it with water. Injects. Floats away for a while.

*

Tuesday 1 November 1977

He wakes early in the morning but stays in bed. He holds the pillow tight but can't get comfortable. His mind repeats thoughts like a dripping tap. Robin reaches for the Diconal.

*

Wednesday 2 November 1977

Robin walks from the train station and down the streets of Cardiff. Hunger and anxiety grip him. Jimmy Andrews awaits. Robin will front it out. He walks through the gates and into the car park.

Every piece of sinew in his body is willing him to walk away. *In his mind, he turns around and runs away.* He feels an oppressive atmosphere as he walks across the tarmac. It's as if he's being pushed back by an imaginary forcefield. Robin reaches into his jacket and takes out his inhaler. He presses and breathes in, holds his breath and breathes out, releasing the gas and some of his anxiety.

Robin walks into reception and carries on down the corridor. He stands tall. He pops his head into the dressing room and sees the lads' clothes hung up on the pegs. He looks at his plastic bag with his boots in.

He heads back out and turns into the tunnel. He hears the shouts and the sound of leather on leather. Robin rubs his neck and heads down the tunnel, towards the shouts.

He walks out into the light, gripping his white plastic bag. The game continues, and Robin makes his way towards Jimmy, who's watching a training match. As Robin approaches, the game stops. Jimmy, confused, follows the stares. Jimmy looks like he's seen a ghost. He's struck by Robin's smile.

'Sorry, Jimmy,' says Robin.

Jimmy turns to the players. 'Get back to it, you lot, nothing to see here. Robin, get yourself changed and get out there. Come and see me before training tomorrow morning. We need to clear the air, but don't worry about that lot out there. I've spoken to them.'

'Okay.'

*

Thursday 3 November 1977

Jimmy Andrews clears his desk, removes the sharp letter opener and locks it in a drawer. There's a knock at his door. He looks at the clock and takes a deep breath.

'Come in,' he says.

'Jimmy,' says Robin, giving a quick nod.

'Morning, Robin, please take a seat.'

Robin sits down. Jimmy moves around the desk and sits down.

Jimmy steadies himself in his seat and sighs. 'Now, Robin, it's good to see you, we were worried. I've got some things to say, but I'm going to let you have your say first. Please explain to me what is going on.'

Robin is taken aback by how calm Jimmy Andrews is. 'I've been having a few problems, Jimmy, as you know.' Robin looks to the floor, fights the tears. 'It's all the stuff with the missus, it's wreckin' my head. After Saturday, what can I say, I just didn't want to face the lads. I feel embarrassed that I done it, and on top of everything else an' all.'

'I'm very sorry to hear that, Robin, and that goes some way to explaining what happened on Saturday, but why skip training?'

'I was trying to work things out after Saturday, and I needed a break, that's all, Jimmy, honest.'

Jimmy reflects on this, for a moment, and knows he must tread a thin red line. 'I'm afraid that's just not good enough. I can appreciate you've difficulties at home, but that does not mean you can skip training. If I let you do it, they'll all be at it – you've got to be fair to me.'

'Look, I'm sorry, I just needed to get my head straight.'

'But your head hasn't been straight since you arrived here ten months ago. It's like there's two Robin Fridays and I never know which one's going to turn up, if indeed you do turn up,' says Jimmy with a sad smile.

'I'll get it sorted.'

'I'm afraid it's too late. I'm at the end of my tether. I'm not even angry any more. I was pig sick on Saturday after that game.' Jimmy pauses, sighs, and leans back in his chair. 'When I signed you I knew that you were a livewire, but I knew from what I'd seen that you had it all – and right now you're wasting that God-given talent. I told you that you could be the King of Cardiff, but it just hasn't worked out that way. Consistency is the key, but that only comes about through commitment. Saturday, in isolation, I could've dealt with, but then the not turning up to training – I can't. You missed the first eleven league games of this season through illness, not to mention your brushes with the law, and I stuck by you, even lied and covered up for you. You should be breaking down doors to get back into this side, but you're not,' says Jimmy, and he feels the red mist rise. 'You're taking a lot of money from this club for very little return, and not turning up for training is a breach of your contract.'

'I'm sorry. I was just pissed off at the sending off – the refs always go for me, and as soon as I give it back, that's it.'

'I know they do, but that doesn't mean that you do over your own teammates. We had to borrow Brighton's tracksuits on Saturday to get home. That lot out there were very upset, but they like you, Robin. They were all asking after you, they're worried about you, as I am and the rest of the staff are.'

‘Look, what can I say, apart from apologise again. Now, what was it you wanted to say?’ says Robin, sitting back in his chair and playing with his wedding ring.

‘I’m afraid that after everything that’s happened, I’m going to have to fine you one hundred pounds. That’s for missing training, three bookings last month, plus *all* of last weekend’s antics – which I won’t go into.’

Robin interrupts, ‘Oh, for fuck’s sake.’

‘I’ve got to do it – if I don’t, what example does that set for the rest of them?’

‘I’m not sure I can afford to do this fuckin’ job any more. It’s just not worth the bleedin’ hassle.’

‘I’m afraid I haven’t finished, Robin. After talking it through with the board of directors, we’re putting you on the transfer list.’

Robin stands up and towers over Jimmy. ‘Fine, I wanna go back to London anyway. I’ve got a contract and you’ll be paying me right up until I leave.’

Jimmy leans back and looks at Robin. ‘We’ll be happy to pay you, so long as you turn up for training. This can’t have come as a surprise, surely?’

‘I’m more pissed off about the hundred nicker that I’m down at the moment.’

‘Look, you know the rules, and I hope you sort yourself out – because you’re no good to anyone until you do.’

Robin lowers his head at the comment, looks down at his hands and sighs.

‘Anything else, before I head back to the hotel?’

‘Yes, I’ll expect to see you for training tomorrow. I can’t select you for Stoke as you’ve got a one-game automatic suspension. There’s an FA disciplinary meeting next Wednesday, and they’ll review what happened at

Brighton. I'll attend that on your behalf. Get yourself some rest, and I'll see you tomorrow morning.'

'See you tomorrow.'

'I hope so,' says Jimmy, hurting for his player.

Robin doesn't look back. He heads down the corridor and out of reception, through the car park, and back to his hotel room. Back to the room with the empty bed – away from Liza, but not away from the thoughts, and the voices. He takes some Diconal and feels better.

*

Reading are in the market for a new striker. A journalist phones Maurice Evans, Reading's manager, and asks if he's interested in signing Robin Friday. Maurice Evans says, 'No, definitely not.'

*

Wednesday 9 November 1977
Welsh FA Disciplinary Commission, Wrexham —

The suits sit at the table, flicking through papers, taking notes, deliberating, concurring, and drinking tea. Players are discussed, and their punishments doled out.

Jimmy Andrews is called into a smoky, oak-panelled room. He is asked by a large man to sit down. Jimmy hears the referee's report. It talks of kicking, punching, of a wild Robin Friday. He listens, waits for his moment, but there is more, much more.

'If we also consider Friday's past conduct, then one can only assume that he's not learnt his lesson…'

'Now hold on a moment, you haven't seen the treatment that is dished out to Friday every time he plays. In the opening minutes of that game he received the ball twice with his back to goal and was whacked both times from behind. To some defenders, it would seem that the ball is an afterthought after taking Friday out first. I can't condone his retaliation, but what other choice does he have but to defend himself from this abuse? It just doesn't seem right to me. It's as if a striker isn't allowed to tackle.'

'Mr Andrews, the rules of the game are quite clear with regards to a player's conduct, both on the pitch and in the ground.'

'We have the referee's report and Brighton's. They allege that Friday threw your team's clothes into the bath, is this correct?'

'What's this got to do with the game or Brighton? It's an internal club matter, and we're dealing with it. I have fined Friday. He has apologised to the players and myself.'

'I'm afraid as it's on the report we've got to deal with it. Taking into account his past conduct, and the incidents at Brighton, the off the pitch incident aside, Friday will be suspended for three games.'

'Brilliant, that's just what I need, another player missing.'

'But Mr Andrews, haven't you put him up for sale?'

'Yes, I have, and not having him on show hardly helps with that cause, does it?'

Jimmy leaves the room and thinks about what he'll tell Robin. Jimmy will wear kid gloves. He wonders how Robin is getting on in the reserve game.

*

The stands of Ninian Park are empty, save for a few fans who watch from the cold, open stands. Robin feels the wind blowing in his face – he feels alive. Queens Park Rangers reserves line up against them, all the way from London, just where Robin would like to be after the game – home.

After two minutes, it's Cardiff City 1 Queens Park Rangers 0. Robin commands the game, commands respect. He sweeps past players with ease, makes his own space, and plays with a smile. The emptiness of the place reminds Robin of playing in the parks of Acton.

Early in the second half, QPR score an equaliser – Robin fires his team up, pulls them together. Cardiff rally and Robin moves into the centre of the pitch, jinks in and out of the QPR midfield – ties them in knots. Robin sees John Buchanan making a run forward and passes the ball with the outside of his foot into his path, and Buchanan rifles home a twenty-yard belter into the back of the net. They celebrate with hands held high. Cardiff City reserves win 2–1. Robin heads out for a few beers before heading back to his hotel room for a kip.

*

He sits in his hotel room and lies on the bed and stares out of the window. He sees the reflection of his room in the dark.

What a fucking week: fined a hundred quid; transfer-listed; a wife that doesn't want to know. There must be a way out of this, must be —

He reaches for his works —

Sets it out —

Uses —

Drifts in clouds of pink cotton wool.

*

Thursday 10 November 1977

Robin paces up and down waiting for Jimmy Andrews outside his office. Jimmy appears in the corridor.

'Morning, Robin, come in, but it'll have to be quick.'

'Mornin', so what's the news?'

'It's not good, they've banned you for the next three matches, so no first-team games until December.'

'Jesus, what did they say?'

Jimmy is surprised at how well Robin is taking the news. 'That you've not learnt your lesson, and that's why it's a three-game suspension – they hope you'll take note.'

'I take a lot of stick out there, and I have to defend myself. Until I'm protected by the referees, then I won't change.'

'I know, Robin, but that's a shame, as the only person who loses out in the end is you. You've a lot to offer a club, you've got bags of ability, but as I've said before you just need to focus on your discipline.'

'Can you lend us a tenner until next week?'

'Aye, Robin,' says Jimmy. He sighs, reaching into his jacket pocket. 'Now go get yourself changed and ready for training.'

*

Robin sits in his hotel room on the edge of the bed pulling on a fag, which glows orange, lighting up the dim room. He looks out of the window and sees the cold November rain running down the windowpane. Robin thinks, deliberates, runs through the options. He stands in front of the mirror and replays past arguments, always winning, always victorious – but he counts the cost. He slumps back onto the bed. Thinks of Max and Nicola; thinks of Liza and Arabella. Thinks it must all be him, because he's the common denominator – thinks of the mess he's making. He twists and turns, trying to nutmeg his thoughts, but they come thick, hard, and fast, and they won't go away today. There is white-hot anger, strangled with bulging veins of blue frustration. He feels his chest tighten and reaches for his inhaler. He pulls on it and lies back. Something has got to change – something has got to go. Robin swills out a glass and fills it up with water. Gulps down its contents. He wishes he was back in London.

*

Suspended, he misses the Hull City game as Cardiff fall 4–1; he misses the Burnley game which Cardiff win 2–1. *The only consistent thing is that I'm not there,* thinks Robin. Jimmy Andrews' nerves are failing him, and the board continue to fight amongst themselves. Cardiff City are becoming easy prey. They sit in sixteenth place in a league of twenty-two. Another relegation struggle looms large.

*

Robin phones Liza and tells her he's now got a flat on Barry Island. That everything will be all right. He's sorry and that he'll change and that he'll pay back her mum, Heather, for the court money and for the house in Bristol. This is a new start, he says. He's two minutes from the beach, he tells her; it'd be great for the kids, he says. He asks when does she want him to send a lorry around to pick them and their things up. Never, she says.

*

He stands on the beach at Whitmore Bay, Barry Island and watches dark clouds move over the Bristol Channel. He sees England in the distance. *I've never been so alone,* he thinks.

*

Wednesday 23 November 1977
Steam rises from the players as they run, shout, and kick in a game of five-a-side. Robin runs but doesn't feel like he's getting out of second gear, breathes in the cold air and goes through the motions. The ball is kicked out of play;

Robin looks off into the distance.
Phil Dwyer collects the ball and gives it a good overarm throw. The ball crashes into the back of Robin's head. Robin is ripped out of his thoughts. He turns, eyes glaring, and sees Steve Grapes laughing. Robin moves towards Grapes with his eyes fixed on his target. Grapes freezes, caught in the headlights. In a flash, Robin releases a fierce right uppercut which jolts Steve Grapes' head back and sends him to the ground. Grapes lies spark out on the floor with glazed eyes. The other players look on with mouths open. Robin spits on the floor, sneers and turns, walks off the pitch, doesn't look back.

Jimmy shouts after Robin, but Robin walks off and heads towards the dressing room. He walks down the tunnel and into the corridor, and goes into the dressing room and pulls his training kit off.

The door opens and Robin looks up, sees Jimmy, pale-faced.

'What the hell do you think you're doing? What was all that about?' says Jimmy in a voice which belies his anger.

'The cunt was laughing at me.'

Jimmy takes a seat on the bench. 'So someone laughs at you and that's the answer?'

'It was today.'

'Now come on, you know that's no way to respond. I know things are difficult for you, but you can't go around hitting your own bloody teammates.'

'It don't matter to me now. I'm on the transfer list, *persona non grata*,' says Robin, pulling his jeans on. He pulls the fly up on his jeans and sits down next to Jimmy.

'Steve didn't deserve that, and I know you'll do the right thing and apologise. And as for you being on the list, what else do you expect me to do? My hands are tied, you're not performing on the pitch in the right manner. Hitting opponents I can partly understand, but your own teammates; it's not right, is it?'

'You're right, I'll apologise, I was out of order, but I wanna get out there and prove you wrong.'

'I'd be more than happy for you to prove me wrong. In fact, I'd be ecstatic. For you to do that though, you have got to sort this temper of yours out. It's ruining your game. You've got a gift, Robin. What you can do with that ball, most players can't, and couldn't if they practised for a hundred hours every week. You should be playing in the First Division, but you're not, you're here, and if you're not performing here then the First Division will never happen for you, and that'd be a crying shame. I really hope you take this on board, I really do. We've enough problems here without you adding to them.'

Robin nods. 'I know, you're right, but it's not that easy. I've got problems.'

'Robin, we've all got problems, son, but it's how we deal with them.'

Robin pulls on his Cuban heels and slips on his blue denim jacket over his T-shirt.

'I better go and see if Steve is all right.'

'I'd leave that for now and get yourself home.'

Robin nods and walks out the door.

*

Robin stews in his guilt. He knows he shouldn't have done it, but it doesn't make it any easier to accept.

*

Robin can't play in the Crystal Palace game at Selhurst Park, gives his tickets away for a few quid. Steve Grapes misses the Palace game too, his neck still aching and in a brace.

*

He sits in a room with a mate, Mark. They start to get busy around their gear; tins clank open, and the works come out. They cook up over a dirty coffee table. Mark injects first, sliding back into a settee. Robin thinks of the ball of anxiety in his chest, almost enjoys it for a moment, knowing that it will soon subside. He dips the needle into the spoon and pulls up the murky pink solution through the gauze. He undoes his jeans and injects into his groin. He sits, jeans still loose around his waist, and falls into a void of comfort. Complete bliss, not a worry in the world. His eyes closed, lids flickering.

*

Robin trains hard all week but aches all over. He tries to blank out the imaginary arguments which run screaming through his mind, attempts to smother them.

*

Wednesday 30 November 1977
Ninian Park —

Jimmy Andrews watches as Robin runs at the Ipswich Town reserve team. A team packed with first-team players as they prepare to play Barcelona in the second leg of the UEFA Cup. Robin is industrious and puts the Ipswich players under pressure. He scores and throws his arms up into the air and smiles.

In the second half, Robin starts to flag: full fitness still out of reach. Cardiff City have a goal disallowed, and it finishes Cardiff City reserves 1 Ipswich Town reserves 2. Jimmy is happy with Robin's performance but still hopes his fitness improves.

*

Robin sits in a toilet cubicle and dabs at some speed; it tastes bitter on his tongue. Robin grunts in training, chases everything, speaks in tongues to himself, goes through the motions and reaches into himself and pulls at everything he's got left. The speed picks him up but doesn't help his coordination as he clatters into fellow players. Sheffield United on Saturday seems a long way off. Jimmy keeps a close watch on Robin and notices there's still a struggle with pace and fitness. Jimmy is running out of options.

*

Friday 2 December 1977

'How much longer am I gonna be in the reserves for?'

'You're still a couple of weeks away from first-team football. I daren't risk you just yet,' says Jimmy.

'So tomorrow I'll be going to Norwich with the reserves?' asks Robin, looking crestfallen.

'Yes, until you can show me a good level of fitness then it'll remain that way.'

'Fine,' says Robin, walking away.

*

Saturday 3 December 1977

Robin wakes early, and by seven o'clock he's on the Cardiff City bus travelling to Norwich City, to play with the reserves. He sits on the bus and dozes. He sits with dark eyes, in the same T-shirt, jeans and denim jacket he's worn all week. The game at Norwich finishes 0–0 and is neither here nor there, and he doesn't care. The game happens, and the players wait to hear the first-team's result: Cardiff City 1 Sheffield United 6.

Serves 'em right – fuck 'em.

*

Monday 5 December 1977

Monday morning ten o'clock, Jimmy Andrews calls a meeting. He's flanked by Alan Sealey and Ken Whitfield, his assistants.

The players sit in their tracksuits; there isn't a sound. Jimmy has a face like a Scottish wildcat chewing a thistle.

'Gentleman, I've been informed that Saturday's game was our heaviest defeat for twenty-two years. A team that have not won a single away game all season came here and bloody murdered us. For twenty-five minutes you held your own, then…bang. It was as if you all gave up. There was no fight, no spirit. Saturday was by far my worst experience as a manager, by a long stretch. I can take losing to a better team if we show character. But where is your character?'

Jimmy looks around the room, at each and every face. 'We're a struggling side, and if we can't win at home, or get something out of a team like that, then we're in big, big trouble. I didn't feel like coming in this morning, but I did because I want this club to survive, to compete. Some of you need to take a long hard look at yourselves. We've got to try and turn it around in training this week. I only want people who give their all, who will spill their guts for this club. If you can't…then we'll show you the door. It's that simple.'

There's silence from the benches. Robin sits staring into space.

'Now get out there and train like your bloody life depends on it,' says Jimmy, pointing at the door.

*

Jimmy watches all week, watches each and every man, looks into their eyes and into their hearts. He needs goals, needs a win. Jimmy looks to the skies for a sign. He pairs Robin Friday and Keith Robson together up front; passes go begging, wide, in front, behind. Robin looks around in frustration. There's no spark, no magic, no understanding – Jimmy makes a mental note.

Robin is paired with Ray Bishop. They run, harry and send the defence into a panic; balls hit the back of the net. Ray Bishop runs for his life. Robin Friday works hard. Jimmy looks into his eyes and knows that Robin Friday is not Robin Friday, but half a Friday is better than nothing on Saturday because at least Friday will fight.

Jimmy thinks…Bishop, the runner, or Robson, the ball player; who'll partner Robin Friday. Jimmy Andrews prays for a miracle.

*

Saturday 10 December 1977

A crowd of sixteen thousand and ninety supporters stand in a ground made for a capacity of fifty-one thousand – Bolton are sleeping giants eager to return to the top flight. They sit at the top of the Second Division, without a blemish on their home record.

Robin sits with dark eyes, his mind playing away.

Jimmy Andrews makes a decision. He chooses experience over youth and picks Keith Robson to partner Robin.

'Can I have a private word, Jimmy,' says Robin. They make their way into the shower area. Robin shakes his head, lowers his voice. 'It won't work with Robson. It hasn't worked all week!'

'It's my decision, and I pick the team, okay. You'll play the target man today, and Robson will feed you.'

'Were you not watchin' this week, have you forgotten? He can't fuckin' run. I'll be on my own up front.'

'I pick the team, and you'll do as I say!' says Jimmy, spittle flying from his lips.

'I think it's a mistake, but like you say, you make the decisions.'

'Well, I'm telling you to play with Robson and score some goals. So do your job, that's what you're paid for.'

Robin folds his arms, walks out of the shower area. Jimmy stands alone, thinks back to this week's training, thinks that Robin may have a point, but he's named his team, set it in stone. Pressure builds.

Robin pulls the number nine shirt over his head. The players line up and head down the tunnel. The whistle blows and the game kicks off. Robin goes hard into a tackle. He catches his knee and the pain shoots up his leg. He tries to run but struggles. The most he can manage is a jog.

At half-time, it's Bolton Wanderers 3 Cardiff City 2.

Robin comes out for the second half, breathes through his arse, his knee still aching. The Cardiff fans aren't enough to heal him: the medicine he craves is not on the pitch, or in the stands. He fails to score, fails to run above a jog. In the fifty-third minute, Jimmy Andrews replaces Robin with Ray Bishop. Robin drops his head, limps off the park, waves at the fans, and leaves the game. He sits on the bench and watches until the final whistle: Bolton Wanderers 6 Cardiff City 3.

On the bus, Robin sits alone drinking from a bottle of Cinzano Bianco. The mood on the bus is sombre. Cardiff City have leaked twelve goals in two games. Robin holds his knee and pops some pink pills.

*

An emergency board meeting is called, not to discuss Jimmy Andrews' contract, not to discuss the team's awful performances, not to discuss anything according to anybody. The door is closed, heated voices and cigar smoke fill the room.

*

Tuesday 13 December 1977

Robin turns up early for training on Tuesday morning. Takes some Diconal for his knee. He goes in hard in training, goes in late. Tempers flare, but no one will fight back. He runs, breathes in and out, heavy. His lungs sting and his heart pounds away. Robin bends over holding his hips. Takes a breather.

*

Wednesday 14 December 1977

Ninian Park, Cardiff City reserves v Southampton reserves.

Robin goes hard into a tackle and takes another knock to his knee. He hobbles on for the rest of the game. His face shows the pain, but he keeps going until the end. Robin knows he's out of the running for the weekend's game against Hull City. He goes back to Barry Island and sits alone.

*

Robin crushes pink Diconal tablets, runs the spoon all over them until they are pink dust. He washes it in with some water, creates a pinky-red paste, like a watery strawberry milkshake. Places a gauze over the mixture, places the tip of the needle into it, pulls the syringe and watches the mixture pull up into the chamber. Holds it up in front of his eyes, presses to clear the air bubbles. Pulls down his pants and injects into a vein in his groin.

*

Friday 16 December 1977

Robin misses training, his knee still swollen and aching.

At Ninian Park, the players train for their game against Hull City.

Alan Sealey pulls up Keith Robson. 'What are you doing? You've got to pick it up, improve your fitness.'

'Get knotted,' says Robson.

There are snarls. 'Do you know how many days' training you've missed? I'll tell you…forty-six bloody days, and we're only in December.'

'Fuck off! I'm not the only one, am I?' says Robson, pushing up into Sealey's face.

Sealey holds back, denies his instinct. 'Go and get changed. I'll speak to you later.'

'Fuck off,' says Robson, leaving the pitch.

The training session continues. The remaining players work hard hoping to be picked for Saturday's game.

Sealey advises Jimmy to drop Keith Robson, but Jimmy is struggling for players as it is.

*

Saturday 17 December 1977

A nil-nil draw versus Hull City. Cardiff City sit in twentieth place in the Second Division, firmly in the relegation zone. There is no Robin Friday.

The dressing room sizzles with grievances, full of worry and sharp elbows. Jimmy takes a deep breath and tries to ignore it all.

In the car park after the game, fans are still milling about, hoping for an autograph, Alan Sealey stands chatting to a journalist. Keith Robson says, 'Goodnight', then he pulls off his jacket and swings at Sealey. Alan Sealey stands stunned, offended. The fight is broken up, and both men drive off in their cars.

*

Jimmy sits in his office, rubbing his chin: Robin Friday, Keith Robson, Robin Friday, Keith Robson. Almost £60,000 spent in transfer fees, plus wages, expenses on top. Jimmy knows his troubled acquisitions are being questioned by the board, by the players. Examples must be made, must be set in bedrock – Jimmy must succeed in taming these men. Jimmy feels the walls closing in on him. Keith Robson is put up for sale and fined. Keith Robson couldn't care less.

*

Monday 19 December 1977
Robin lies in bed, his body aching, like he's got the flu, his ears ringing. He'll see Jimmy tomorrow. Robin phones Liza and asks if he can spend Christmas with her, but she says no. He tells her that he's something very important to do, but he won't say what it is. Robin tells her he'll change, and asks, again, if he can spend Christmas with them, but she still says no.

*

Robin packs his gear into a suitcase and leaves Barry Island.

*

Tuesday 20 December 1977
Jimmy Andrews stews in his office. He looks at his phone.

Jimmy thinks he's been too soft on his bad boys. He sends Keith Robson to training with a hefty fine and asks him to improve his attitude, to play to his full potential. Jimmy is tired. He must now deal with Robin Friday.

Jimmy clears his desk and hides his sharp letter opener.

There's a knock at the door…

Jimmy: Come in.

Robin enters with a meek smile and dark eyes. Has the feeling he's been here before: déjà vu, déjà vu.

Robin: Alan said you wanted to see me.

Jimmy: Yes, take a seat.

Jimmy fidgets in his seat. Robin sits down.

Jimmy: Where've you been?

Robin: I didn't feel well, so I thought I'd get myself right before coming back in.

Jimmy: So why didn't you call me?

Robin: I didn't feel well enough to.

Jimmy: This just isn't good enough. I've stuck by you, and this is how you repay me. What a bloody few days it's been, sat here, in my shoes. We've put Robson up for sale, and I'll put the whole team up for sale if I have to. But you, you're already up for sale, and that hasn't shaken you, so I've no choice but to suspend you for breach of contract, without pay for the next two weeks.

Robin: Are you fuckin' serious?

Jimmy: I'm deadly serious. You've pushed it too far this time.

Robin sits glaring at Jimmy, his face dark, his mind whirring – an uncomfortable moment's silence.

Robin: Then I quit. *Robin slams his hand on the desk.*

Jimmy, startled, looks through frozen eyes, sits up in his chair, not quite believing what he's just heard.

Jimmy: You can't.

Robin: I can, and I fuckin' am.

Jimmy: Don't think you'll be able to turn out for anyone else. We retain your registration; you know that, right?

Robin: I don't care. I'm done. I don't want to play again. I'm fuckin' sick of it all. You can shove it!

Jimmy: Before you do this, do anything, think. You might not get another chance in the game.

Robin: I don't want another chance. I'm finished with it all.

Jimmy: What are you going to do?

Robin: I'll work in London, get back on the asphalting, anything but *this*. I'm fuckin' sick and tired of being told what to do. I just can't settle here; I don't belong here.

Jimmy: This is a huge decision, and it leaves us right in the lurch. If you walk out that door, that's it, you know that? There'll be no second chances.

Jimmy waits, hoping that Robin is calling his bluff.

Robin: I'm fuckin' done.

Robin walks out the door, no season's greetings. Jimmy sits with his head in his hands, feeling like he's been run over by a lorry. Jimmy has no address for Robin: he has lost Robin Friday.

*

Robin sits on the train looking out of the window. A grey sky looms outside. His mind wanders as he pulls on a fag. *No money for Christmas, I've got to get money for Christmas – I'll sort it, even if I have to beg, borrow, or steal. Things are getting dark.*

The train enters a tunnel. The lights flicker. Robin looks at his reflection in the window; his reflection sneers back at him, eyes like pools of oil, cheeks pointed through a thinner face. His smile has gone. He looks down at his hand, touches the scar where the tattoo of the blue swallow used to fly. The bird is gone, but the scar remains.

*

Wednesday 21 December 1977

Jimmy Andrews picks up the phone and dials. The phone rings out.

'Yes, Bob Paisley, please…Jimmy Andrews, Cardiff City…yes, thank you.'

'Good morning, Jimmy,' says Bob Paisley in his Durham accent, his voice warm and welcoming.

'Morning, Bob, how are you?' asks Jimmy.

'Thankful for small mercies, Jimmy. What can I help you with today?'

'Well, I've had one of my players walk out, so I'm here to see if John Toshack might be available on loan.'

'I'm sorry to hear that, Jimmy, who was it?'

'Robin Friday. We've had problems all along, but it got worse this season, much worse, such a wasted talent.'

'I remember, tall lad…with hair. We looked at him at Reading – good player, but a fiery temperament.'

'I knew buying him at a modest fee meant there would be problems, but it just didn't work out. I just couldn't fix him.'

'You can only do so much, the rest is up to the player. You're a good man, Jimmy. Now, John Toshack…yes, we can spare him. I don't have a problem with you talking to John. He'd be a good addition and help you shore things up a bit. Dependable is John.'

'We need dependable right now, Bob.'

'It's over to you then, Jimmy, and if he agrees, then we'll speak again.'

'That'd be great, absolutely great. Thank you. Cheerio, Bob.'

'Goodbye, Jimmy.'

*

John Toshack doesn't want to return to Cardiff City: he sees his future elsewhere.

*

Robin goes back to Acton for Christmas, smokes, drinks, injects. Doesn't see or speak to any of his family. Signs on for social security payments. Goes to his doctor, gets more Diconal. There's no football, no crowds. The only thing he craves is a high.

PART FOUR
1978–1990

Robin sits in his room in Acton, looks out the window, past the rooftops, and wonders where Liza is. Feels jealousy rise, thinks of her doing what he's always done. Thinks of her with other men. *Got to find her.*

*

Wednesday 25 January 1978
Piccadilly Circus —

Robin sees a kid, twitchy, a punk with a dirty leather jacket and orange hair. 'You need some gear, mate?'

'What you got?' asks the kid.

'Two Diconal, or pinkies as they're known, you tried 'em?'

'Nah, any good?'

'It's like a speedball. It'll light up your brain like a fuckin' Christmas tree, before setting you down on a bed of feathers. One tablet, one hit. Snort it, swallow it, inject it, whatever you want.'

'Sounds, fuckin' great, mate. How much?'

'I'll do 'em for a quid each.'

'All right, I'll 'ave 'em,' says the kid, reaching into his

pocket.

Robin grabs the kid's hand. 'Not here, we'll head down to the underground, too much chance of getting nicked up 'ere. I'll head down, just follow me,' says Robin, looking around, checking for coppers.

'Yeah, got it, mate.'

Robin tramps down the stairs, mixes in with the crowds. His shadow follows him a few steps behind. He heads around to the left, pops his hand into his pocket and pulls out the two tablets still in their packet, pushes the tablets from the foil. The kid steps up, looking around.

'Here you go,' says Robin, with the two pink tablets in his palm.

The kid fumbles for his money, puts his hands in his pockets, and pulls out two £1 notes. The kid looks at Robin with his mouth wide open as a big hand reaches out and grabs Robin's shoulder.

'Right, you two, what have we got here? A bit of a deal going down?' The copper holds Robin by his arm. 'Open your hand, sunshine.'

Robin opens up his hand, showing two pink tablets.

'What are they?'

'Diconal.'

'Where'd you get them?'

'They're prescribed to me,' says Robin.

'Why are you selling them to snotty here?' says the copper, pointing at the punk kid with his thumb.

'I just needed a couple of quid.'

The copper looks at Robin in disgust and shakes his head.

'What's your story?' says the copper to the kid.

'I was just getting some change out for this bloke.'

'And I suppose he was giving you a couple of magic beans for this *change*, was he?'

'No.'

'Listen, this isn't "Jack and the Beanstalk". Now take your bloody jacket off.'

The punk kid removes his jacket, and his arms are covered in marks, tramlines in his elbow creases, silver scars and bruises.

'Junkie?'

The kid looks down at his feet.

Robin watches passers-by looking on with eyes that judge.

'I'm taking you both back to the station,' says the copper. 'I am arresting you for supplying drugs. You are not obliged to say anything, but anything you do say may be given in evidence.'

As the copper pulls out handcuffs for Robin, the kid sprints away up the stairs and disappears into the crowd.

'You lot can move when you want to, can't you?'

The copper puts handcuffs on Robin and pushes him up the steps. Robin ambles up the steps of Piccadilly Underground up into Piccadilly Circus with his head down.

A dark blue police van arrives, and he's goes into the back of it with the copper. The driver turns and asks, 'What's he done?'

'Caught him selling his tablets to junkies.'

The driver shakes his head. 'Drugs, drugs, drugs, all we see now.'

The copper says, 'Right, what's your name?'

'Robin Friday.'

'Address?'

‘Thirty-seven Fordhook Avenue, Ealing.’

‘What do you do for a living, or is this it?’

‘I can’t work at the moment, I’m on the social.’

The copper nods, and there’s quiet. Robin bumps along in his seat to the rhythm of the road.

*

Bow Street Police Station —

He stands in a cell.

Kicks the wall with all his might.

‘*Fuuuuuccccckkkkkkk!*’

He hops around holding his foot, the pain taking his mind off the shit soup he’s in. He sits down, holds his foot, rubs his foot. Hears the hum of distant traffic and voices from within Bow Street. There are heavy footsteps and then a rattle of keys in the cell door. Robin looks, waits.

‘Evening, Mr Friday,’ says a heavyset older copper with a tray, two cups of tea on it.

‘Evening,’ says Robin, with an inquisitive look.

‘Brought you a cuppa, you want one?’

‘Yeah, please.’

‘Sugar?’

‘Yeah, two please.’

‘I hope you don’t mind me intruding, but I noticed your name on tonight’s booking sheet, and thought I recognised the name.’

‘It’s not like I’m going anywhere, is it?’ says Robin, laughing.

‘No, I suppose you’re not,’ says the copper, laughing. ‘So what’s going on?’

‘How long you got?’

‘As long as you want.’

Robin takes a slurp of his tea, puts the mug down on

the concrete floor. Sits back on his bed.

'I don't know where to start, I really don't,' says Robin, picking at his jeans. 'Women, and my taste for the high life, and I ain't talkin' about luxury goods. I've been divorced once, and now my second wife has left me and wants a divorce. A mess, a right fuckin' mess.'

'That's what they call complicated.'

'I'm trying to get off the hard stuff, getting meds off the doctor, like.' Robin frowns. 'This all off the record, guv?'

'Yeah, don't worry.'

'I shouldn't laugh. I could be going to chokey for a while for what I done today.'

'Let's hope not. Now, what about football, you going to play again soon?'

'Once I get out of this mess, yeah, I hope to, but I've got to get my head together first.'

'I heard about your debut for Cardiff. That was some bloody going. You're some player, you know.'

'I was some player. Now look at me here with you – no offence, like.'

'None taken, you still are a good player. No one can take that from you, can they?'

'I've taken it from myself.'

'You're right, but only you can sort yourself out, get yourself straight.'

'I wish it was that fuckin' simple.'

'It can be as simple or as complicated as you want it. There are people out there, millions of them, with dreams of playing football, or old buggers like me, who once had that same ambition but didn't get the break, gave up, or were just not good enough. You kept yourself going, through it all, and achieved those dreams. You're a good lad, but you've got to sort yourself out, just you, not for the docs, not for the women. It's your choice – think about it.'

Robin listens, nods. 'I will try and sort it out.'

'I mean…what's it like to score in front of a crowd?'

'A buzz, a real fuckin' buzz, and I always like to entertain 'em too, make 'em laugh, give 'em something to remember, even in the boring games.'

'It must be bloody great, and you've got that with you forever, haven't you?'

'Yeah, great memories, particularly Reading – loved it there, the lads and the camaraderie. Elm Park was magic. The fans at Cardiff were great to me too.'

The copper laughs, and says, 'I could talk to you all night, but I've got to get back to work. It's been a pleasure chatting with you.'

'Likewise,' says Robin, passing his empty mug to the copper.

'You need anything, just shout, and I hope to see you playing again soon. If I don't see you again, good luck.'

'Cheers,' says Robin.

The cell door closes, and Robin lies back on the bed, folds his arms and looks up at the grotty, tobacco-stained ceiling.

*

Robin is released and told that he must attend Bow Street Magistrates Court on 24 February 1978.

*

He wakes up late in the morning, but the first thought that enters his head is a fix, each day, every day, day after day. A buzzing monotony that he can't escape.

*

Friday 24 February 1978
Bow Street Magistrates Court —
Here we go again —

The charge is read out: 'That you, Robin Friday, were charged for an offence committed on the twenty-first of September nineteen seventy-seven at Piccadilly Circus, where you did with intent to deceive make a statement to falsely suggest that you were a member of a police force, contrary to section fifty-two, subsection one, of The Police Act nineteen sixty-four. You were found guilty of this original offence and conditionally discharged for twelve months on the twentieth of October nineteen seventy-seven, here, at Bow Street Magistrates Court. But did subsequently breach the conditions of the discharge by committing a further offence on the twenty-fifth of January nineteen seventy-eight, where you, Robin Friday, unlawfully supplied a controlled drug of class A, being two Diconal tablets containing dipipanone and cyclizine, to another at Piccadilly Circus Underground, contrary to section four, subsection three and one, of the Misuse of Drugs Act nineteen seventy-one.'

'How do you plead?' asks the chief magistrate.

'Guilty, Your Honour.'

'Have you anything further to say?'

'I'm really, really sorry. I never done nothin' like this before, and I certainly won't again. I made a very poor decision. I became very depressed after my wife left me, you know.'

The now familiar whispers of clerks and magistrates seem to echo off the oak-panelled walls.

'I will be assigning you a probation officer, and you

will be the subject of a medical examination. You will be remanded until the twenty-second of March nineteen seventy-eight, when your case will be reviewed.'

Robin shuffles out of the dock, head down.

*

Robin tries to get clean, and he goes back to train with Hayes. He'd love to play again, but he can't: Cardiff City hold his player registration. He starts to work part-time as a painter and decorator.

*

Wednesday 22 March 1978
Bow Street Magistrates —
Like a second home —

Robin enters the dock; the chief magistrate looks over his glasses and asks Robin to explain his conduct.

'I'm sorry for everything I've done, and all the trouble I've caused, but my life is a mess. At the time of the incident I was low on funds, and someone asked if I had anything, and I had two tablets, so I sold 'em for two quid. I know I shouldn't 'a' done it, but I'm not a drug dealer. My wife has left me and I can't play football at the moment – it all just got on top of me. I've been very depressed. I made a stupid decision of which I'm not proud. I want to be free of drugs and lead a respectable life again.'

'What are you doing for income, Mr Friday?'

'I'm drawin' social security and workin' part-time doing a bit of paintin' and decoratin', as I can't play football at the moment cos I'm injured.'

The magistrates deliberate.

'Taking into account your guilty plea, and some of the difficulties you have encountered, you have got three months to sort your life out. I want to see if you can get yourself free of your drug addiction, and I will defer sentencing until then. You will be recalled here on the twenty-second of June nineteen seventy-eight, which means you have three months to get help and sort out your drug problem,' says the chief magistrate.

As Robin leaves the courtroom, a press photographer snaps him.

*

'All right, Mum,' he says, planting a kiss on his mum's cheek and holding her tight.

'So glad to see you, Robin.' She holds him tight and doesn't want to let go.

'Come on in, get yourself comfy,' she says, pointing at the settee.

She busies herself and sets the kettle to boil on the gas cooker.

'Any news then?'

'Yeah, I made the news,' he says, pulling out a copy of the *Evening Standard*. He finds the page and passes it to her.

She looks down and sees his photograph: his eyes stare out from a thin face; the familiar Robin smile isn't there. She is silent for a moment as she reads the small article.

'I'm sorry, love,' she says, shaking her head. 'What are you going to do?'

'I'll get clean, sort my head out, all this stuff with Liza. I'll pull through – get back on that pitch and play again.'

'You're always welcome here, you know that, don't you, Robin. There is always a bed for you here.'

'Yeah, I know, thanks.'

The kettle begins to whistle from the kitchen.

Memories of childhood spring forth and tug at his heart strings.

*

Robin attends drugs counselling.

'So how are things?' says the middle-aged lady with a soft voice.

Fuckin' shit, trying to a put a lid on this habit, up and downs, shakes, and sweats. Going through the mill. The missus has gone, and I've kids I don't see. I can't play football. Yeah, things are tip top.

'Yeah, sort of all right…like, you know, just trying to get by.'

'How are the cravings, Robin?'

Like a fuckin' tiger's claws are in my back!

'Hard sometimes, but what the docs got me on helps, stops the cravings, and I'm out running trying to get fit, eating well.'

'That's good, positive, you're starting to make that important journey. Are your parents supportive?'

What's with these fuckin' stupid questions, talking through things, dredging up the past, over and over, the same bullshit conversations, without any answers, just a reassuring smile as I stumble through my words. I wanna move forward.

*

Robin trains with Hayes and tries to get himself fit. Runs, but not like he used to; runs in the heat, and sweats, and hopes that somewhere in all of this he can return to football.

*

Thursday 22 June 1978
Bow Street Magistrates Court —

Robin sits with his solicitor Miss May, and the chief magistrate calls Robin to the dock.

His charges are read through by the magistrate, and he sits watching them tumble off the magistrate's tongue.

Miss May stands to defend him. 'He is sufficiently recovered now to be able to view with horror the results of getting involved in drug-taking.' She pauses. 'We've all heard about the stress a professional player can face, and Mr Friday is sure that it was this, coupled with the break-up of his marriage, which led to his drug-taking.' She looks at Robin, then turns her attention back to the magistrate. 'He's now training with Hayes and hopes to play in a charity match for them in July. His only wish is to keep on training and return to the professional game.'

She's played a blinder, touch wood, he thinks, gripping the wooden bench.

The chief magistrate beckons Miss May towards him. There is whispering, and the clerk of the court listens in. There are nods, but no smiles, just straight faces.

The chief magistrate looks at Robin, and says, 'When considering this case, there's been a lot to deliberate on, but it would seem that you, Mr Friday, are at last trying to turn your life around. You will be fined seventy-five pounds for the supply of class A drugs on the twenty-fifth of January nineteen seventy-eight, and twenty-five pounds for being in breach of a conditional discharge. You will pay these fines back at five pounds a week; failure to do so will lead to imprisonment. I hope that you've learnt a valuable lesson and that you will not fall back into the trap of drug-taking again. Do you have anything to say, Mr

Friday?'

'No, Your Honour, and thank you,' says Robin, and he walks out of the dock a free man.

'Thanks, Patricia,' he says to Miss May.

'That's a good result. Are you pleased?'

'Relieved is the word, I think.'

They walk out of the courtroom, side by side, and Robin sees a man coming towards him.

'Robin Friday?'

'Yeah,' says Robin, frowning.

'I'm officially handing you this notice on behalf of your wife, Liza Friday,' says the man, pushing a brown envelope into Robin's hand. 'This notice is being officially served to start divorce proceedings.'

'Fuck off!' says Robin, throwing the letter to the floor.

The man turns on his heels and is gone.

'Were you expecting that?' says Miss May, looking on with concern at Robin.

'I don't know…yeah, probably. A bit of a shock, you know, especially today. I get up from one knock and then there's another one waiting.'

'Chin up, Mr Friday. I wish you luck, and please try and stay out of trouble,' she says with a smile.

'Cheers, Patricia, and thank you. If it weren't for you I'd be back inside, no doubt.'

'Goodbye, and I hope not to see you again.'

'Likewise.'

*

He goes for runs in the park, does press-ups, and keeps himself busy. *The devil makes work for idle hands.* He's got to get back to playing again.

*

Robin phones Jimmy Andrews but the phone rings out.

*

Wednesday 12 July 1978
Ninian Park —

Robin knocks on Jimmy Andrews' door.

'Come in.'

Robin opens the door and says, 'All right, Jimmy, how are you?'

Jimmy coughs and collects himself. Eyes wide. 'Bloody hell, Robin, I'm good, thanks. This is very unexpected, how are you?'

'I'm much better, thanks – been trainin' down at Hayes the last few months. Startin' to feel fit again.'

'I'm glad to hear that.'

'That's the reason I'm 'ere. I'd like to come back to Cardiff, to make up for last season. I just had too much going on, but I've sorted it now. What about it, Jimmy?'

'We can't have you back here, not now. I stood behind you and then you let me down when I needed you most. When you walked out you told me you couldn't settle here and you wanted to go back to London, remember?'

'Jimmy, I'm so sorry for what I done. I wasn't thinkin' straight. I was very depressed. I fucked up. There was just too much going on. I could play on an appearance fee-only basis. That way, if I don't play, I don't get paid.'

'That sounds like a raw deal for you, and I'd feel pressured to play you…and what if you got injured? That's no way to live, is it?'

'I just wanna play again, and you hold my registration, so I can't play for anyone, can I?'

'If I can help you get back into football, I will, but not here. We're strapped for cash as it is. *You* know, and *I know* you'd be better off nearer home.'

Robin nods. 'So if I find a club, you'll help me?'

'If you find a club, then yes, I will, but you're going to have to work very hard to build up trust with any new club. I hope you're ready for that challenge.'

'I'm ready, and I know I can still do it on the park.'

'Okay,' says Jimmy.

'Cheers, Jimmy, and no hard feelings, like.'

'No problem, and you take care, Robin. I wish you the best of luck.'

Robin and Jimmy shake hands, and Robin walks down the corridor and out of the doors, Ninian Park behind him.

*

Wednesday 19 July 1978

Robin picks up a newspaper, flips the paper and turns to the back pages to catch up on the latest from the world of sport. He turns the page, and his eyes are drawn to the headline:

DRUGS IN SOCCER INQUIRY STARTS.

The investigations into whatever drug abuse may exist in English football began today when the chairmen of the 92 league clubs received questionnaires from the FA League joint committee of study.

The chairmen of all 92 league clubs, today, received questionnaires regarding the use of drugs by players and to find out whether or not drug abuse exists in the English game.

The lines he reads, and he thinks of the lines he's done, the lines he's run, and the lines he's crossed.

The letter signed by FA chairman Professor Harold Thompson, explains that due to recent events it has become necessary to ensure medicants are not used by professional players to gain an unfair advantage over their opponents.

This may mean the introduction of random drug tests by the FA next season, and comes after Scotland and West Bromwich Albion winger Willie Johnston was sent home during this summer's World Cup in Argentina after he failed a drugs test.

The main questions are:

1 – Have any drugs in the enclosed list of drugs prohibited by FIFA ever been used by your players in training or matches?

2 – Can you state whether any other medicants have been used by your players?

3 – Do your players receive pain-killing drugs? What kind are they?

4 – Can your manager give his general views on the subject?

Thompson has urgently requested that all replies must be received at FA Headquarters by the 5th August.

Robin closes the paper and throws it into the nearest bin. He knows that if he's to get himself back into the game he'll have to be dope clean, clean of anything, and in a moment of clarity he looks into himself and feels that the world of professional football may have shut its doors on him for good.

*

Robin asks questions, follows up on leads, and finds out Liza's working at the Playboy Club in London.

'So, what you gonna do?' asks Mark.

'Go there,' says Robin.

'As soon as she sees you, you'll be kicked out, mate.'

'That's where you're wrong. I'll go in disguise.'

'What sort of disguise?'

'You know Dick Emery, when he dresses as that bird with the wig and boots?'

'Are you fuckin' serious?'

'Yeah.'

'Fuckin' hell, you nutter, they'll lock you up and throw away the key.'

'Just you wait and see.'

*

Robin puts a tiny paper tab of LSD on his tongue and swallows —

He looks up and applies mascara to his eyelashes, adds a spot of rouge to his cheeks. Paints his nails red. Laughs. Pulls on a long, curly brown wig, adjusts it. Pulls out the red lipstick and draws it onto his top lip, closes his lips, rubs them together, and pouts, admiring his handiwork.

He stands in front of the mirror: fur coat, frock, bright red cowboy boots, wig, and made-up to the nines.

'Oh, you are awful, but I like you,' he says, swinging his handbag and laughing at himself in the mirror. *I've had worse*, he thinks.

He goes down the stairs.

'What do you think, Mark?'

Mark turns and shifts back in his seat.

'Jesus Christ, mate, you look mental,' says Mark, laughing. 'You can't go out like that.'

'Just watch me, son,' he says, heading for the front door.

*

Playboy Club, London —

He winks at the doormen. 'Evening, gentlemen,' he squeaks.

They look at him, nod. 'Er, good evening…love.'

Robin thinks about hitting them with his handbag and telling them they're awful but he likes them, but he thinks better of it, smiles, and heads up the stairs.

The room is busy, men and women at the bar, people working at the card tables, and the roulette wheel spins. Bunnies walk amongst the tables. He looks around trying to find Liza amongst the bunnies. He spots her dealing at a card table surrounded by men. He takes a deep breath and heads over to the table.

He stands behind the card players, watches her deal. Stares.

She looks at him but looks away.

She carries on dealing, finishes the game, then looks up again with a frown. She looks him up and down, looks at his shoulders, looks at his eyes. He winks. She shakes her head, steadies her hands, and takes a sip of a drink. She signals to the bar, and another bunny comes and replaces her. She runs off towards a back room, closes the door shut.

She doesn't want to know.

Robin walks out of the Playboy Club and heads into Soho.

*

He hasn't eaten for days. The only nourishment his body craves is junk. He heats up a spoon and watches the mixture bubble.

*

July 1978 —

'We can't have a talent like you sitting around doing nothing,' says Allen Batsford, manager of Hillingdon Borough of the Southern League.

'So what'll we do?'

'I'll talk to Cardiff, try and get your registration released,' says Batsford. 'We've a good little side here, Robin, and you'll fit right in. We'll get you sorted.'

*

He eats what he can, scrapes food off the plate, but his real hunger still needs to be fed. He sits upon his bed and binds a rubber cord around his bicep.

*

Saturday 29 July 1978

Hillingdon Borough v Northampton Town —

Robin watches from the sidelines as Hillingdon trail Northampton Town.

In the seventieth minute, Robin is brought on as a substitute. He runs onto the pitch in the heat of the afternoon. Chases the ball. Goes through the motions, doesn't feel part of this, feels alone. He starts to flag. The final whistle blows and it finishes Hillingdon Borough 1 Northampton Town 3.

Robin walks from the pitch breathing hard. Looks into himself: *I've lost the desire, lost my belief, replaced it with something else. The drugs, the women, the lack of training. I've no belief, I know I don't. Too many problems. My head is fuckin' fried. My debut against Northampton, when I was unstoppable, when I changed the game.*

'Here you are,' says Allen Batsford, giving Robin his

wages.

'Thanks, Allen,' says Robin, bundling the brown envelope into his back pocket.

'We'll see you Tuesday evening at training.'

'Yeah, sure,' says Robin with a smile.

*

Tuesday evening comes and goes. Three weeks come and go. They seek him here, they seek him there, but they cannot find Robin Friday anywhere. Robin thinks of Allen Batsford, feels the guilt, but he must get his fix. The torment ends when he slides the needle in.

*

A petition takes off in Reading and is signed by three hundred supporters demanding that Robin Friday be re-signed by manager Maurice Evans.

*

Thursday 10 August 1978
Elm Park, Reading, Annual General Meeting —

'What is the possibility of bringing Robin Friday back to Reading?' asks a supporter.

Maurice looks back, straightens his tie and says, 'I am not denying the talent of Robin Friday. He's the most naturally gifted player I've ever worked with, but I've spoken with both Jimmy Andrews at Cardiff and Allen Batsford at Hillingdon, and Robin is simply not physically fit enough to play football at the moment, and I'm also informed that his attitude has not improved since he left us. As far as I'm concerned the matter is closed.'

*

Wednesday 23 August 1978
'Hello Allen, it's Bob Holmes here from the *Evening Standard*,' says Holmes, holding the telephone receiver.

‘Hello, yes, Bob, what can I do for you?’ asks Allen Batsford.

‘I hear things are shaping up well for you at Hillingdon. You’ve got Robin Friday with you, haven’t you?’

‘No, it appears we don’t, Bob. We signed him from Cardiff three weeks ago, and I had to pull a lot of strings to get his forms released. He hadn’t eaten for three days when he first turned up to training, so we wet-nursed him. He played about twenty minutes against Northampton, we paid him a week’s wages, and then he disappeared.’

‘Really?’ says Holmes, enjoying the detail for a moment. ‘What would you do if he turned up again?’

‘Well, I doubt I’d take him back. He’s burnt his bridges here.’

Bob Holmes has got a story, but he doesn’t smile.

*

Thursday 24 August 1978
Robin receives a decree nisi from Liza.

*

Robin tries to get his head straight. Fights against his addictive body. Sells his watch and gold pinky ring but keeps his wedding ring. Buys packets of white and brown powder, and gets prescriptions for Diconal.

*

Tuesday 5 December 1978
Robin opens the door and signs for a recorded delivery. He opens it. It’s a certificate making the decree nisi absolute (divorce) with Liza. Robin scrunches up the letter, drops it to the floor, and heads out of the door.

*

He works with Tony, his brother, for a while. They decorate and plaster, and then Robin needs to get away.

Needs to get some proper money coming in again. He gets back on the asphalting.

*

He's down on his hands and knees. He spreads the black mastic asphalt into the roof. A hot tarry air surrounds him, clings to his clothes. Swirling steam climbs in wisps. Robin works the asphalt into the surface, over and over. One coat, then two. Sand is sprinkled down, and a mate pushes a wooden float and rubs the sand into the mastic. Robin looks on, admiring his handiwork, and pulls on a fag.

*

He's up on the roofs, down on his knees, taking the piss, telling his stories, always telling his stories, making his workmates laugh and spill their tea.

*

September 1980
Tony Friday gets into an argument with Lebert Cummins. As the argument turns into a fight, Tony grapples with Cummins, who rips Tony's gold chain from around his neck in the mayhem. The red mist rises and Tony slashes Cummins with a Stanley knife across the face and stabs him in the back. He appears at Acton Crown Court and is sent down for thirty months for malicious wounding and due to his previous violent conduct.

*

Time passes, and Robin meets Mary, marries her in Fulham on the fourteenth day of August 1981. The registry office seems familiar, its oak-panelled walls and desks look like a magistrates' court, but that's all in the past; this is a different type of sentence. Time to settle down. They stay together and live in Fulham.

*

Monday 17 December 1984

He climbs up the stepladders, reaches up and slaps on the plaster, pushing into the ceiling, levelling it out, smoothing it.

The transistor radio plays, covered in plaster and paint: a well-travelled companion. The news comes on and Robin listens:

> *The former footballer, George Best, appeared at Southwark Crown Court today, and is set to spend his Christmas in gaol.*
>
> *Best was appealing against a twelve-week sentence for driving while three times over the legal limit, assaulting a police officer, and failing to answer bail.*
>
> *His appeal against the original sentence, which was imposed by Bow Street magistrates earlier this month, was dismissed. Best had argued that he felt the sentence was overly harsh. Judge Gerard Butler QC told Best that the original sentence was 'neither excessive nor unduly severe'.*
>
> *Best stood clutching the rail of the dock as his appeal was dismissed and showed no signs of emotion. He was taken down by a prison officer and will spend his Christmas at Pentonville Prison.*

'Fuckin' hell,' says Robin, pulling on a fag and coming down the stepladders. He looks out of the window, down the street, at the cars coming and going past Victorian terraced houses. He doesn't envy George's Christmas, thinking back to his own Christmases past. *Why do things always seem to fall apart at Christmas?*

*

After a while, Robin starts to struggle again, begins to dabble with junk. Mary leaves Robin, and after seven years, the marriage ends in divorce. Robin works less and claims the dole. He moves in with his twin brother Tony.

*

'Come on, you've got to sort yourself, Robin,' says Tony.

'I'm trying. You don't know how fuckin' hard it is,' says Robin, looking up from the settee.

'Why don't you move back to Mum and Dad's for a bit…you know, try and get yourself straight?'

'You kickin' me out?'

'Look, I'm just saying why don't you go back home for a bit. No harm is there?'

'Oh fuck off,' says Robin.

'I'm trying to help you, mate.'

'Trying to help yourself, don't you mean.'

'That's out of order, and you know it.'

'Tony, I'm sorry, I'm gonna try. A new start. Get myself sorted like you say.'

'I hope you do,' says Tony, staring out of the window.

*

Robin sits at home and watches the football results come in. He's taken back to his childhood, when he'd listen to the results on the radio and close his eyes and try and guess the results. Afterwards he'd be desperate to get outside to play football on the Scrubs, in the street, anywhere he could kick a ball.

Mum cooks him a fried egg sandwich with brown sauce. His old man sits with his pools coupon, waiting, the warm voice of the BBC announcer enunciating the names of all those famous clubs, the syllables rising and falling.

His old man curses. 'No good so far,' he says, ticking and crossing with his biro.

The announcer reads out the results, sounding like he's got a few marbles in his mouth.

The flowing names from faraway places doesn't settle Robin – he's got the needle again; he needs a needle again.

'Look at your old lot Cardiff. Relegated. Fourth Division now; what division were they in when you left 'em?'

'The Second,' he says, looking out the corner of his eye. Then he mutters under his breath, 'Like you didn't fuckin' know.'

'So, what're you gonna do, son?'

'About what?'

'A job, a flat, you know.'

'It'll get sorted; I've a few decisions to make.'

Robin sits squirming in his seat. He stares past the TV and out of the window; he feels his old man's eyes boring into him. Robin coughs. 'I've gotta go out and meet a mate,' he says, pulling himself out the chair, leaving the half-eaten fried egg sandwich. Mum pops her head out the kitchen door. 'You off out, dear?'

'Yeah, just off to see a mate for a swift one.'

'All right, mind how you go.'

'Yeah, course I will. If anyone calls, tell 'em I'll ring 'em back.'

'Will do.'

He looks back and melts with the smile of his mum, looks at his old man sitting there in the chair, eyes fixed on the TV; his numbers haven't come up, so it's back to work Monday – hope lost for another week.

*

Robin goes in and out of St Stephen's hospital for infections and problems with his chest and problems stemming from his habits.

*

Summer 1990 —

Robin's mum helps him to secure his own flat through Ealing Borough Council. A flat for those with substance abuse issues or mental illness.

He moves into 5c Burlington Gardens, Acton, and tries to get by, tries to sort his head out. Keeps himself away from his neighbours, calls them 'arseholes'.

*

In July, Chloe, his niece, is born in Ruislip. Robin thinks of his own daughters and feels a bruise deep in his heart. He turns thirty-eight years old.

*

Wednesday 21 November 1990
Griffin Park, Brentford: Hayes v Cardiff City, FA Cup, first round replay —

He arrives just before kick-off. It's eighteen years since he played for Hayes against Bristol Rovers in the FA Cup first round – almost half a lifetime ago. He gets to his seat, collars up without being recognised, his face older, but still with that trademark smile.

He watches Hayes play in their red-and-white shirts with black shorts versus Cardiff in their blue shirts and white shorts and blue socks. Hayes of the Conference and Cardiff of Division Four.

You've still got time, time to fix the things that've been broken, time to forgive and to forget. To let bygones be bygones.

He warms himself on the thoughts of the good times, the goals and the giggles.

Sentimentality drifts into him, and he feels a pique of overwhelming sadness – lets it settle, focusses back on the game. Kicks and heads every ball, his knees twitching and his elbows digging into himself.

He's seen so much here, from the first game he ever came to with his grandad; he can see himself there with Tony and his old man.

He watches Hayes' number five, Reg Leather, at thirty-seven years old, cut inside and go around the Cardiff left back before powering in a shot that the keeper fumbles before gaining control of it.

Then, with seven minutes left, Hayes break on the left wing and the ball is crossed low into the box, and the number seven, Paul Clarke, is there to prod the ball past the helpless Cardiff City keeper. Hayes 1 Cardiff City 0. The ground erupts, and Robin is out of his seat, hands in the air cheering Hayes. The Cardiff fans stand still, frozen behind the goal, and many look at their watches knowing that time is running out.

The final whistle goes, and claps and cheers ring out around Griffin Park, the magic of the FA Cup still alive. A voice talks over the tannoy but nobody listens, and nobody cares because Hayes have done it.

Robin stays for a while in his seat, lets others pass him by, and they disappear down the steps and away. He sits quietly, enjoys the silence, the peace, but knows the jubilation that's going on in that Hayes' dressing room, and the dejection that is pressing on those Cardiff players. He wishes he was down there, but then wishes he wasn't; he's seen both sides of that coin.

I did it my way, and there'll never be another me. I did what I could with what I had – I could've been one of the best but just never quite got there, almost, almost, but not quite, he thinks, then smiles with melancholy.

Robin reaches into his jacket and pulls out a straight, lights it up, turns his collars up and walks down the steps and out into the street. Gets the train back to Acton, back home to his flat for a cuppa and a spliff.

The chemist, must visit the chemist.

He looks out of the window, down at the street lights, starts to feel edgy, wants to score again.

*

Robin goes to his contact, swaps his pound notes for heroin and coke wrapped in clingfilm.

*

Sunday 16 December 1990

In the evening he sits at the table with his mum and dad, the smell of roast chicken and steamed vegetables clinging to the fabrics in the house.

'Your first Christmas in your new place, son,' says his mum.

'Yeah, it's all right, you know. Can't complain.'

'Any news on the job front?' asks his dad.

'Nah, it's pretty rough out there to be honest, not much about.'

'Well, maybe Tony can put some more work your way?'

'Yeah, maybe. Look, I'll sort it in the new year.'

His mum starts to clean the plates away from the table.

*

Wednesday 19 December 1990

5c Burlington Gardens, Acton —

Robin sits alone. The biting cold, framed, but moving, as sleet melts onto the windowpane.

The radiator pushes out its heat into the room. He sits on a red Chesterfield. There's a coffee table scattered with newspapers with a thick white candle burning at the table's centre. The candle flickers and makes shadows dance on the walls of the room. A Courage pub ashtray sits peppered with old ash and the dog-ends of old straights and spliffs. A blue inhaler lies on its side with its cap open. A golf-ball-sized chunk of Moroccan black solid sits with mustard-coloured pockmarks and scratches, its rich, musty aroma clinging to the furniture. A cup of tea sits half-empty and cold with a warm can of Breaker lager for company. A line of music albums nestle in a wooden side-table, old but immaculate. The stereo plays an old tune from the 1970s, the vinyl spinning black at 45rpm. The music is low and quiet, the drums and guitar just audible but still beating and fighting to be heard.

Robin stretches across to the side of the settee nearest the door, where his black leather jacket is draped over the arm of the Chesterfield. Reaching into an inside pocket, he pulls out a small bag of Afghan brown. He sets it down and lays his works out in order. Picking up a teaspoon, he half fills it with water from a bottle. He opens the bag and taps it carefully into a teaspoon, fighting against his shaky hands. Tap, tap, just a bit more. The powder rests on top of the water for a moment before being soaked up. Just a bit more. He adds some lemon juice. Holds it. Tap. The bag is placed onto the coffee table while both eyes stay fixed on the teaspoon. Robin reaches down and picks up a syringe; he uses its needle to stir the brown mixture in the teaspoon. Moving the teaspoon over the candle, he watches as it starts to bubble; he pulls it away for a moment and stirs it again with the needle. He draws a fist and opens his hand, pushing hard with his muscles. He tenses and ties a rubber cord around his bicep, close to the elbow. A swollen vein pushes out. Older marks, now healed, show as tiny scattered silver lines, but they're just visible in the low light of the candle. Looking back to the spoon, Robin passes it from his right hand to his left. Steady and in control. Focussed. He places a gauze over the mixture. Dipping the needle into the spoon, he pulls at the sandy brown mixture; it flows up the needle and into the vial. Robin presses on the syringe and squirts a little of the mixture into his left hand. Then wipes it on his jeans. Sitting hunched, he takes care to push the needle into the throbbing vein in his left arm. Enjoying the sharp scratch, he pulls back on the syringe and watches as a tiny red cloud of blood blooms inside the vial. Breathing in, Robin pushes the syringe top and watches the muddy mixture empty out into his vein. His eyes are now closed. A colossal breath pushes out from his lungs as he falls back into the comfort of the Chesterfield. The warm pink blanket of the drug wraps around Robin. Euphoria. A thousand holidays; all the orgasms he's ever had; all the goals he's ever scored. He pulls the syringe away and loosens the rubber tie from his arm. Floating in buzzing tranquillity. His thoughts are paused and all restlessness gone. High. Higher than ever. On a rooftop and staring back on all that has gone before.

*

Robin comes to and reaches for a fag. Lights up and inhales. He puts his works away back into the tin and puts it away in a drawer next to his bed.

*

Cheating death —
Playing against Death —
Playing with Death —
Death.

*

Robin walks to the kitchen and feels a flicker of static fuzz, holds his chest. He stumbles forward, reaches out but falls to the floor. His eyes roll back in his head. His breathing is shallow. *He hears a crowd. Arms wave in the shadows; they surround him. A fuzziness appears before his eyes. Static fizzes. There's a crackle and he falls again. The blackness draws Robin to its centre. Quiet, still, and waiting.*

Then he is blinded by floodlights and an emerald green sparkle from the ground. He watches a ball flying towards him. He flicks the ball up, turns at the exact moment it passes over his shoulder, kicks out, and it flies from his foot with a whoosh and ends up in the far right-hand side of the goal. Players run at him and fans vault the terrace wall, and he's surrounded by the warmth of their cheers. He sees his family and waves with a smile. Janis sings a lullaby. Robin stands, arms outstretched. Death wraps its arms around Robin and takes hold, but this time it doesn't let go.

*

After several days, the front door crashes open. Robin Friday has already left, but only for a while, like.

AFTERWORDS

It has been an absolute pleasure, and a challenge, to write about Robin Friday, and it has taken me on a journey I never thought possible. I have tried to do both his memory and legend justice but in a realistic and authentic way. At times it has felt like he has been watching over my shoulder, saying, 'Put this in…put that in.'

I knew from the start that there was a lot more to Robin's story, and I felt compelled to investigate further, as if something was driving me on. I wanted to hold his story up to the light and see what I could find out. Furthermore, I tried to search for the truth of what had happened to him during his life. In fact, it got to the point where I had to decide what to include and what to leave out – there was so much information.

*

Robin Friday, the player, could've played in the old First Division, of that there is no doubt. Still, Robin Friday, the personality, couldn't have played at that level for long unless he'd made drastic changes to his lifestyle and attitude. He was supremely talented but had come into the game late, age-wise. Jimmy Andrews, the Cardiff City manager, suggested that this is why Robin was the way he was. Jimmy said that when a young player joins a club at fifteen or sixteen, like any apprentice, they learn the trade and they learn the discipline. He went on further to say that because Robin didn't come into the game until he was twenty-one, he had become accustomed to a particular way of living, and that's what went against him. The move to Cardiff was taking him further away from London and didn't suit Robin. Cardiff City was and is a very proud club, but at the time of Robin's signing, there were a lot of issues going on at the club which I have tried to portray in this novel. Robin wanted to be nearer home, and he would disappear off to London most weekends to see his friends.

Jimmy Andrews wanted Robin to succeed and gave him every chance, but by the start of the 1977/78 season it had all spiralled out of control. Jimmy Andrews was a lovely person, a great coach, and had an excellent knowledge of the game, but as a manager there were question marks. Signing Robin was the biggest gamble he ever made in his managerial career, and it didn't pay off at the time, unfortunately.

*

When Robin was at Cardiff City he was really struggling with his addiction issues. Robin had become disillusioned with the game, due in part to his own actions, which impacted upon his mental and physical health. Jimmy Andrews said that sometimes Robin would turn up full of beans but the next day he would be listless. In Robin's words, 'My head was fucked.' Writing about a footballer who had an addiction problem has had its own challenges. Just how did Robin do it? How could he play professional football with everything he had going on? Robin had a penchant for a pink pill called Diconal, a pharmaceutical opiate, which he said was prescribed to him, and sometimes not prescribed to him but procured nonetheless. People's perceptions of heroin addicts are that they 'walk around off their nut' all the time, but this could not be further from the truth; heroin is like a safety blanket for many. Addicts can function without too many issues. In fact, the problems only arise when they can't get heroin; they get ill from withdrawal –the 'clucking' or 'flu'. We also hear of addicts, be it alcohol or opiates, who are able to keep such habits hidden from friends, partners, and families for years – so it can't be ruled out that Robin may have 'chipped' at his habit for many years, and I believe he did. As things started to go south for him, then so his intake of heroin increased, particularly around the time that he moved to Bristol, a city known for having its own drug issues.

*

The information in the press and elsewhere suggests that Robin had been arrested for impersonating a police officer in the 1980s. Searching the court registers for Robin was like a game of cat and mouse. I turned over pages and pages of these huge registers, but there was no sign of Robin. I went to the British Library and searched through the *Evening Standard* looking for him too, but there was no trace. After a bit of further detective work, I decided to go back to the court registers and look at the year 1977. I ploughed through the registers and it was there that I found an entry for Robin on 21 September 1977. The charge was for impersonating a police officer. Stunned into excitement, I took in the moment and decided I had to go to the toilet, so I left my bag and the court register open on the desk. I wanted to savour the moment, as I'd found something that had been hidden for decades. As I left the toilet, the fire alarm went off and we had to evacuate the building. The timing was perfect and, though coincidental, was also very much in line with Robin's sense of humour. I had to wait outside for an hour wondering if I'd be able to get back in. Luckily, I did and was able to follow the trail and see that Robin was sent to Pentonville but was bailed after a short time. Jimmy Andrews had kept that story hidden from the press and from the entire playing staff at Cardiff City and probably the board of directors too.

Then, of course, on 25 January 1978, after Robin had walked away from the game, he was arrested, near the same spot at Piccadilly Underground, for selling his Diconal pills, which he said were prescribed to him. Robin managed not to get sent down again, even though he had breached a conditional discharge: evidence of his mesmeric charm once more.

*

Robin did ask Jimmy Andrews if he could return to Cardiff City in July 1978, but that door was already closed to him. In fairness to Jimmy, he did help Robin by releasing his player registration so he could sign for Allen Batsford's Hillingdon Borough, but as we see, that didn't last long. Robin had known Batsford at Walton & Hersham, where he had a brief association before trialling with Reading, going back to Hayes and then signing with Reading in the 1973/74 season. There were rumours that Robin had trained with Brentford at the start of the 1978/79 season, and that is entirely possible as John 'Minty' Murray had signed for them and could've put a word in for his old friend, but perhaps after they realised that Robin was registered with Hillingdon Borough and had walked out on them then the door to the professional football world was finally slammed shut.

*

Robin wanted to entertain the fans, and that's why they loved him. He was different on the field and off it. He often spoke out against managers in the game who, he argued, didn't like players that entertained the crowd. Robin said he didn't want to be a robot and just run about for ninety minutes without any hint of individuality or flare. Robin just wanted to enjoy himself and play without the pressure of the professional game.

*

If *Man Friday: the first half* is the story of Robin overcoming challenges and making his way towards the pinnacle of his short football career, then *Man Friday: the second half* is about Robin's battle with himself and his demons. Robin could in one moment be funny and charming, then reckless and uncompromising in the next. He was a very complex individual.

In the 'Afterwords' of the first book, I suggested that *Man Friday: the first half* was about a man who loved to play football and who really did give a fuck. I still believe that, but there were definitely times when he really didn't give a fuck; we can see that in this novel. But you don't do the things he did to himself if you're in a good place either. At the start of the chemical ride it might be a bit of fun, but then it gets dark and Robin wasn't the type of person to play about with half measures – he just didn't believe in them and by then it was too late. There was a change in Robin's persona, so says his second wife Liza, and the Robin Friday at Cardiff City is very different to the Robin Friday who played for Reading. Sadly, he never fulfilled his true potential, and that is a tragedy and perhaps why I have written *Man Friday* as a tale of two halves.

Robin loved his music and was a big fan of Frankie Miller. There's a song that Robin never got to hear called 'I'll Never Be That Young Again' and it could almost have been written about him. It's a beautiful song with soul and spirit and in it are many lessons, just as there are lessons in Robin's story.

Finally, whilst very well researched, *Man Friday: the second half* is purely a work of fiction.

I hope that you have enjoyed my work, and as I write these words I bring to a close five years of research and writing about a man called Friday. Here's to Robin Friday. *Shine on...*

Stuart Kane, October 2020

Sources & Acknowledgements

The following have all helped inspire or have aided in the research of this novel:

Acton Gazette (1965-80)
A Kestrel for a Knave by Barry Hines (1968)
Beatlebone by Kevin Barry (2015)
Biscuits & Royals by David Downs (1984)
Charlie Hurley: The Greatest Centre Half the World has Ever Seen by Mark Metcalf (2008)
Daily Mirror (1972-90)
Dancer by Colum McCann (2003)
Blood's a Rover by James Ellroy (2009)
Crisis? What Crisis? Britain in the 1970s by Alwyn W. Turner (2008)
Hayes & Hartington Gazette (1989-94)
I Believe in Miracles by Daniel Taylor (2015)
Libra by Don DeLillo (1988)
Lonely Boy by Steve Jones with Ben Thompson (2016)
Mr Cardiff City: The Autobiography of Phil 'Joe' Dwyer by Phil Dwyer with James Leighton (2011)
Middlesex County Times (1980)
More Than a Job? by Roger Titford with Eamon Dunphy (1992)
Only a Game? By Eamon Dunphy (1976)
Poor Cow by Nell Dunn (1967)
Red or Dead by David Peace (2013)
Saturday Night and Sunday Morning by Alan Sillitoe (1958)

Shankly: My story by Bill Shankly (1976, 2011)
South Wales Echo (1976-78)
The Changing Room by David Storey (1972)
The Damned Utd by David Peace (2006)
Evening Standard (1974-90)
The Grass Arena by John Healy (2008)
The Greatest Player You Never Saw by Paul McGuigan and Paolo Hewitt (1997)
The Loneliness of the Long Distance Runner by Alan Sillitoe (1959)
The Legend of Robin Friday by Roger Titford (2017)
Reading Chronicle (1973-91)
Reading Evening Post (1973-97)
The Rocky Road by Eamon Dunphy (2013)
The Rothmans Football Yearbook (1974-79)
The Unfortunates by B. S. Johnson (1969)
The Savage Detectives by Roberto Bolaño (2007)
This Sporting Life by David Storey (1960)
Trainspotting by Irvine Welsh (1999)
Wondergoals and Cowboy Boots by Jamie Carter (2006) DVD
Western Mail (1976-78)

Some of the stories and scenes which appear in this novel have been inspired by the many fan forums dedicated to Reading Football Club and Cardiff City Football Club.

This book would not have been possible if it were not for the journalists and unnamed photographers who recorded or captured Robin Friday.

I would like to thank the following people who have all helped with this book in some way. Former Cardiff City player, John Buchanan, for talking to me about his own career as a professional footballer and life at Ninian Park during the 1970s. David Giles, former Welsh international and Cardiff City player, who was able to share some fascinating stories about Robin's adventures and share some of the finer details of the goings on at Ninian Park in 1977. Alwyn Evans for his support and assistance. Mark Denham at Cardiff City FC for his kind permission regarding the 'Letter of the week' from the Cardiff City v Charlton Athletic programme. The brilliant journalist and author, David Owens. Michael Lackey for his continuing research on the biographical novel. David Peace and Kevin Barry for agreeing to interviews with me about their works on Bill Shankly, Brian Clough, and John Lennon respectively. Richard Sheehan for his copy-editing. Malcolm Bell, for his continuing encouragement. Edward Lishak for his avid support of 60s and 70s football history. Amal Chatterjee for his inspirational teaching. The staff at Reading Central Library. The British Newspaper Archives. The London Metropolitan Archives. The staff at the British Library, London. Natalie Jones at Reach Licensing (Mirrorpix). My mother, Susan Kane, and my father, Jim Kane. My wonderful girlfriend, Romina. My cousins out in San Diego, Cal Walker and Terri Stevenson. My friends: Alex Götschel, Jonnie Irwin, Pete Weston, Simon Chopra, Brian Williams. The Cornish family, Becconsall. Kingsley Peters and Adam Lloyd of Kingel Limited for their work on the cover design. I would also like to give a special mention to the fans of Reading FC and Cardiff City FC and their passion for their respective clubs. A mention too for the many kind words of so many people who actually saw Robin Friday play back in the day and contacted me to say how I'd brought his memory back to life for them. Thank you to all of you!

Printed in Great Britain
by Amazon

83776838R00192